USA TODAY BESTSELLING AUTHORS

TERRI E. LAINE
& A.M. HARGROVE

A BEAUTIFUL SIN

Published By Wicked Truth Publishing, LLC

Cover by Sofie Hartley at Luminos Graphic House
Cover photo by Sara Eirew Photography
Chapter headers by Max Henry of Max Effect

ISBN-13: 978-1533671844
ISBN: 1533671842

To anyone who has suffered abuse
at the hands of another,
this book is dedicated to you.

Prologue

CANAAN

Bless me, Father, for I have sinned…

Words I've repeated how many times? It doesn't matter. What matters is the confession that comes now. God and the church are my life, but sometimes we are given choices—choices that are neither good nor evil, but weigh heavily on one's soul. Mine walks in the form of something so beautiful, she is the temptation I never thought I'd have. Or perhaps she is my salvation, my deliverance from my skeletons, the invisible chains that bind me, the very ones that have constricted my heart for far too long.

Believe me, I have no regrets, but I know I have sinned. When she stepped into my life, I didn't see how much we would become entangled with one another—or how hard it would be to untangle those bonds. But I must admit the truth to myself, and to God.

This isn't a love story. For that would go against my vows. Yet the sins we've committed could mean the end…or the beginning of everything.

Father, this is my confession…

One

CANAAN

Fourteen Years Ago

I was a sinner, taught from an early age that I would fall short of perfection. If not by actions, I would eventually succumb to impure thoughts. And what kid my age didn't have random thoughts that would contradict the laws of God? What I hadn't known that day was how much of a sinner I was and the price I would have to pay.

"Canaan Michael, get out of bed now! Mass starts in forty-five minutes. You're going to be late," Mom shouted.

Blinking my eyes open, I glanced over at the clock and groaned. As much as I loved being an altar server, my bed felt so awesome right then.

"I'm up!" I called out as I threw the comforter off and climbed out of bed. I managed to do the necessary things in only a few short minutes in order to join my parents in the kitchen.

Dad glanced up from where he poured a cup of coffee. "That was fast," he said. "Want some breakfast?"

"No, sir. Communion, remember?" As Catholics, we needed to fast an hour before we took Holy Communion.

Dad proudly glanced over at Mom. They were used to me spouting off rules of our faith and occasionally scripture, for that matter.

"You have plenty of time. By the time Communion comes, it'll be way past an hour," Dad said, patting my shoulder.

I glanced at the clock to check the time. "Okay, I'll have some toast."

Mom poured orange juice and milk for me while Dad handled the toast. As soon as it was set in front of me, I scarfed it all down, and they both laughed.

"What?"

"You act like you haven't eaten in a month." Dad shook his head and his tone changed. "If I didn't know better, I might have thought you were a glutton."

I nodded, realizing my mistake. "And gluttony is a sin."

Dad gave me an approving nod.

"Sorry. It's just that I don't want to be late. I'm the lead server today." I took my duties very seriously, more so than any of the other servers.

Dad winked at me. "Gotcha. Well, let's go then. You ready, Susan?"

Mom smiled and nodded.

We pulled into the church parking lot and I eagerly got out. On my way inside I remembered something. "Oh, before I forget, don't wait on me afterward. Father O'Brien asked me to help him clean up the sacristy after Mass. I think Sister Rita, the one who usually does it, has been sick. So I said I could help. I'm pretty sure he'll give me a ride home."

"Okay. We'll see you later then. Dinner is at five."

Not wanting to be late, I hightailed it to the room where the altar servers changed into their robes. While we were getting dressed, Father O'Brien stuck his head in. "Are you still planning to help afterward?"

Some of the other boys gave me curious looks, but I ignored them. "Yes, sir."

He nodded and left. A few minutes later, we went out to light all the candles before the start of Mass. During the service, I kept my posture straight as I listened to the introduction rites, the Liturgy of the Word, and said all the prayers during the Liturgy of the Eucharist, which I had memorized by heart. My mind drifted a bit as I tried to pinpoint when church had become more than a place my parents hustled me to every week. Every time I entered I felt God within my soul. I never shared this with anyone, except my parents, because I was already the odd man out at school. When you're fourteen, even in Catholic school, love for the church is fuel for bullying. My parents, along with Father O'Brien, were the only ones who knew how important my faith was to me.

As I stood at the altar waiting diligently for my part, I watched the other boys robotically go through the motions. They didn't get it like I did.

Even though it wouldn't be until next year that I would enter high school, I was pretty sure I wanted to become a priest. Leaving behind the elementary school here at Holy Cross was just one step closer to that goal. When I graduated from the eighth grade, I would move on to the Catholic high school clear across town. My parents had agreed to bring me to early Mass every morning before school because they understood how important it was to me. Church was my home and someday would be my life.

When Mass was over and my robes were hung in the altar server's room, I reentered the sanctuary. Inhaling, the lingering scent of incense flooded my nostrils, and I thought of how much I loved that smell. There were items on the altar that needed to be returned to the sacristy, so I gathered them and picked up the soiled linen that was used during Mass as well. When I walked into the sacristy, Father O'Brien was waiting for me.

"Is everyone gone, Canaan?"

It was a strange question, one I didn't think too much of at the time. Father O'Brien was someone I trusted.

"Yes, Father. The church is empty. I grabbed these on my way here." I nodded toward the items I held.

"Good. Put them down there." He pointed to the table where his vestments were usually laid out for him prior to Mass.

I did as I was told and turned to go collect the other things.

"Lock the door, Canaan."

"Sir?" I faced him, only to find his eyes were dark as though he were angry.

"I said, lock the door." The chill in his voice made me frown.

"But—"

"You heard me," he snapped, pointing at the door.

At first I thought he wanted it locked because maybe he had the money collected at Mass, and he didn't want anyone coming in.

"Yes, Father." So I went and locked the door. I turned around to find his hard stare. He loomed before me, tall in stature, much bigger than me. And for the first time in his presence, I felt uneasy.

"Come here, Canaan."

I did as he commanded. It was Father O'Brien, my pastor and priest, and to disobey him would've been a sin. Besides, I was always taught that priests were God's ministers who represented Christ and the Church. Why would I not listen to him?

That day he gave me my first lesson as to why I was a sinner.

I stood there with my head hung low. My hands clenched the table—the table I had once revered because it was where the Holy Chalices rested—and I feared my knuckles would burst through my skin. I stared at the floor, where red wine from the cruet had been knocked off the table and seeped into the rug like blood. As the stain grew larger and larger, it seemed symbolic somehow—

"Clean up, Canaan."

Father O'Brien's voice was the knife that flayed my soul. His approach was silent, and I only knew he was near when his breath fanned across my neck from above. Spikes of fear chilled my blood. Although his tone was low, I heard him clearly. If only I were taller, like my dad, maybe I could have overpowered him.

"Canaan, this is God's way, his path for you."

His meaning burned a trail of confusion mixed with hatred into my heart. Foul air locked in my lungs and I was unable to breathe without choking on the scent of my own filth.

When his hands landed on my back, terror would have emptied my bladder. Only that had already happened. I prayed to my God who hadn't come to my aid that I wouldn't have to endure more penance for my sins. Father taught me a lesson I never wanted to learn again. My skin crawled as his hand slid down my back closer to a place I couldn't bear to think about. I shuddered for what seemed the hundredth time.

"Now, clean up. We have work to do."

He couldn't be right. My teeth clenched together and I tasted dirt and rust. I spun around so fast Father O'Brien stepped back in surprise. I ignored the ache in my body and in my soul and found my spine instead.

"God would never do this to someone." Tears threatened to spill over and I forced back the sob in my throat.

He stepped forward, towering over me, and I flinched. He was no small man. Large and intimidating, he reared up over me with his arms extended. I shrunk into myself, fear freezing me in place. His hand landed on my shoulder much like my father's had that morning. However, Father O'Brien's touch sickened me.

"You will see this is the way to become closer to Him." His tone was hard and unyielding, much like he had been.

Him? God? I didn't want to believe it.

"Now clean up," he demanded before leaving the room.

His voice was like a whip across my skin. I wanted to hate him with all my guts, but I was afraid. Afraid that hate would consume me more than the fear that held me in place. Shame made an appearance too. It turned out to be the key that locked my mouth tight. And somewhere deep inside, a voice kept screaming at me to forgive. Forgive. FORGIVE. I grabbed my head in anguish because I wanted to scream out my pain. Then I looked at the wine stain on the floor. And much like the rug, I knew I would never be the same again—a prisoner of my own heart and soul.

Somehow I managed to put myself to rights before a soft knock came at the door. I still glanced around, knowing Father O'Brien wasn't there. So I went to the locked door and opened it. Standing there was a young girl I recognized as one of the many faces that attended school and Mass every Sunday. She rubbed at her arms as if she were cold.

"Excuse me? Do you know where Father O'Brien is?"

I turned my head in disgust as bile rushed up my throat. "No." My voice was bitter and cold, bordering on rude.

"Oh, okay," she stuttered.

Her soft footsteps retreated and I wondered if she saw the humiliation that was etched in my skin. Then another thought hit me. How could I possibly leave her to find him alone?

It took the strength that Samson possessed for me to

scramble after her.

"Hey," I called after her.

She stopped dead and turned to face me with skin so pale she looked like she'd seen a ghost.

"You shouldn't be here." Somehow I managed to get my voice to boom out and not squeak from the terror that still coursed through me.

"But I—"

"Father O'Brien is a busy man. He doesn't have time to see you today."

My gruff words stole what little light there was from her eyes and I watched her face fall. The awful feeling in my gut forced my eyes closed for a second as I willed back the anger I shouldn't have directed at her. I tried again and managed not to sound like the wretch I was. "Can I help you with anything?"

She hugged herself tighter and started rubbing her arms again.

"No, thanks."

Her soft words were choked off at the end. She tore out of the church and headed toward the rectory, leaving me unable to apologize for my rudeness.

"Canaan, who was that?"

The bile I'd held back threatened to rise again.

"No one," I said, wanting to run out the same doors she had.

"Are you ready to go home?" he asked, his hand landing on my back.

I jerked from his touch but nodded anyway. Quickly, I led the way out of the sanctuary I'd once thought of as my home. Only now it felt cold and forbidding, a place where I didn't want to be.

Two

HAVEN

Putting as much distance between that boy and me was my goal. Father O'Brien had been my final hope—the last person who I thought could help me, but it was plain I wasn't worthy of him. I was a nobody, like my uncle kept telling me. Not only that, my heart had been shattered by Canaan, the boy whom I had secretly crushed on.

I needed to hustle home, to that place where the devil himself lived. I snuck out and hadn't told Aunt Kathy where I was going. If Uncle Kent caught me, I would pay for sure. After the other night, I was positive he would kill me if he discovered I wasn't there. Pain seared the backs of my thighs each time my feet hit the ground, but I prodded on. My dress rubbed against the welts and open wounds on my shoulder blades, but that didn't slow me down. If anything, it urged me forward. The house was only four blocks from the church. I bit back the sting of that boy's words—I had counted on Father O'Brien's help. Without it, my situation was doomed. Because if he wouldn't help me, who at the church would or could?

When I rounded the corner, any spark of optimism I held

was immediately extinguished when I saw Uncle Kent's police car in the driveway. He must've popped in for lunch, something he rarely did. Maybe I could sneak in through the back door and he'd never know. As soon as I made it to the driveway, I heard him yelling at my aunt.

"Where is she?"

"I don't know, Kent. I thought she was in her room."

"Goddammit, you can't even do one thing right, can you?"

My aunt cried out. He probably hit her. We were both used as his punching bags. I hurried around the back and slowly opened the door. I'd learned the trick of how to do that so it wouldn't squeak. As I was closing it, I thought I was in the clear until his voice boomed across the kitchen.

"Where the hell have you been? Are you sneaking around seeing boys already?"

His question caught me off guard. Boys? What boys? He never let me do anything, other than go to school. It was dumb of him to think otherwise.

The only boy I thought wasn't gross was the boy who'd sent me back to this hellhole. And he was older than me. No way he thought my twelve-year-old self was even alive. I'd seen it in his blank expression not ten minutes ago. And our Catholic school was pretty small and strict. There wasn't much time to be chasing around boys anyway.

"Answer me when I ask you a question, goddammit!"

Crap! I need to pay attention to him when he speaks. "No, sir. I haven't been sneaking around seeing boys." My voice shook as I answered.

"Then where were you?"

"Church."

His beady eyes darkened and nailed me to the floor. "Church? You expect me to believe that?"

"Y-yes, sir," I stuttered.

His lips clamped together and that muscle in his jaw

twitched. I knew I was in for it. "Why'd you go to church? You went last night with your aunt."

A trapdoor opened in my gut as I recoiled in dread. He believed I was lying, and I had no answer. I didn't know what made me do it, but I turned and tried to run out the door. I never made it two steps. He snatched a handful of my hair and yanked me backward. I flew right into the brick wall of his chest. My uncle was huge compared to me and I was no match for what was about to happen.

To my horror, he opened the basement door and practically threw me down the steps. My hand grabbed the railing, saving me. Still, I landed in a heap at the bottom. Wincing, I collected myself and struggled to my feet. He'd never done this before, but my instincts told me it was going to be bad.

"When you came to live here, I told you never to lie to me. You're a slow learner, Haven. Maybe this time, you won't be so quick to forget that rule of mine."

I didn't bother to plead or beg. It wouldn't help and sometimes made it worse. He unbuckled his belt and watched me as he took his sweet time taking it off. That was what he wanted. He hated me so much that he loved to see my fear. His eyes glowed with the anticipation of it. And then he smiled when he knew he held me in the grips of terror.

"What are you waiting for?" he asked snidely.

Air moved in and out of me so fast, my vision became spotty. I was still sore from his beating last night and hadn't had time to heal. This one would surely put me in the hospital.

"Please, Uncle Kent," the words slipped out, though I hadn't meant for them to.

His crooked teeth gleamed in the dim light of the dank basement. "You trying to piss me off even more, Haven?" he taunted. "Get that dress off, or I'll yank it off of you."

I had precious few things to wear as it was, so I couldn't

afford for it to be ruined if he tore it. It was one of the only nice ones I had. I reached behind me, wincing, to unzip it.

"Hurry it up. I haven't got all damn day," he sneered.

His tone had changed and I understood what that meant. I made quick work of undressing. I stood in my undergarments, rigid as a rock. I crossed my arms over my chest, trying to keep from shivering in the cool basement. In that moment, I hated him with every teeny bit of me. If I had the means, I would've killed him, right there.

My throat was so dry; I tried to swallow but couldn't. I went to lick my lips, but all my spit was gone.

"Turn around."

When I did, stupidly I tried to make another break for it. I never gave it a thought. My feet just took off. I heard a growl, followed by a bellow. Then I found myself pushed to the floor. No time to watch the stars dancing in front of my eyes with the cold floor embracing me. Blows rained down, tearing into my flesh. At first I screamed, but my throat became so raw that after a while, they were nothing but hoarse whimpers. I retreated into that place where nothing could touch me...that place where numbness ruled. A land where Mom waited for me and soothed me in her warm embrace.

"Kent, stop. Please stop," my aunt begged. She'd come to save me. "She won't be able to go to school if you continue."

His blows slowed but didn't subside.

"Come on, honey. Come upstairs with me. Leave the girl alone and let's spend some time together. You look tired, and I know how to relax you."

Aunt Kathy's voice lulled me out of my safe space.

"Oh yeah? And what do you have in mind?" he asked.

"Whatever you want."

I heard them mumbling, but all I cared about was he'd stopped. When their footsteps carried them upstairs, I knew what they were going to do. It was the only thing Aunt Kathy had in her arsenal. They were going to have sex.

When I'd explained to Macie about the noises that came from their room at night, she told me what they were doing. And that was the only time my uncle was truly nice to my aunt, when she promised to go to their room with him.

God, why did you take Mom from me and send me to Hell? What did I ever do to deserve this? Was it because I had a crush on that boy? Well, you don't have to worry. I hate him as much as my uncle. I never want to marry, ever.

The shouts in my head were louder than my beating heart. I shivered on the damp floor, longing to move but couldn't. When I tried, pain surged like an eruption of a volcano. My neck, shoulder blades, all the way to the backs of my thighs felt like lava coursing through my body.

The buckle must have dug into me good this time. Why had I thought Father O'Brien was the answer? The only things I'd gotten from my trouble were welts and more bruises I would have to hide.

Tears dripped from my cheeks onto the floor. It was sad when you were so weak you didn't have the strength to sob for the movement would prove worse than the release of emotion.

It wasn't what I expected my life would be when I moved in with my aunt and uncle after finding out Mom had died. I'd cried plenty that day. She'd been the best mom in the world. So sweet and pretty; I could remember brushing her long, blond hair.

I wished I could erase the day I came home and saw Uncle Kent's car in the driveway. If I'd known then what I knew now, I would've kept walking right on past the house. I could've slept in the woods, like those fairies you read about in books. Anything would've been better than this.

That day he declared he was the new sheriff in my life. And he'd been right. The horrid man controlled everything from what I wore to who I hung out with. My life under his rule became a literal prison. Only his continuous punishment would eventually shatter me into nothing. And who could I tell? The only living relative I had was my aunt, and she already knew.

Sometime later, I gathered myself together and pushed up from the floor. A wave of dizziness rose with the pain. If I didn't get in the shower to rinse the blood off soon, it would dry and then I'd have a mess. It took most of what strength I had, but I made it to the small bathroom, partly on my hands and knees. The shower was as bad as the beating with the water singeing my raw and open wounds. I shivered under the cool water. It hadn't taken me long to learn that cold was better than hot after one of my uncle's sessions. The air dried my back and thighs, saving me from rubbing the damp towel over the welts and open sores. I found the mirror and braved a peek at the damage. When I saw what my back looked like, I buried my face in a towel. There were so many places that scars covered me now I would never be normal again. From my shoulders to my waist I looked like latticework.

The knock startled me. "Haven, are you okay?" It was Aunt Kathy.

"Yes," I choked out.

"He's gone. Let me put some salve on for you and get some ice on that."

I opened the door so she could come in. When I spun around and allowed her to see, she gasped. "Oh, God, sweetie. I'm so sorry."

"Did you call him?"

"What?"

"Did you call him to tell him I left?"

"No! I would never do anything like that. I had no idea you were gone. He came home for lunch," she said. "I wasn't expecting him."

I had to believe her. She was the only tie to my mom, and why would she lie? She was going through some of the same things I was.

I hissed as her fingers applied the salve. "I hate him, and I don't know why he does this," I said.

"I'm sorry. He's just like that." She finished working on my back. "All done, honey. Don't forget to take some ibuprofen."

"He's not just like that. He's cruel. And how am I supposed to go to school tomorrow acting like I'm fine?" I didn't wait for an answer because I knew she had none.

"I wish I could be more helpful to you." She hung her head. I hated it, but she got her due from him like I did. What I couldn't understand was why didn't she leave and take me with her?

"I can't wait until I'm old enough to leave. When I turn eighteen, I'm gone from this place." But that was six years, six awful years, from now. And if he were to keep it up at this rate, there'd be a good chance I wouldn't make it that long.

Three

CANAAN

Present Day

The paper rattled in my trembling hand. After reading the letter for the third time, the words still hadn't changed. I wanted to believe that somewhere in there was a greater plan, which at first seemed like a bad joke. My initial thought was to ask the bishop, the head of the diocese, who had sent it, if he was intentionally trying to be cruel. But he would have no idea my reasoning for not wanting that assignment.

It couldn't be happening. As much as I wanted a parish of my own, going back had never even been a consideration. I stood there as a dark part of me, the one I kept hidden in the furthest reaches of my soul, threatened to escape. The edges of the letter crumpled in my balled hands. Images I kept locked in the recesses of my mind burst through my impenetrable walls and flooded my thoughts like a tidal wave, chilling me to the depths of my bones.

Closing my eyes and opening them again hadn't changed the first words of the letter.

It is with deepest sorrow that I write this to inform you of the sudden passing of Father Thomas O'Brien. My breath hitched. *You have been selected as Associate Pastor at the Holy Cross Catholic Church*. What should have been joyful news made my skin crawl with what felt like a thousand biting ants. I rubbed the back of my neck, a motion I hadn't found necessary in years.

Even in death, the mere mention of the man's name sent me into a tailspin. Holy Cross was a place I vowed never to return to and hadn't. I'd made excuses not to come home, forcing my parents to visit me when they felt the need.

If not for my love and dedication to God, and knowing that everyone in the church hadn't punished me for my sins, I might not have continued my pursuit of the priesthood. But I needed absolution and what better way than giving my life over to the Lord and somehow making a positive difference in the life of others.

I scrubbed a hand over my face. What was I supposed to do? One didn't refuse the bishop's orders, especially one so young as I. To gain an associate pastorate at the age of twenty-eight was relatively substantial, at least with the Congregation of Holy Cross. I would have a lot of explaining to do if I tried to get out of the appointment.

"Canaan, you okay? You look like you've seen a ghost," my mentor, Father Tony, asked.

I glanced up and dropped my hands to my sides and tried to find calm I didn't feel.

"I'm good, thanks."

Reading me well as always, he asked, "What do you have there that's rattled you so?"

I tried to laugh, but it came off more as if something were caught in my throat. "My orders."

"Really?" His eyes sparkled as they should. It should have been a joyous occasion.

I nodded and handed the letter to him, unable to share the news in words, lest he figure me out.

His eyes flew across the page with a frown then a blossoming grin.

"Sad news about the father. May his soul rest in peace."

May his soul rot in Hell.

"It's not the best way to get an assignment, but you'll do fine."

He patted my back to congratulate me. *Act happy, Canaan.* I pasted an acrylic smile on my face as he rambled on about how great this was. All the time he talked, I could feel the snake twisting inside of my guts. If only he knew the truth.

"Why so glum? This is your home parish. Were you close to this Father O'Brien?"

Acid burned my throat, forcing me to clear it.

"He was there, yes."

He studied me and I knew I'd blown it. He would see the stain that would forever mar my soul no matter how much penance I paid for my sins.

"You know you can talk to me about anything."

When his hand lightly touched my arm, I nearly jumped out of my skin. To cover up my reaction, jumbled words left my mouth in haste.

"It's going to be strange going back there, to my hometown. I'm a little more than nervous to face family and friends as not the boy, but the priest."

"Canaan, you'll do well there. You're a great counselor, and your heart is in exactly the right place. Of all the seminarians that have passed through here, you have been the ideal everything. I'm going to selfishly miss you."

The sad, forced smile shouldn't have convinced him of anything.

"I'll only be a little over an hour away. I'll come back to visit or you can come visit me."

"True," Father Tony said as he patted my shoulder, "but I have a feeling you're going to be so busy, you won't have time for us back here."

"Never. This is my home," I objected.

He grinned. "Not anymore. Since this is a death, you're needed now. You'd better start packing."

"It's a good thing I don't own much."

We both laughed.

"Canaan, one thing is true—your parents are going to be very excited about this news."

"That they will. I better give them a call. And Tony—thanks for everything these past few years. You've been the best mentor I could've asked for."

"It's been my pleasure."

We hugged for a few seconds, and I watched him walk away until he disappeared around the corner.

I reached for the wall to hold myself up. I couldn't imagine the fate I was facing. Going back there would be like facing Hell. But it looked as though I had no choice.

Pulling my phone out of my pocket, I called Mom and Dad. They were shocked. None of us thought I'd end up back home. My mom kept giggling like a schoolgirl, while Dad talked about all the father/son things we could do.

"Dad, that sounds great, but keep in mind, I'll have a lot of parish obligations too."

"Oh, right, son. Someday you'll take over the parish and be like Father O'Brien was. He'd just asked about you recently."

My blood froze. I barely formed the coherent question not much louder than a whisper.

"What did he want?"

"The usual. He's been asking about you off and on over the years. Wondering how you were faring and if you planned to come back home. He was very fond of you."

When I didn't respond fast enough for fear I would gag on

any words I tried to say, Dad called out my name.

"I'm—I'm here. Do you know what happened to him?"

"You know, that's the strange thing. He took a bad fall. He was healthy as could be, but they say he could have had a heart attack. The man took great care of himself, so it's hard to believe."

There was something disquieting about Dad's thoughts regarding Father O'Brien's death. Perhaps there was something more to the story. Had my dreams of the pits of Hell opening up and swallowing the man whole come true? And if so, how much penance would I have to do to cleanse myself of the stain of relief from my belief that the world would be a better place without him?

"Sometimes those things just happen," I said to fill the silence. "I hate to cut this short, but I need to get my packing started."

"Okay, Son. Do you need us to come and help?"

"No, I've got this. I don't own very much."

"Right. But will it all fit in your car?"

"Dad, I'll be living in the rectory, so I don't need furniture. Remember?"

"That's right. You let us know if you need us."

"I will, and thanks, Dad. I love you both."

"Same here."

By the time I made it to my quarters, which really only consisted of a bedroom and bathroom, my thoughts had drifted back to my days as an altar server at Holy Cross. Father O'Brien haunted my dreams for years, and I hoped I could be free from those nightmares that were my reality. Only I wasn't. Immediately, I fell to my knees to beg for God's forgiveness in being relieved over the demise of the man.

A few days later, I drove from what had been my home at the Moreau Seminary, located at the University of Notre Dame. That was where I had been educated, ordained into the priesthood, and then served in different capacities on staff. It was going to be a huge transition for me, one I doubted I was prepared for. My soul had been permanently cracked and scarred by the things that had transpired in the bowels of the church. I wasn't sure what my reaction would be when I entered the place. The day I left, I secretly vowed never to return. Was there another lesson I would be forced to endure upon my return? Or perhaps not a lesson but a test? Whichever the case, I would discover it soon enough.

It didn't take long to drive from South Bend, Indiana, to Bloomville, Illinois, a suburb of Chicago. The new pastor, Father William Cernak, would be there when I arrived. He'd known my parents since he had been the associate pastor to Father O'Brien. I didn't know him, but Mom and Dad had nothing but good things to say about him. I wondered if he had any idea about Father O'Brien's sacrilegious use of the sacristy and his depraved methods of punishment. Probably not. Father O'Brien would've been too smart to let that slip out of the bag.

On the way, I stopped by my parents' for dinner having not seen them in some time. Mom made my favorites and Dad was happy to have someone to talk about sports and politics to.

"I can't believe this day has come," Mom said. "For a while there I thought maybe you would have chosen a different profession."

"And that would have been okay," Dad added.

Although I knew they were very proud of my choice.

Mom's smile warmed me where cold had seeped into my bones from the topic of conversation. "I was so worried about you. You pulled back from wanting to attend Mass. Thank heaven for Father Rose. When he started Saturday evening service, you seemed brightened by the prospect. It's a shame he had to leave to take care of family. He was young and I thought he really helped you reconnect with God."

Father Rose had been a godly man. But I was more grateful not to serve as altar boy when Father O'Brien gave the service.

I'd almost lost faith, but had come to accept who I was and trusted God's plan for me.

I didn't stay long, much to Mom's disappointment. I said my goodbyes and drove to the rectory to meet Father Cernak.

When he ushered me inside with a friendly and easygoing manner that I liked, I knew instantly we would get along great. We sat and talked about what my goals were, which, to his surprise and my own, I told him truthfully that I'd been prepared to stay on staff at the seminary.

"I'll be honest. I had no idea this was coming. I was happy where I was, so this took me by surprise," I said.

He smiled gently. "God often works in mysterious ways, Canaan. There's a good reason He brought you back here. I'm sure it will be revealed to you soon enough."

My guts twisted at the thought. The idea of counseling people I knew and the potential things I might learn chilled me. I questioned whether I would be capable of that. Worse, I both dreaded and feared my first visit to the sacristy. What should be a revered room was a place of horrors for me.

"I'm sure you want to get settled. Let's get your things."

The robust man was probably in his forties and moved with speed. It only took two trips to get all my things inside and deposited into my new room. It was decent—a small bedroom with an attached bathroom, much like my rooms at Notre Dame. I unpacked and put all my things away, which took no time at all. When I finished, I joined Father in the den.

"Father Cernak, the nice thing about not owning a lot is it makes moving easy."

We both chuckled.

"So, Canaan, I think first off, we ought to be on a first name basis, if that's good with you."

"Absolutely."

"Good. Call me Bill, then."

"Bill it is."

"Tomorrow is Saturday, and I thought it might be best if you celebrated our five-thirty evening Mass. Does that work for you? It's well-attended and it's casual. You're young, and I think you'll be a hit with the youth. They're the ones who frequently attend that service."

"Sounds good. I guess I need to work on my homily then."

"I was going to suggest just that. You can introduce yourself instead of focusing on the message from the gospel. It will make it easy on you, and it will satisfy the curiosity of the parishioners. And the Saturday attendees expect an abbreviated homily anyway. Now, Sunday, I was thinking you could do the early service and do the same thing. Is that okay?"

"Yeah. It sounds good."

"On Sunday, I'll do the nine thirty and eleven thirty. Then next week, we'll move it around to give you a bit of exposure. Of course, you'll be present at all."

"Sounds good."

Bill nodded, then added, "Great. Then why don't I show you the office here so you can get acquainted with things? Tomorrow morning I'll give you the grand tour of the church. Of course, I'm sure not much has changed since you left."

"Sounds good." Why did I keep repeating the same phrase? *Pull it together.*

"One other thing."

I glanced back at him. "What's that?"

"Father O'Brien." I froze, unsure of where the conversation was leading. "The police have been around asking questions."

When he didn't go on further, I prodded him. "About what?"

"About his death. He fell backward and landed right on his head on the concrete, fracturing his skull. Even though he had a heart attack, they have to investigate if the heart attack came before or after the fall. They believe that it's probably the former. They tell me it's all as a matter of course for these things. I don't think they will be back, but I thought it best to warn you."

Four

HAVEN

Present Day

He was moving fast, which I liked. His hand burned a trail down my back before he worked the zipper on my skirt.

"God, Haddy, you're so hot."

"Haven," I said, correcting him.

"Yeah, whatever," he said, fumbling with my zipper.

"Don't talk, okay?" He was totally blowing this for me. I needed to get off and had made my choice for the night. I hoped I hadn't picked wrong.

"God, your body is amazing."

Whack. He slapped hard against my ass.

The slap wasn't actually that painful, but it rattled me. "Don't hit me. I'm not into that."

Whack. "It's a love tap, and your ass is off the charts."

That was it. I shoved him away from me and started buttoning my blouse.

"What the hell, baby?"

"Don't 'baby' me. I told you I'm not into hitting."

I turned back, and his hands were palm up toward me with his pants around his ankles and his condom-covered cock pointing at me in accusation.

"Okay, fine, fine. Don't go."

His slightly smaller than average dick wasn't worth my time.

"Too late for second chances," I said after zipping my skirt back up. With my clutch in my hand, I was out the door. I was up for a lot of things, but *love taps* weren't one of them.

The whole *love tapping* thing had unnerved me more than I cared to admit. I dropped my clutch twice before I was able to get in the elevator. During the ride down, I felt the burn in the back of my eyes. Shit. Where was that coming from? I rarely cried, yet tears dripped off my cheeks. I exited the building and quickly hailed a cab. Thankfully, the ride home was short and I grappled with the keys to unlock my door. It took me several stabs before I hit the damn slot and once I stumbled inside, I hunted for my phone and dialed Macie's number.

Her sleep-heavy voice indicated I'd woken her up. "Yeah? What's wrong?"

She knew me too well and had since our younger days at Holy Cross Catholic School. It was one thirty in the morning. I would never call her if something wasn't wrong.

"I just had a really bad one."

"A bad one what?"

I wanted to tell her all about the memory that threatened to bowl me over, but instead I heard myself saying, "A date."

"Jesus. What happened?"

So I told her about the dude who slapped my ass.

She chuckled. "Okay, this is not funny in the least, but you left him standing with his dick ready to go." She giggled some more, then sobered. "Do you think it wasn't so much the slap, but the memories it triggered that had you heading for the hills?"

She knew me better than I was willing to admit to myself. But I couldn't find words to answer her.

"I'm going to ask you this one more time. Are you sure you want to come back to Chicago?"

I let my head fall back on the sofa.

"I don't know if the possibility of going back to Chicago was the trigger."

She was quiet. Too quiet.

"Macie, you there?"

"Thinking."

I sighed, needing her to talk me down from the ledge. "Well, can you think verbally?"

"So, you know how I feel about your random hookups."

"Damn, you make it sound like I'm on the prowl every night. It's like every blue moon when I get an itch."

"But can't you find a steady guy to scratch you?"

"Now that just sounds gross. Besides, I don't think I'll ever trust anyone enough to claim him. It's all because of fuckface. He's the reason I refuse to put my trust in anyone."

"You trust me?"

I wasn't sure that was a statement or a question. "Of course I do. You've been in the trenches with me. And you've never betrayed my trust."

"And maybe there's a guy like me out there."

"Then you can have him. I like keeping things simple."

"And what's that? Casual hookups so you can avoid something serious?"

"Exactly," I agreed.

She sighed and I knew she'd given up the relationship talk with me for tonight. "Fine, but back to the initial problem. Has anyone ever slapped you before during sex?"

"Yeah, and I don't like it. At all. And I've dealt with it."

"And?" she prodded.

"And what?"

"Any memories, flashbacks, anything ding-a-ling?"

I took a minute and thought about it. "No. Not that I recall."

"Then it's definitely Chicago. So, back to my other question. Are you sure about this? This could totally fuck with your head."

It could, but this was a golden opportunity that didn't come around often.

"Yeah, I know. But if I don't take the risk and do this, I could totally screw my career over."

"I know this may sound harsh, but is your career worth your sanity?"

I groaned. I'd worked so hard ever since I left Chicago to escape my uncle. My art was what kept me focused—that and my mom's memory. I did it for her too. I knew she would've wanted me to follow my dream, and art was my dream.

"Yeah. It is," I admitted.

"Then you have your answer. And I'm here with open arms and a sturdy shoulder if you need it. You are going to stay with me, right?"

"If you can stand me."

"Do you even have to ask that?"

"Yes."

But she ignored my moment of self-doubt and moved on. "So give me the details."

"Macie, it's almost two in the morning."

"Hey, you're the one who woke me up."

And she was right. A small laugh escaped from my now happier face. I was thankful for her. She had a way of doing that for me. She was my shining light who managed to pull me through all the hell I was forced to endure. Without Macie and her mother, I was damn sure I would've never survived with a shred of sanity left. She helped me play the game with Uncle Kent so I wouldn't get as many beatings. She taught me to keep my mouth shut when I would've sassed back. Macie taught me to be a thinker. And it paid off in the end. The abuse, though bad, wasn't as frequent as it could have been. And even though Macie's mom had no idea of what I was going through, she knew things weren't good at home, just not why. I swore Macie to secrecy because I knew it would only cause more problems if her mom tried to intervene.

In retrospect, I wasn't sure there was anything I could have done differently. Uncle Kent was still on the police force and did a lot in the community. Aunt Kathy sent me tidbits over the last few years of all the accolades he'd been awarded for stellar service. If I'd accused him, he probably would have had a lot of his friends to help him out. I could've been sent somewhere else where it would've been just as bad or worse.

"So? I know your show runs for six months, and I know when you're coming, but are you going to give me the scoop about how you got hooked up with this deal? You've been super tight-lipped about it." Macie's voice pulled me back again.

"Sorry. I was just thinking about how lucky I am to have you."

"Aww. I love you too, Have. But like you said, it is early in the morning, so talk."

"Fine." I laughed but got right to the story. "Well, a friend of mine was selling her jewelry in Central Park, and she asked me if she could take a few pieces of mine to spruce up her little booth. So I said yeah and while she was there, this rich guy approached her and asked about them, then gave her his card and said he was an art broker."

"Seriously?"

"Yep. Turns out he's this broker named Jonathon Houston, who's a pretty big deal in the art world. So I called him and he told me about this gig he's setting up in Chicago. I have to do this, Mace. It's all about the new breed of artist breaking out. I met with him and showed him my work. He was, or acted like he was, totally into it. He says I'm that blend of impressionist and eclectic. Whatever the hell that means. I just paint what I want to paint." I didn't have a degree in art but worked with whatever talent I was born with. "I don't have a particular style and I told him that. But he said that I didn't see what he did. So I'm coming. I have to see where this can take me. It could be my big break. Plus, he's giving me an advance because he thinks my work is going to really sell. Like big time. And I can use the money."

"Why didn't you tell me all this earlier?"

"I don't know. I guess it still hasn't really sunk in."

"Jeez, this could totally be your ticket. But you love New York. This would mean leaving it all behind."

"It's just temporary right now. The show runs for six months. And then it's back to reality and New York. Who knows if this is the catalyst for my career and I won't have to be that proverbial starving artist. Besides, I could work anywhere if I chose to stay in Chicago longer, and travel back and forth when necessary."

"Oh my God, this is so fucking cool. Okay, I am so on board with you coming back here. I have to admit I was going to try and talk you out of it, but after hearing this, you're right. This could bust your career wide ass open. Your room is ready for you. And you haven't mentioned, is this Jonathon hot?"

I laughed. "He's okay. Not really my type. He's all starched shirts and suits. I'd never fit in his world. Besides, he had a ring on his finger. Anyway, it'll be a couple more weeks before I come. I have to close up shop here since I'll be gone for six months and that's a long time. You haven't had a roommate for quite a while. You're sure about this?"

"Totally sure. I have everything. All you need are your clothes and stuff."

"Thanks, Macie, you really are the best friend anyone could

ask for. I wouldn't be here today without you."

"Hey, remember our pact? We've got each other's backs, right?"

"I'd fist bump you if I could." I could see her putting her fist in the air.

"After all this great news, I think it's safe to say I'm going to sleep well and not worry about you now. You almost gave me a heart attack earlier."

"I almost gave *me* a heart attack earlier. Thanks for talking me off the ledge, again."

"It's what I do best."

"Good night. I'll call you tomorrow." As I curled up around my pillow, I thanked God for her again. I closed my eyes and hoped sleep claimed me for the few hours that it normally did. Only I woke up covered in sweat. The fear that consumed my unconscious mind pulled me out of bed and into my spare room where I worked out all the hurt and pain of the past on a blank canvas. Art was still and always had been my escape, my therapy. If not for it, I was pretty damn sure my mind would've cracked by now. Well, art and Macie.

Five

CANAAN

A fine sheen of moisture covered my skin as I jackknifed up in bed. The dream resurfaced from time to time. I shouldn't have been surprised by its reappearance. His voice rang in my ear, as it had been then, only now it was a whisper. I blinked away the memories and prayed that I hadn't called out and awakened Bill. He would only ask questions I had no answers for.

The dawning day meant I would be forced to face my demons in that room of Hell. I searched for the instrument I needed to pay my toll of penance. I found the stretch of leather that was worn with age and teeth marks. I stared at it with despair, remembering. Then I removed my robe before I whipped my arm over my shoulder and let the sharp sting take me away. One day, the sinner inside me would be purged, or so I prayed. One day, I would be cleansed and worthy of God's love.

Much later and after showering, I found my way to the kitchen for a small breakfast. Stomaching any more wasn't possible if I were to face that room.

"Good morning, Canaan. I hope you slept well in your new room." Bill's cheery greeting reminded me to turn my frown into a smile.

Hoping my fudging the truth some sounded sincere, I said, "I did, thank you. And good morning to you."

"Excellent. I see you've already eaten. So how about we take our tour of the church then?"

"Sounds like a plan," I said, my guts clenching in protest. I swallowed back the miniscule breakfast that tried to bully its way back up my esophagus. My sweaty palms felt like they oozed moisture so I rubbed them on my pants, hoping they didn't leave dark streaks behind.

Following Bill's long strides, we left the rectory and followed the walkway that circled the parking lot, then entered the church through the side door. It was early, only six a.m. There would be an eight o'clock mass that morning Bill would conduct, but currently the church was dark and empty. He flicked on some lights, casting the altar in a heavenly glow.

"Look the same as you remember?" His voice came from my left. I looked at the scene, remembering how I served here all those years ago.

"It does. I always thought the wood carvings in the front were something else. Even as a kid I used to stare at them."

"The altar you mean?"

"Yeah." It was hand-carved and made out of oak, or so I'd been told many years ago by one of the nuns.

"I think it came from Italy," Bill said.

"I think so, too. We're lucky to have it here."

"Yes, we are. So, the tabernacle is the same, I'm sure."

I walked up the steps and moved behind the altar, opening the doors of the tabernacle, the small enclosure that held the chalices of hosts and wine. Of course now it was empty.

"It is." I smiled. "As is everything else, it appears."

"Good. All the books, missals, and so on, are too. So you should be fine. Just like an adult altar boy."

Like a fist to the diaphragm, all the air expelled from my body, and I felt punctured in the worst way. What should've been a glorious moment was instantly sullied and turned to something dirty and shameful. I quickly turned away to hide my face. There wasn't a way to cover up my emotions, so the only thing to do was hide myself.

"Ready to move on?" Bill asked, unaware of my turmoil.

"Uh huh."

He led the way to the room where the altar servers changed. It was nothing more than an area where a series of multi-sized long red and black cassocks and white surplices hung. There were also hooded albs with several colors of cinctures, which could be coordinated with the colors of the priest's vestments.

"I remember wearing these," I said.

"I remember wearing similar ones in the parish I grew up in," Bill added. "We ask the servers to arrive thirty minutes early and we have a lead server. Is that how it was when you served?"

I nodded.

"Good. Then shall we continue? By the way, you were educated here, too, weren't you?"

"I was."

The school was connected to the church. The server's room had a dual exit. One went to the school, and the other to the church. It was designed for the students so after mass on school mornings, they could scoot right into the school.

"I bet you have some stories."

"Not me. I was the good kid, the one who wanted to be the priest, the nerdy one."

Bill stopped and looked at me. "So you knew that young, huh?"

"Yeah. And you?"

"Not until college, actually. I saw everyone around me going to parties and chasing girls, and I wanted to connect with Jesus. I became the nerdy guy then."

"We all find our way, I guess."

"On to the sacristy."

His words chilled me. I rubbed my arms as if that would somehow help, left with no choice other than to follow him. My eyes stayed trained on the grain of the wooden planks on the floor, reminding me of the marks I had embedded into my own back as my discipline. I clenched my fists so hard that even my short nails made their way into the flesh of my palms. When the dark wooden door loomed before us, I shuddered, praying Bill didn't notice. Thankfully, I stood behind him. He unlocked the door and walked through as though he didn't have a care in the world. And why should he? The room wasn't Hell for everyone. It was mine and mine alone.

Bill's voice faded as my eidetic memory brought forth image after image of Father O'Brien. Even with my eyes open, a playback of what had happened in there continued in my head. Searing pain, not just physical but psychological, gripped me, forcing my feet back toward the door. Tremors racked my body, and I knew I needed to get control of myself, or Bill would soon discover my secret. I slumped against the wall I'd backed into and mopped my brow with the back of my arm. Bill turned when he heard the sound.

"Canaan, are you all right?"

A lie buried in truth erupted from my mouth. "My stomach."

"What is it?"

"I'm not feeling well. I need the bathroom." I clamped a hand over my mouth as breakfast made its way to the back of my throat. His arm shot out in the direction I already knew in which to go.

Slamming the door behind me, I made it to the counter and gripped the edges to stop myself from collapsing. I hung my head over the sink half bent over. The past I thought I could bury forced its way front and center.

My knuckles tightened around the edge as the memory of the stench of his skin punched into me along with his grunts as he held me prisoner. Instead of the basin, I saw the wine stain that had become my only focus, my pinpoint of sanity during that first time.

I panted as I did my best to wash the pictures out of my head. As I stared, drops of my own sweat trickled down the drain. Hauling in air through my nose, control slowly came back to me.

Bill's voice came through the door. "Canaan, are you okay in there?"

Clearing my throat to make way for some air, I said, "Getting there."

"Do you need to go rest?"

"Maybe. Give me a few more minutes." I flushed the toilet for effect. Then I flushed it again.

Running the cold water, I splashed my face until it felt chilled, and I was finally able to breathe easier. The question would be whether that debacle would recur once I left the safety of the bathroom. I had no choice but to see.

When I walked out, I felt guilty for the concern that was imprinted in Bill's face. "Son, are you feeling better? You gave me a bit of a scare."

"I'm not sure, to be honest." I allowed myself to gaze around the room. When no further video replay threatened to undermine my ability to carry on a normal conversation, I said, "I think I'll be okay."

"Are you sure? We can do this later."

"No, let's go on."

He looked skeptical, but nodded. "This is where we keep all

the vestments. Someone, either Sister Grace or one of the women from the Altar Guild, will have your vestments laid out for you before mass. It was something Father O'Brien always insisted upon. Since the Guild has taken it up as one of their duties, I think we should continue. Are you good with this?"

"Yes, that's fine. As long as they don't mind doing it."

"They've indicated to me they enjoy it. I think it makes them feel a bit more needed around here."

I glanced at the table upon which the vestments would be set out and my guts twisted. *The table.* It was his favorite place of administering penance. I couldn't prevent the shudder that ripped through me.

Bill saw it. "Still okay there?"

"I guess I'm not as good as I thought." I wiped a layer of sweat off my forehead. I hoped it got easier being in here because if it didn't, my life would be its own Hell on Earth.

"We're almost finished, and then I think you may need to go rest." He showed me the closet where all the chalices, cruets, communion wafers, and everything else needed for Mass were stored. And then finally, he showed me the padded kneeler where I could pray before or after Mass, if I wanted. With a jolt, another memory crashed into me. That kneeler was used for many things by Father O'Brien, none of them being prayer. I didn't want Bill to see me make a fool out of myself, so I made a flimsy excuse and bolted out the door.

Only when I opened it, a woman with haunted faint blue eyes stood on the other side. I was shocked considering the early hour. So we stared at each other for a moment.

"Can you help me?"

Her words triggered a faint memory. But it fled as fast as it came, leaving behind the ever-present need to run.

I shook my head. "I'm sorry," I said, rushing off.

When I got to my bathroom in my quarters, the meager breakfast I'd eaten earlier finally succeeded in making its reappearance. My declaration of not feeling well came to life. I was sick. Truly sick. I only hoped and prayed that I could turn things around and become the associate pastor Bill believed I could be. Right then, I wasn't so sure I had it in me.

Six

HAVEN

It was weird being back. The skyline was different, but the city itself was so much like New York—busy and never truly asleep. But being so close to home haunted me. After a few days of settling in, Macie talked me into calling my aunt. Macie's mom told her that she'd run into my aunt and she hadn't been feeling well.

As much as I hated my uncle, my feelings for my aunt were different. She hadn't set out to make my life miserable and had tried when she could to make my pitiful existence better. Weak and frightened were the best ways I could describe her through my adult eyes. And who was I to judge her because she couldn't stand up to her husband? She had been his punching bag as often as me and had intervened during many of the times he beat me. I would learn later that she used sex to calm him or entice him away from me. If not for that, I wasn't sure how I would've survived. In retrospect, she most likely put herself at great risk doing what she did, only I was a kid and didn't understand that at the time. Since I'd moved, I had traded a few holiday text messages over the years, but if

Kent hadn't been in the picture, I would've done a lot more. Back in the city, I texted her that I wanted to see her. I didn't have to specify that I didn't want to run into my uncle. Her response stated he'd be working the day shift for the next two weeks. He was usually gone by eight in the morning.

Because I would soon be busy with the gallery, I took a chance and stopped by in the morning. Only, after taking the elevated train, or the L as it's known, and a bus, I arrived to find his cruiser parked out front. Not sure what to do, I walked away, not wanting to stand at the bus stop near their house as I made my decision. I ended up walking farther and passing Mom's old house and was struck once again by her loss.

Even after all this time, the overwhelming sense of her absence lassoed me and pulled me to the church without conscious thought.

I stood staring at the spire when a hand touched my arm and nearly scared me out of my skin.

"Sorry to scare you, my dear. I'm not as spry as I once was."

At first I saw no one and had to glance down until I saw a tiny older woman. To my artist's eye, I beheld a face sketched with kind lines that revealed her age, much as tree rings did. A warm smile greeted me from beneath her nun's habit.

"It's okay," I reassured her.

"The Lord works in mysterious ways, and it looks like he sent you to help me. Would you mind going in search of Father Cernak to help bring in donated baked goodies?"

I nodded, and she moved exactly the way her shoes sounded—squeaky, slow, and steady. I almost offered to open the front doors of the church when her very shaky hands were taking forever. I headed through the church in search of the priest. After finding the sanctuary empty, I decided to make the sacristy my next stop. Before I could knock, the door swung open and a tall guy in dark pants and a button-up shirt burst through with a light mist of sweat on his brow.

"Can you help me?"

His head moved side to side causing his hair to dance with his movement. "I'm sorry," he spit out and disappeared before I could say any more. A flashback, déjà vu, or a distant memory from years ago hit me, and then it wisped away as a voice intruded upon my thoughts.

"Hi, can I help you, miss?"

Unlike the first guy, his face was kind and genuine. "Um, yes, if you're Father Cernak." I glanced back at the retreating figure. Something struck a chord, but I couldn't quite place it.

"I am."

I shook my head, bringing my attention back to Father Cernak. "One of the nuns asked for help carrying things in."

I felt sort of silly. I should have helped her myself. But when we found our way back outside, the extra pair of hands was needed for the amount of baked goods that needed to be brought in.

"Oh, Sister Grace, I see you brought the food for the soup kitchen," Father Cernak said.

"Yes, and the bakery gave us so much more than I anticipated."

Father Cernak turned to me and said, "We run a soup kitchen here on the first Saturday of every month for lunch. This is our day and Sister here has picked up all the donations. Would you mind helping us carry this into our cafeteria?"

"Not at all."

"And I didn't catch your name," he said.

"Oh, I'm Haven Richardson. I went to school here at Holy Cross."

His face lit up. "How wonderful. Do you live around here then?"

"No, I'm here temporarily for a gallery showing of my art work. But I came to pay my aunt a visit." I explained who Aunt Kathy was.

"Oh, I know Kathy. She's a wonderful parishioner," he said with such a kind smile.

"Yes, I'm sure." I returned his grin.

"So, your aunt wasn't home at this hour?"

"The truth is, after I came all this way, I became a little nostalgic and decided to pay a visit to the church first, and then light a vigil candle for my mom. She died when I was only eleven and was a parishioner here." My deflection served its purpose.

"Oh, I'm very sorry." His frown felt kind and not pitying, and his voice carried deep sincerity. "You must've been devastated."

"Yes. I still miss her very much."

Father Cernak stopped walking and touched my arm. "Haven, that's not something a young child easily dispenses. I'm sure it still touches you. If you ever feel the need to talk, I'd be happy to listen."

I liked the man, which surprised me. I wasn't usually endeared with anyone so easily. His warmth and kindness thawed my bitter heart with those few simple words, and to like someone was one step closer to trusting them. And trust was a rare thing for me.

"Thank you, Father. I'll keep that in mind."

We walked toward the cafeteria again. It took us a couple of trips to get all the donated food inside, but when we were finished, Father Cernak and Sister Grace thanked me profusely.

Waving away their unnecessary gratitude, I said, "It was nothing, really."

"Haven, will you join us for Mass sometime while you're here?" Father Cernak asked.

The question caught me off guard because I hadn't attended Mass in years. He read the hesitation in my expression.

"Don't feel pressured, but I thought if you were here, you might want to pay a visit with your aunt."

The pause lasted too long, and I blurted out the words, "Oh, I don't know."

He was thoughtful when he said, "Can I ask you something?"

I knew he was going to dig a little deep. But how could I have refused a question from him?

"Sure."

"Do you still go to church? And it's okay if you don't."

I stared at my shoes when I answered, "Not really."

He didn't chastise me, or condemn me to the fires of Hell, like I thought he might.

He only said, "Many people have their reasons for walking away from the church, and I suspect you have yours. You may find that as you get older your ideas change, so I hope you don't walk away from it forever. But I would also add that one should never be forced or pressured into going to church. Maybe while you're in town, you'll visit us here for our Saturday evening service. Just remember something, Haven—God loves everyone, no matter what."

I finally pulled my eyes away from my feet, which no longer held any interest for me, and glanced up at Father Cernak. His light brown eyes were compassionate and sincere, and for some reason, he made me stop and seriously consider coming back to attend Mass.

Smiling, I said, "Maybe I'll take you up on that, Father."

"I hope so. You have yourself a good day, Haven. And thank you again for your help this morning." He shook my hand and I walked away, feeling as though I had encountered a true man of God.

As I walked toward the bus station, again I passed by my old house. My steps slowed and Mom's voice came to me from years ago. Then I remembered running through the door, that awful day she died, and finding Aunt Kathy and Uncle Kent there. Welcome to my new house of horrors. I picked up my pace and passed my old Hell. Uncle Kent's car was there, so I just continued on to the bus stop. It would have to be another day that I visited my aunt.

On the ride to Macie's, my thoughts traveled back in time. The run-in with the guy with green eyes had me thinking about that day I'd come to church looking for help. Anger boiled as I thought about the inconsiderate but beautiful boy who'd sent me packing. There was something about the guy who fled the room that reminded me of him. But that couldn't be. There was no way he was a priest, so why would he be in the sacristy?

When I returned to Macie's, she was just getting up with her hair plastered to one side of her head.

She yawned before she spoke. "You went all that way for nothing?"

"No," I said absently. I was thoughtful for a second "Not for nothing. I met a priest who might have returned my faith in mankind."

"Really?"

"No," I said, laughing, "but he was easy to talk to."

"The new guy?"

"New guy?"

"Holy Cross has a new priest because Father O'Brien died. That's what my mom said."

"Father O'Brien died?" I remembered him. He'd been the one I'd wanted to reach out to. My mother thought so highly of him. And he'd come to visit her a couple of times when she was so sick and couldn't go to Mass.

"Yeah, he like tripped and fell or something. Had a heart attack." She waved the thought aside and moved to the coffee maker.

"Well, I met Father Cernak. Is he new?"

"No, he's been there a while."

"He's was really nice," I said. "I don't know, Macie, but I might go to Mass. And you know me, I'm not a church person at all."

"Yeah, everyone loves him. He's been great, I think. But I don't pay too much attention when Mom talks about it. I haven't attended Mass since probably last Christmas, or was it New Year's? But they just got a new priest to help Father Cernak after Father O'Brien died. But I can't remember his name."

"No rumors about him?"

"None that I've heard. Why?"

"While I was there, I ran into this guy. He could be the new priest. He left in such a hurry, I can't be sure. But he reminded me of that asshole, Canaan, who told me to scram that time I went to the church to get help."

"Have." She placed a hand on mine. "I haven't heard anything. And if the new priest used to go to school with us, that would be like big news Mom would have shared with me."

That was true.

"I guess so. If I ever run into him, I would have some choice words for him. None of them would be good to say in a church."

"It would get you banned from church." She chortled. "Anyway, why'd you think it was him?"

"He was pretty hot. Remember how we practically drooled over him when we were, what? I think it started in the fifth grade or something?" We both cracked up. "But there is no way he's a priest. I mean, a guy like that could get anyone he wanted. Most guys that hot are full of themselves and not the Holy Spirit."

She laughed and so did I.

"Have you seen him? Canaan?" He might not be the priest, but he could still live in the area.

"No, not since he graduated. He, like, disappeared. Wherever he went for college, he never came back. Of course there were rumors. Everybody claimed they had a secret love affair with him. I don't know. He seemed so shy for a guy who looked the way he did."

As hot as he had been, I had to let it go. My childhood crush had crushed me. And he was no longer important. He was a stain on my life I should have washed away a long time ago. I wouldn't give him another minute of my thoughts. I switched gears back to Uncle Kent.

"Oh. Whatever. But yeah, the devil was home by the time I got there, so I'm going to go another time."

"Maybe you should just confront him." My hands instantly rubbed my arms. It was something I did all the time back in the day. Macie caught it. "Forget I said that."

"No, you're right. It might as well be while I'm here. My therapist told me I needed to confront my fear of him one day."

"You've held on to this for far too long. It's fucked with you, and it's time for you to kick it the hell out."

I chewed my nail as I thought about what she said. She was right. It needed to be addressed. The question was, would I have the nerve to do it when the time came or would I wither up like a dead flower?

Macie nodded in what I imagined was agreement. Then she said, "Since you're back so early, why not grab some breakfast?"

"Sure, why not."

We went to a local place around the corner and filled our starving bellies with yummy food. Macie was a foodie, so she knew all these great local places to eat. I had an amazing omelet and she ordered sweet potato pancakes that I tried to steal from her.

"Oh, God. I've died and gone to heaven. I've never eaten anything this tasty," I said, stabbing and filling my mouth with another forkful of her pancakes.

"I told you this place was awesome."

"I don't know how you stay so skinny." I looked at her, as much as I could with the table between us.

"Running. You should try it."

"What? Am I fat?"

"No, you fool. It helps with stress and you're always loaded with it."

I dragged my fork though my omelet as I thought about what she said. She was right. Stress ruled my life and had since my mom died.

"Okay. I'll give it a try."

Later that afternoon, after our food settled down to our ankles, she convinced me to go for a run. As we ran, Macie suggested again I should toss my fears of Kent to the wind and confront him.

"He can't hurt you anymore."

I looked at her and stubbed the toe of my shoe on a crack in the sidewalk. She had to grab my arm to keep me from biting the concrete. Once the world was back on its axis, I said, "Says who?"

"Huh?"

"Who says Kent can't hurt me anymore? He's still a brutish asshole and still has that cop status he can throw in my face."

"Maybe. But would he, knowing you've established yourself on your own now?"

"Mace, that wouldn't stop him and you damn well know it. Why do you think Kathy is still with him?"

"You have a point."

This discussion was beginning to give me a headache. Or perhaps it was the fact I was so out of shape that the simple act of breathing was like climbing Mt. Everest.

"I think I'm gonna head home to lick my wounds. I'm dying."

"Okay. I'll be back in an hour."

"An hour? What the hell are you? A machine?"

"Haven, this was supposed to be therapeutic for you, so you could talk about your uncle. It wasn't supposed to kill you." And she broke down laughing at me.

I flipped her off and headed for home.

By that night I crashed, exhausted from the run. My intentions were to wake up early and text my aunt, but I didn't wake until after eleven. It was so late, I had to scramble to make it to the gallery by noon.

Seven

CANAAN

Wretchedness filled me, like it always did. Being in the sacristy had thrown me back to the beginning all those years ago. The dreams I tried for years to expunge nailed me harder than the leather strap I used for penance. That had sufficed for so long, but not anymore. More physical exertion would be necessary for me to work out my demons, along with my frustrations. I needed to increase my daily workouts with weights and find a place to hang my punching bag so I could take it out on that. With the move, I'd missed a few, and that hadn't helped at all.

A light tap on my door preceded Bill's voice. "Canaan, are you feeling better?"

I cleared my throat as I got to my feet. "Somewhat. I'm not sure what got me."

I opened the door to let him in.

"You look a bit peaked. Probably a virus." He sighed. His expression conveyed his sympathy for me. "I hate to tell you, but I failed to mention it last night with everything else I had to fill you in on. Today is our turn for the soup kitchen. I'm getting ready to go say early Mass. I think it's best you stay here for the morning."

Nodding, I said, "If you think so. I should probably clean the sacristy bathroom."

He waved a hand. "I'll handle it. Just get to feeling better soon. And the soup kitchen is off limits too. If you're contagious that could cause an epidemic. Maybe even Mass this evening. Giving out Communion would spread it as well. You need to rest. I'll be back later."

"Thank you."

The only problem with being shut in my room was it allowed my unoccupied mind to fill with unimpeded thoughts of the lessons Father O'Brien taught me about sin. I lay in bed assaulted with the memories of the first one. I could almost feel his hands on me. My shame then was still unimaginable. The sounds he made during his mini homily to me about how it was my beauty that made me a sinner by creating temptation in others, caused my nausea to return with a vengeance. He had to plant the seeds of righteousness into my very soul so I could be cleansed, or so he said. As I begged him to stop the pain, he reminded me that Jesus himself endured suffering in order to save our souls.

I blinked away the memory, forcing back the bile, still wanting to hide from everyone, especially my face, which turned heads even to this day. Women and even some men gave me ungodly glances despite my collar. I was unworthy of their attention and didn't want it. Lust was something I learned to fear because I saw it every time *he* looked at me. I was afraid everyone knew my secret and my sin, even my parents. I hated myself as I got out the leather, in need of pain to dull my thoughts and pay the price for the debt I continued to owe my Lord for being that sinner.

On my knees in front of the crucifix, I prayed for assistance from God the Holy Father on this new journey of mine and that He would absolve my sins, every one of them. I begged Jesus our Savior to forgive me, and I repented once again, and I asked the Holy Spirit to help guide me in the truth of things. How was I to guide others when I could barely function myself?

I was certain the Almighty had a purpose for me, but I wished he'd soon show me what it was. My belief in Him was as strong as it ever had been, and I would never give up on Him. But it was my patience that was wearing thin.

Later in the day, I convinced Bill that I was sure whatever had gotten a hold of me must've passed because no other incident occurred. I felt confident I could say the five-thirty Mass, but if he could be on call, just in case, that would be great. He agreed. With great trepidation, I made my way to the sacristy around four thirty. I wanted to get there early to give myself a few extra minutes so I could chase away my demons.

When I entered, it wasn't as bad as the first time, though it was surely no walk in the park. The odor of the place was what seemed to throw me for a loop. It wasn't necessarily the incense, either.

It didn't take me long to figure out what it was. I could smell *him*. Violent shudders tore through my body, almost propelling me back out the door. I prayed for strength, knowing he was gone and couldn't hurt me anymore.

After long seconds, I opened my eyes. The vestments were already laid out and neatly arranged in perfect order, as I knew they would be. It took another few moments to get my feet unglued from my spot. With slow careful steps, I made it to the prayer station, the one I had abhorred for so many years. I vowed then that it would become a place of new meaning for me. In that moment, I knew what I had to do. I fell to my knees and, for the first time ever, said a prayer of forgiveness, not just for me but for Father O'Brien. I'd long since learned that his method of teaching and punishment wasn't wholly right. But it didn't absolve me of being a sinner.

I left the sacristy having survived, and maybe one day I could make peace with the room that had broken me. I went to check the altar, ensuring that everything was in its place for the epistle and gospel. I wanted to have the missal prepared as well, so I checked to see if everything was as I wanted it. When I was satisfied, I checked the time and saw that it was already five o'clock. That meant the lead altar server would arrive soon. It was time to stick my head in and introduce myself. When I did, I was surprised, which I shouldn't have been, to see the server was a girl. She gave me a toothy grin glowing in neon braces. I let out a breath I didn't know I was holding and grinned back.

"I'm Father Canaan, the new priest." I stuck my hand out.

"I'm Shelby. I'm the lead server today, so I hope I don't screw things up for you, Father." She giggled.

Her joy reminded me of how I'd felt my first time being an altar server. My smile slipped as I remembered how all of that enthusiasm had been stolen from me by one act. I managed to work the curve back to my lips before I spoke as Shelby didn't deserve the shadows that still lived in my heart.

"I'm sure you'll do great. I have to admit, I'm just a little nervous. You'll have to help me out." She nodded. "If you ensure I have the water, wine, and communion wafers when I need them, then hopefully *I* won't mess up."

I gave her a conspiratorial smile.

"What about the bells?"

"See? You're already a winner. We can't forget to ring the bells during the consecration. And I know you won't," I said with a wink.

"You know, Father, you're young for a priest. I thought you had to be old to be one."

I laughed at her frankness. "No, not all of us are ready for the nursing home."

"That's good. Everyone will be happy to see you, then."

"Oh? Why's that?"

"'Cuz Father O'Brien was a little like Kanye West. You know, never liked to have any fun. Always grumpy like. Never smiling. You look like you're more fun. You actually laugh."

Youth and ignorance were bliss. And I was glad I actually knew who Kanye was. "I hope so. At least I think I like to have fun."

"Cool. Well, I'll see you around the narthex."

My raised brows let her know I hadn't any idea what on earth she was talking about.

"You know, right before Mass?"

"Oh! Gotcha! And, Shelby. I'm counting on you to help me make my first Mass a success."

It was time to get dressed. Most people, even Catholics, didn't realize the ritual involved in donning the vestments. But I loved this part or so I had until I opened the door to the sacristy. I held my breath and waited for the anxiety to pass. I pushed through it because the garments awaited me and I didn't have much time.

I walked straight to the bathroom sink and while I washed my hands I prayed out loud. "Give virtue to my hands, O Lord, that being cleansed from all stain I might serve you with purity of mind and body."

Once my hands were cleansed, I placed the alb—the long white robe—over my head, and let it fall to my feet. Saying the required prayers, I continued to place each article of clothing carefully and reverently on my body. The stole—a long slender decorated band of cloth—came next. It was a symbol of the Yoke of Christ and was always adorned with a cross. I wrapped the cincture—a rope-like belt—around my waist, tying it tightly over the stole, and I said the prayer, "Gird me, O Lord, with the girdle of purity, and extinguish in me all evil desires, that the virtue of chastity may abide in me." This was the symbol of chastity. And last came the chasuble—the colorful poncho-like outer garment that can be ornate in some churches. Holy Cross's were beautiful but not very fancy, which I liked. This symbolized charity and also the Yoke of Christ.

I was ready to celebrate my first Mass as associate pastor at Holy Cross. Leaving the sacristy, I joined the altar servers in the narthex, chuckling to myself as I remembered what Shelby had said.

"Everyone ready?" I asked.

"Yes, Father."

"Lead the way then." The first server walked into the aisle, cueing the music, which was modern Christian music for this contemporary Mass. I started singing along, as I knew these songs from the contemporary Masses at Notre Dame.

Participation was excellent and my introductory homily went smoothly. I saw the interest in the faces of the congregation. It was the same on Sunday. Mom and Dad stopped by the rectory early Sunday afternoon and brought us dinner, including dessert.

As I settled into my new role, the rest of the week was without incident. Or so I thought. It was Saturday afternoon, and I had just wrapped up listening to the good people of Holy Cross confess their sins to me. Over half of them were young kids whose parents had brought them in, I was sure, and they confessed silly things that made me smile. Arguments between siblings were probably at the top of the list, then came lying, followed by disobedience. I absolved them of their sins, doled out the usual Hail Marys and Our Fathers for penance, and sent them on their way.

As I left the confessional, I caught a glimpse of blond hair out of the corner of my eye. The fact that it was blond wasn't what I noticed. It was that it was the palest of blondes I'd ever seen. Then I realized from her profile it was the young woman who'd come to the sacristy door on the first day I was there with Bill—on the day I ran out because I was ill. A shadow of a memory passed through my mind, but fled quicker than I could put a finger on it. I watched her as she carefully lit a vigil light and then prayed for a moment. When she finished, she stood and turned.

It's been said that priests are immune to beauty. I say whoever came up with that statement was a blind fool. The woman possessed the rare type of beauty that one never forgets, and I'd come across attractive people throughout my life, but never one that gave me pause. Not noticing her that day was proof of how affected I'd been by a return to that room. I shook myself out of those thoughts as God was the only beauty I could allow myself to admire. Instead, I went to speak to her, to apologize for my rapid departure, only I never got the chance.

"It *is* you. You're Canaan Sullivan, aren't you?"

Smiling, I said, "Yes," as I reached out to shake her hand.

She ignored it and unleashed a fury I'd never experienced before.

"How dare you call yourself a priest? A man of God?"

Her disdain for me made me hesitate, as I was confused by her ire. Words I wondered myself a million times made me unable to hold her glare. I glanced about in search of an escape or to see if anyone had witnessed the exchange. Only I found we were alone as embarrassment infused me with heat.

"No one is perfect, but I've given my life in service of our Lord."

Her expressive eyes narrowed. "Of course you did, with your holier than thou attitude."

I'd been accused of things before, but never that. My competence wasn't in question. So what had her spitting mad?

"I'm terribly sorry. You have me at a loss."

She barked out a mirthless laugh, which only added to my confusion. Her eyes, beautiful ice blue, were shooting sparks. And the golden skin of her cheeks was dotted with two bright spots of crimson. What in the world could I have possibly done to anger her so?

Shaking her head, she said, "Unbelievable. But why would you ever remember? Let me clue you in, *Father*." She said the last like it was a curse. "When I was twelve, I came to the sacristy looking for help...and you"—she pointed a long, slender finger in my direction—"sent me away. You told me Father O'Brien didn't have time for anyone like me. That he was too busy. So I left. I was twelve fucking years old."

As flabbergasted as I was, I needed to calm her down.

"You have a right to your anger, but this is the house of the Lord," I told her. She was practically shouting now and cursing in this most sacred place and that was completely unacceptable. I made a quick decision. Even though it filled me with dread, I reached for her wrist and moved toward that room of torture, the only place that would afford us some privacy.

"Do not hush me." She pulled her arm free from my hold, unwilling to walk with me. I needed to get to the bottom of this, so I glanced around to ensure we were still alone.

She looked like she wanted to scratch my eyes out and leave me for dead. So in the calmest voice I could muster, I said, "Can you please explain everything? From the beginning, because I have no idea of what you're speaking. You seem to know who I am, but other than last week, I've never seen you before that I'm aware of."

Her accusatory glare made me shrink, and I was no small man. She was furious, no doubt, and I needed to get to the root of it. Her words were spoken softly, but their meaning rang out loud and clear. "You're an asshole. I was twelve years old when I came here for help. *You* turned me away. You said

Father O'Brien was too busy for me. Right there." She pointed to the door of the sacristy.

Oh, God, no. The image was as vivid now as it had been then. The young girl who came here *that day*...right afterward, had been her. *The soft knock at the door.* Oh, I should have remembered those eyes, her hair.

Oh, God. I shook my head back and forth. "No, no, no, it wasn't like that. That's not what it was. I didn't turn you away. You have it all wrong. I sent you away, yes, but not for the reason you think."

"Yeah? Well, you sentenced me to Hell for six more years."

What was she talking about? "To Hell? What do you mean by that?"

"My uncle, the devil. Straight to the Hell of living with him. I came here for help that night. I came to see if Father O'Brien could help me escape the beatings I was getting from that fucking bastard. I could barely walk that night. I..." She wiped her cheek that glistened from her tears. "But no! *You* sent me away. And you know what?" Now her voice lowered to almost a whisper.

"What?"

"I believed you. I didn't think I was important enough for Father's help. I didn't think I mattered."

Guilt stabbed pain into my head. I pushed back my hair, hoping for relief. Because of what he'd done to me, I had ruined this girl's life—sent her home to live with her own monster. I wanted to scream and curse, louder than she had.

"I'm sorry," I muttered.

"You're damn right you're sorry. You're a sorry excuse of a priest."

I shook my head in defeat. "You don't understand—"

"What I understand is you ruined my life."

"You're right. And I'm sorry," I said again. "This isn't much of an excuse, but I wasn't much older than you. I sent you away because I thought it was the right thing to do at the time."

It wasn't much to offer, but it was all I had. What I really wanted to do was to offer her the comfort of my arms, but I was sure she'd rather see me lifeless on the floor.

"What? What does that mean? That it was the right thing to do?" She looked at me like I was crazy. And I was closer to it than she thought.

Lifting my head, I found her blue eyes targeted on me. "It doesn't really matter now, does it? I did you a great disservice, and for that I'll ask God to forgive my grave sin."

I shielded my eyes from everything as my head bowed. The idea that my actions hurt this woman drove a knife into my heart. My sins deepened as my soul grew darker. The prayer I said for years popped in my head like a beacon. *"Merciful Jesus, please forgive my sins, cleanse me of the darkness within, and give me Your strength to rise above my weaknesses."*

"You think it's that easy? To ask for forgiveness and then move on like nothing ever happened? Well, I'm sorry, *Father*. It doesn't quite work that way for me. The belt buckle and the pain I felt when it gouged into my flesh each time he laid it across me, I don't think I'll ever forget, much less forgive. I don't buy into your Catholic ways that easily."

Her words slayed me, making me feel the sting of the buckle like I was the one who'd been beaten. I jerked as though the fires of Hell had burned me. And surely they were burning me—burning my useless soul and turning it to ash. She had the face of an angel, and I was the one who ruined her life.

"I'm sorry, and I know that's not enough. I will regret my words to you that night for the rest of my life."

"Small compensation, don't you think?"

"I don't know what else to say," I said. My chest constricted as though iron claws were squeezing the very life out of me. I could barely get a breath past my lips. I didn't want her to see me like this. She stared me down and for a moment I thought

I saw her eyes soften, but then it was gone, replaced by anger again.

"There's nothing left to say." She spun and slammed the door behind her, leaving me to fend off the anxiety attack I tried to hide. I hadn't had one in years, but now it was on me in full force. I thought about Father O'Brien and the hell he had inflicted on both of us. May God forgive me, but I hoped the flames of Hell were burning his black soul.

Eight

HAVEN

My run-in with Father Canaan Sullivan didn't affect my opening night at the gallery. The designers were amazing at staging my art, using my largest piece as the anchor. It was nearly life-sized, reaching to my shoulders when I stood next to it. But they'd hung it on a wall, leaving it close to the ground so it could be seen and inspected by anyone wanting to get a closer view.

"This anchor piece won't last," Jonathon said as he inspected everything the afternoon before the show.

"I don't want to sell it."

He whipped his body around so fast, it almost knocked me over.

"What do you mean?"

"It's more than a painting to me. I have an emotional attachment to it."

His mouth was slack. He stared at me as though my words were utterly ridiculous. And maybe they were. To him. But not to me. It was a painting of my mother and the first and best I had ever done. I could never let it go.

"Haven, you need to rethink what you just said. That piece is why you're here."

"I'll replicate it."

"Buyers don't want copies and you know damn well why. People who come to these showings want originals. They'll want a Haven Richardson. *Original.*" He spit that last word out. "Got that?"

"Yes, I get it." My annoyance rang out with my words.

He stomped away, anger radiating off him. Maybe I should've told him it wasn't for sale before today, but I didn't. Now I was going to have to deal with his wrath. Shit. I took out my phone, snapped a few dozen pictures, and then left before I had to cope with any more of a pissed off Jonathon.

When I got home, I relayed the incident to Macie.

"Paint another one, change the background and you keep it. Make it different enough so the original will be original and the owner won't know or care if he did know. Put your mom in a different color dress, too."

"You don't understand. That was my mom and my best memory of her. I am emotionally attached to that piece. It's not just a painting to me. It's almost as though it's a part of her. It may sound absolutely crazy and ridiculous, but it's how I feel about it. I painted it right after I left the hell I was living in. It was my very first major piece, too."

"Then I don't know what to tell you. If you don't sell, you risk Jonathon sending you packing, and there goes your career."

I held my finger in the air. "Unless I can talk the buyer into a different painting. I can explain the significance to me and maybe he or she would be willing to negotiate. If not, I won't have a choice."

"Sounds like you've got it figured out."

"It's my only chance, Macie."

As Jonathon promised, a car showed up at five thirty to pick us up. When we arrived at the gallery, I walked her around and witnessed her stunned expression at my work. She'd seen it, of course, but not on display in such an elegant fashion.

"Oh, Haven, you're amazing. Look at this. All those years of sidewalk shows have totally paid off for you. I'm so proud of you." She wrapped me in a huge hug.

"Doesn't it look fabulous?" Jonathon asked as he approached us.

We agreed and I introduced him to Macie.

After placing a kiss on her knuckles with his eyes never leaving hers, I watched my best friend blush.

"So nice to finally meet you, Jonathon. I've heard great things about you."

She nearly stuttered out the words. Jonathon's amused expression showed that he was well aware of his effect on women. Hadn't I been dazzled by his handsome face and pretty words?

"Haven, do you want to take a look at the studio to make sure things are in order? I know how you artists are with your brushes. I wanted to have all of that stowed safely away."

"Sure. Let's go," I said to Macie. "I'll show you around."

Soon people filled up the gallery and before I knew it, Jonathon was pulling me every which way. He introduced me to those who wanted to meet the artist who painted the showcased collection. And there were many. As soon as I finished meeting one person, another was there to take the last one's place. My head spun. When the showing ended, I didn't know if I was up or down. My throat was parched and I was losing my voice.

Macie brought me a bottle of water, which I guzzled in one long drink.

"Another, please," I croaked.

One more appeared in my hand, this time from Jonathon. I downed that one too.

"I need to sit. Is this how they always are?"

Jonathon bellowed out a laugh. "Oh, hell no. I knew you were special, Haven. The Chicago Tribune wants an interview tomorrow. I told them that you wouldn't be in until noon tomorrow. You need to rest after this. We had all sorts of offers. And the large piece went into a bidding war before it sold."

The news punched the air out of me. "Wait. You sold my large painting and didn't check with me first?"

He only shrugged, as if it were nothing. "You were tied up. It's in your contract, but you probably didn't bother to read it. I'm fair, Haven. This is your big ticket. Soon you'll be able to name your price on anything. You can paint whatever you want."

It was not anger that consumed me but raw anguish. Feelings of abandonment and loneliness invaded my soul. Once again, someone I thought I could put some faith and trust in proved me wrong. "That's all fine and good, but I told you I didn't want to sell that piece."

"I thought you'd reconsider when you heard the price it brought in."

"No amount of money would have been worth it."

There wasn't anything to say to him anymore. Maybe Macie was right. I could recreate it with the photos I had taken of it. Right now was not the time to argue. I was too tired to make any sense, and besides, the damage was done. The dang thing was already sold. And it only reinforced another hard lesson I'd learned long ago. Don't ever trust anyone because they'll only kick you in the face.

"Whatever," I said. "But I'd like the name of the buyer, please."

He eyed me suspiciously. "You're not going to do anything stupid, are you?"

"Not in my opinion."

A glass of wine appeared in my hand, along with a small plate of food. My appetite was nil, though I should've been starving.

"You know, I don't seem to be hungry. I would like very much to go home and crash." I looked pointedly at Macie.

"I'm ready when you are."

Jonathon nodded. "I'll call the driver. And, Haven, you should know this was the most spectacular gallery showing I've ever had. You were amazing. Congratulations."

As pissed as I was, he was going to give me the buyer's name. And maybe I could convince them to take another painting. Meanwhile, I hated to admit it, it was all because of him I was standing in that moment.

I bit off the snarly reply hovering on my tongue and instead forced out the plastic response, "Thank you, Jonathon." Though I didn't feel thankful at the moment.

"No, you owe it to yourself. Go home and get some rest. I'll see you tomorrow."

By the time we got home, I barely had the strength to get undressed and crawl into bed. Exhaustion plowed into me and sleep stole every conscious thought.

Three weeks passed and my anger toward the esteemed Father Sullivan hadn't diminished in the least. At least he'd had the courtesy to act contrite. No doubt thoughts of him sent my blood pressure soaring. And if that weren't enough, he was one more man who had shown his true colors.

The whole Jonathon issue with him selling my painting from under me still rankled, and I didn't quite know what to do about it. He saw it as nothing but a giant dollar sign, but to me it was a part of my past that will forever be lost. Losing that piece almost felt like my mother died all over again.

So I threw myself into my work, like I often did. Escaping into my canvases was my therapy. My production was off the charts according to the asshole Jonathon. Small pieces were scattered all over my workplace like litter on the streets of Chicago. It didn't take long for Jonathon to come and collect them, claiming how spectacular they were. I ignored him. They meant nothing to me except they were a way for me to release the emotions that had built up inside me in the few short weeks I had been back in my hometown.

Wrath fueled my artistic hands. Canvas wrapped around a giant frame so large I needed to get help from the gallery employees. It was almost the size of a wall. And then my hands went to work.

Dark colors emerged, forming splashes in the sky. Reds, purples, grays, and navies blended into a cloud-filled sunset that looked as ominous as my life was back then. Soon the background had been shaped. Days later, as I painted, I knew what was manifesting. It was a memory.

A young girl stood with her back facing me, posture hunched as her arms hugged her frail body. What should've been a shelter of the church in front of her proved to be no shelter at all. And facing her was a boy, not much older than herself. Dark-haired and handsome, whom she thought to be carefree with the world at his fingertips, turning her away and sending her back into an Inferno.

I hardly ate and slept as my hand continued to wield colors of paint, mixing and adding touches here and there, until the memory was complete. Only the painting wasn't quite an accurate representation of the truth. Reality had happened during the day, which wasn't stormy. My anger had fueled the colors to create the tempest in this reflection of the past and I was positive why.

As I inspected the finished product, I began to notice something. Canaan's eyes. How could I have painted him and not been aware of his pain? His brow was drawn and furrowed, and his green eyes matched the incoming storm. Did I do that intentionally or did I pull that from memory?

"Holy shit! Where is all this coming from, Haven?" Jonathon stepped in front of me to scrutinize my work.

I was so engrossed in examining my own memories that I hadn't noticed his arrival. "Yeah, uh, I…" There was no adequate answer, so I let my voice trail off.

"Jesus, Haven, this is brilliant. It's like you've had an epiphany or something."

"Or something." The fury that had driven me could be partially laid at his feet. But I had to reserve some of it for Canaan.

"When will it be ready?"

"This afternoon," I muttered.

I put my final touches on the painting. It loomed large and foreboding before me. I couldn't get Canaan's eyes out of my mind. He said he thought he'd been doing the right thing. Maybe so. He had been just a kid himself.

Stop this! Let it go! There was no resolution so it was time to move on. He was the one who screwed up, not me. I'd been an innocent then, not so much anymore. I'd lost that label long ago.

As I stared at the painting, the pain of the beatings nailed me. I flinched, imagining the bite of the buckle as it bit into my flesh. Squinting, I looked again at Canaan's eyes. Were they a reflection of my own? Did I displace my pain onto him? Or was it there all along?

The brush lifted as if it had a life of its own, adding the final strokes to him before I felt it was complete. I stepped away to take my final assessment. I always looked at my work with one eye closed. It gave me perspective to make sure I didn't miss anything. Satisfied everything was in order, I considered the painting finished.

Grabbing my bag, I walked down to the private bathroom that was in the back for employees and artists. The first thing I noticed was the reflection in the mirror. It reminded me of my mother with her haunted eyes. Since I was planning on meeting Macie for dinner later, I changed into my extra clothes because the ones I had on were paint splattered.

Running some gloss over my lips, I headed up to my workspace. The painting drew my attention as soon as I entered the room. It sparked with life, almost as if lightning were going to strike from the cloud-streaked sky. Once again, Canaan's eyes pulled me in. Pain spoke loud and clear, making me want to soothe it away.

What the hell is wrong with you, Haven? I shook myself, tearing my gaze away from the gigantic piece of art.

"Miss Richardson, we're here to move the painting." It was one of the workers.

"This is the one. Be careful because the paint is barely dry."

It took four men to move it and they placed it with the rest of my work. Jonathon was there to supervise along with the display expert to figure out where to place it. They decided to showcase it in a separate space since it was so unique and large. Undoubtedly, it would be an attention getter. How could it not?

"Unbelievable. Just look at it, Haven." It was Jonathon who spoke.

"I am. It's kind of hard not to. The thing's so damn huge."

"First your interview with the Chicago Tribune, and now this—you're going to be at the top of the A list, my dear."

The interview. That had been interesting. They wanted me to talk about myself. And I wouldn't. It made for an interesting hour, the reporter trying to pull information out of my bared teeth hidden behind my fake smile.

"Don't try to make nicey-nice with me. You're still on my *shit* list."

He chuckled. "It's okay. I'll make us both a lot of bank on this."

And that was that as he walked away, leaving a trail of

dollar signs. I wondered if in the end it would be worth it.

Unfortunately, he was right about one thing. The painting attracted all kinds of attention, even as soon as it was staged. Like moths to a flame, every patron who walked through the door stopped in front of it as though they couldn't resist it. During a lull, I took a picture of it with my phone so I could show it to Macie that night. I needed to ask her a question about it.

It was five in the afternoon when I made another round, chatting with customers, answering questions. Then I turned around and saw him.

Nine

HAVEN

Father Canaan Sullivan stood bathed in light as if he were haloed. Only I knew better. I watched him for a second as his pensive expression fixed on what essentially was himself. Caught up in the intricacies of my work, he didn't notice my approach. I took in his handsome physique. He was certainly still as striking as he'd been when we were in school, despite the fact that he was dressed in black and had that little white thing around his neck, informing the world that he was a priest.

"What are you doing here?" I asked coolly.

My tone wasn't pleasant. I couldn't care less about his station in life. His head whipped around as my frank words startled him. Composing himself took a second as his eyes dug into mine briefly before he addressed me. That gave me a moment to assess how tired he looked, exhausted, in fact. Then he turned back to the painting.

His words were quiet, but clear. "You did this?"

My lip curled as I hurled back a snarky response to his idiotic question. "I am H. Richardson as you can see by my name on the painting."

He bowed his head for a second, his eyes closed. When he opened them, I could see recognition. "That's...it's..." He ran his hand through his hair as he stared at it. "That's us, isn't it?"

"It is."

My tone had lost some of its bluster. He was clearly rattled, maybe even more than me.

"From that day. Long ago. The day I destroyed your life."

I hadn't expected him to be so blunt. But his words only reminded me of all the hurt I'd endured.

"Yes." My tone was unfriendly and clipped. "Why are you here?"

"I, uh...I saw the article. The...the interview with you in the paper. I wanted to see your work."

I brushed aside his stuttering words. He wasn't the victim here; I was.

"Well, you did. You can go now." I moved to leave him.

"Wait, please."

Just like that night, his voice caused me to stop and face him.

"I also came to tell you it was wrong of me."

He turned and studied the painting. His hand reached out to touch it.

"Don't," I warned.

He quickly drew it back.

"I only finished it today so it's not quite dry." I didn't understand why I felt it necessary to explain that to him, but I did.

"The likeness. How did you—"

"Memory, obviously." My tone indicated he was an idiot, yet he said nothing in response to that.

He shook his head. "How could you know?"

"Know what?"

He flicked his head toward the painting. "Nothing. Never

mind. I'm so sorry for everything I caused you."

"I think it's best that you leave."

He shifted from one foot to the other. "I want to...no, I *need* to tell you some things."

"I don't want to hear any *things* from you."

"Haven, is everything all right over here?"

It was Jonathon. Of course he would come and check on me, his new moneymaker.

"Yes, I'm fine."

Jonathon stood there, waiting for an explanation. When one wasn't given, he asked, "Is this man causing you trouble?"

I released a long slow breath. "As I said, I'm fine. This is Father Sullivan, and he was just leaving."

Canaan turned to Jonathon and they exchanged a few words. I didn't pay attention to what was said. As it was, I could barely focus on staying on my own two feet.

As he moved to leave, Canaan said, "Your work is magnificent, Haven. It is truly a gift from God. I'm sorry to have distressed you. Have a nice evening." And he slipped out the door before I could think of a response.

"That's a first," Jonathon remarked.

I had forgotten he was standing there. "A first?"

"I can say I've never had a priest visit one of my galleries before."

"Oh." It was the only thing I could think of to say. I felt like a zombie the rest of the evening, walking aimlessly, unable to think. I planned to meet Macie at eight for dinner and drinks. In the state of mind I was in, I was fairly useless, so I told Jonathon I was leaving early. I sent a text to Macie to let her know I was on the way.

The restaurant we decided to meet at was only a short distance from the gallery. It was an off the beaten path place that we knew wouldn't be crowded and had great food with cheap drinks. When I walked in, the first thing that greeted me was the huge bar. Since I spied some empty seats, I decided to wait for Macie there. The room was dimly lit and I was texting a message to Macie as I walked. I grabbed the first seat at the bar and planted my butt on it.

"What can I get you?" the bartender asked.

"I think I'll just have whatever hard cider you have on tap to start with."

"Coming right up."

As I waited for my drink, I scanned through my emails. I felt eyes on me and glanced up. He was staring at me. Of all the places in Chicago, what were the chances of me running into Father Sullivan again?

"Mind if I join you?" he asked.

"I sort of do," I snapped.

He was sitting two seats away.

"I promise I won't do anything to bother you."

"You're already bothering me. And is it normal for priests to hang out in bars?"

"Not really, but given that I'm Catholic, Irish, and that ever since I learned the truth about what happened to you, I'm finding I'm doing a lot of things I probably shouldn't be." I noticed a bit of hope spark in his eyes.

Before I could stop myself, the sharp retort flew out of my mouth. "I am aware that Catholics drink. I lived with my uncle who drank on a regular basis. And I paid dearly for it."

My words extinguished his spark of hope like a bucket of water tossed on a flame. "It seems I keep digging a hole for myself where you are concerned."

"That hole you're digging? You dug it for me years ago. You're welcome to jump into it anytime. At the very least, it's probably best if you go your way and I go mine."

"Haven, that's not possible for me. You see, I'm in the business of forgiving and helping others do that."

"Yeah, well, excuse me, Father Sullivan, if I don't buy into that crap. My soul doesn't believe in God, nor does my mind, because He abandoned me a long, long time ago. And forgiveness? I'm not sure that's even a word."

You would have thought I'd slapped him the way he recoiled from my words.

"Haven, you can't mean that."

"Oh, but I do."

"But God's love is so great and vast. To not believe is...well, you must. You're missing out on the greatest glory." His convictions were so obvious.

"That's your path, Father, but it's not mine. And don't try to impose your values on me."

"That's not what I'm doing. I only want to open your eyes and fill them with the light that should be there."

A rueful laugh busted out of me. "Oh, don't worry. See these blues?" I directed my thumb up to my eyes. "They were opened at the ripe old age of eleven."

Canaan hung his head for a second. "There are things...things you don't know."

I swiveled in my seat to glare at him. His face was in shadows, though I could see the lines furrowing his brow. The purple smudges beneath his eyes sketched a picture of insomnia. I recognized the signs of this ailment, since I'd suffered from it for years. There were times when I wouldn't allow myself to fall asleep, afraid *he* would come into my room and beat me for the hell of it.

"Yeah, I'm pretty sure you said that before."

"It has to do with why I told you what I did that night." Then he hit me with those eyes of his—deep green and dark as a stormy night. I found myself leaning into them, almost falling into their depths. "I thought I was protecting you."

"There you are! I was looking for you in the dining room." Macie's voice interrupted what he was going to say next.

I was rattled, to say the least. Macie leaned down to hug me, and I felt like I was on another plane. When she stood up, she asked, "You okay?"

"Fine. Let's go." I jumped off the bar stool.

Her eyes darted back and forth between Canaan and me, but I refused to supply her with an explanation. Not then or there anyway.

As we walked away, I glanced over my shoulder to see Canaan's eyes following us. Guilt rained over me. His mouth was slightly open as if he had more to say, but I didn't give him the chance. Was it because I didn't want to hear, or was it because I was afraid he may deserve my forgiveness?

"Who was that? And why is he a priest, for fuck's sake?"

"I can't answer the second question, but as for the first, he's Canaan Sullivan. From Holy Cross."

"No! Really? He's that Canaan?" She glanced over my shoulder to look at him again. "The boy everyone crushed on in school, including you, who ended up crushing you?"

"The same."

"He sure has grown up," she said wistfully.

We arrived at the hostess station, so the rest of the story had to wait until we got our table, which only took a few minutes.

Once we were seated, Macie struck again with wide mischievous eyes. "So, don't leave me in suspense. You know I can't stand that."

My hand moved to my forehead. I knew this was going to be painful. "He showed up at the gallery."

Her jaw dropped, which was the same feeling I'd felt. "What? You're joking?"

"Why would I joke about that?" I asked. Macie craned her neck. "What the hell are you doing?"

"I'm trying to get another look at him. You rushed me out of there. I didn't get a good chance to really check him out."

My jaw would've hit the table had I let it. "So, one, he's a priest, for Christ's sake. You don't check out priests, Mace. Two, that's totally creepy, so stop."

"No, it's not creepy. He's still hot, maybe even hotter if that's possible. But why would someone so good-looking become a priest in the first place?"

My hands flew up in the air. "How the hell would I know? I mean, maybe he loves his faith and the church. Have you thought about that?"

She sank into her thoughts and nodded. "I suppose so, but I never gave it much thought. I always thought of priests as sort of stodgy and nerdy. He is none of those things. Although wasn't he an altar boy or something? But damn, did you get a look at his biceps? He must work out a lot."

It might have been the fact that I agreed with her that my head started to pound. Still, I couldn't keep up with all her thoughts with my own in a chaotic state. "How the hell did you manage to notice all of that in, what, two or three glimpses? Are you the body detective or something?"

"Or something. So go on." She waved a hand to get me to talk.

"Go on?"

Macie huffed. "Yes. The gallery."

"There's nothing to tell. I told you about seeing him a few weeks ago. And he showed up today. Said he read the interview and wanted to see my work. He did say there were things I needed to know about that night."

"Hmm. Interesting. Maybe he likes you."

The glee in her eyes was recognizable. She got it every time there was a guy she thought would be perfect for me.

I gave her an exaggerated eye roll. And it made my head hurt worse than it already did. "I'm gonna pretend I didn't hear that."

"But it's true. Why else would he stalk you?"

"He's not stalking me. And he's a priest," I said slowly as if she hadn't seen or heard me earlier. "He took a vow of celibacy and all that."

Macie squinted at me while giving me a shrug, dismissing my words. "Then why did he come here?"

"I don't know, but he was here when I got here. So there. No stalking." I felt like sticking my tongue out at her, but refrained.

The waitress came and took our order. But that didn't deter Macie one bit. She jumped right back in where she'd left off.

"Then it's that damn Catholic guilt they ingrained in us at Holy Cross. He feels bad for sending you away that night."

I rubbed my head again. "I know, but can we get off this subject? What's done is done. I don't even want to talk about it anymore. But I do want to show you something." I pulled my phone out and showed her my painting.

"Oh...oh...Haven. When did you do this?"

Although Jonathon had praised me, I knew it because he saw it as saleable. Macie's wide-eyed wonder was truth I could trust.

"I started it a week and a half ago and finished today."

"Jesus. It's giving me goosebumps just from your phone. I can't even imagine how I'll feel when I see it in person."

Suddenly, all the emotion I'd felt while painting wanted to rear its ugly head through sobs. I blinked furiously to ease the burn of tears that threatened to spill. Macie looked up at me and saw raw emotions exposed.

"Hey, babe, what's going on?"

"Nothing," I said with a shake of my head.

She knew me too well for an answer like that to get past her.

"Don't bullshit me. You and I have been around way too many blocks together for that."

"Mace, I don't really know. That painting, take a hard look at it and tell me what you see."

That had been what I wanted to ask her about.

Her eyes searched mine for a time and then she did what I asked. Her fingers spread the picture, enlarging it so she could study it better. "Well, shit. It's Holy Cross. And is that Canaan when he was young?"

"Yeah, and that was me. Only you probably couldn't tell since it's my back facing you."

"So, this piece of art is the result of your anger at him for what he did?"

I tossed a hand in the air. "You might say that."

The waitress brought us our food then, but I wasn't sure I could eat a bite.

Macie reminded me of a ravenous dog as she dug into her cheeseburger. "I'm sorry, Have, but I'm starving."

"No, eat. That's why you ordered food." I was glad someone was hungry. I picked at mine.

"You know what I think?" she added.

"You're going to tell me anyway, so what?"

"You need to talk to him and hear him out. If he says there are things you need to know, then you need to listen to what he has to say." I went to say something, but she held up her hand. "Wait, I'm not finished. He's a priest, Have. He's not going to spin a web of lies and tell you some trash like you'd expect from others. He'll tell you the truth. Go to him and give him the chance."

I chewed on her words and maybe she was right. But I wasn't ready to accept that.

"I don't know, Macie."

Before she could answer, a dark shadow loomed over our table. I looked up into the deep green eyes of Father Sullivan.

"Father," I breathed.

"Haven. Once again I regret upsetting you. That was never my intention. I hope you have a good evening."

Macie kicked me under the table.

It was enough to spur me to speak. "Um, I was wondering if there would be a time we could talk."

The way his eyes popped told me more than I needed to know. His hand trembled as he handed me a card. It was white and simply said in plain black letters, Father Canaan Sullivan. Directly beneath his name was his phone number.

"You can reach me at this number, day or night. Have a good evening, ladies."

Ten

CANAAN

Going to the gallery was a mistake, but I'd felt drawn to it as if a siren had lured me there. Looking at her paintings was an even bigger one; it was as if she'd painted my soul. The expression she captured on my face, the pain reflected in my eyes—how could she have known? But then she couldn't have. She must've pulled it from her memory, from that long ago day. I stood on the platform, waiting for the train, so consumed by my chaotic ruminations of the beautiful and talented woman that I never heard the L pull in.

"Mister, aren't you getting on?" a voice asked behind me, taking me out of my internal confession.

"Sorry," I mumbled as I moved through the open doors.

Falling into the seat, I reflected on my memory of that piece of art. Her vision of that fateful day included a stormy cloud-filled sky, as if lightning were about to strike. I got the impression that Haven was sending a message to me. She wanted the heavens to strike me dead for what I had forced upon her for all those years.

The impending issue was how could I explain myself without revealing my personal truths? Or did she deserve the knowledge of my shame in payment for how she'd been wronged? What would I say to her if she called? I couldn't possibly expose the truth. But I couldn't lie either. The spinning web of deception grew larger every day. First Bill and now Haven. Soon I would be wrapped in a cocoon so massive, I would be trapped by my own falsehoods. What kind of a priest was I?

I wiped the sweat off my brow and stuck a finger under the neckline of my shirt in an attempt to loosen it. The saintly collar that used to bring me comfort and even joy had turned into a noose and threatened to crush my trachea. I reevaluated my role as a priest. In the little time since I had returned to Holy Cross, my life had taken a one hundred and eighty degree turn.

A grim-faced Bill greeted me when I walked in the rectory door.

"I hate to be the bearer of bad news, but Kathy Frederick's condition has become unstable, and she's been hospitalized. I've been at the hospital with her this evening, and I told her you'd be there sometime in the morning, if your schedule is open. You have the six-thirty Mass so I thought you could go sometime afterward."

Kathy had been diligent in her attendance at Mass since my arrival a few weeks before. We'd spoken a few times before she'd gotten sick in the last week.

"That's awful. Of course I can go." Immediately, I thought of Haven. "Hadn't her condition improved some?"

"She'd been stable, but apparently her lungs seem to have worsened."

"I see. Is she critical?"

Bill shook his head. "No, not critical. It looks like her disease is progressing and affecting her heart now too, though. It's times like this, they often like to have more than one priest to talk to."

"Yes, that's true." It was terrible news. In our short acquaintance, I've found that Kathy was a lovely person. "I'll be happy to go in the morning." I wasn't sure if Haven even knew her aunt was sick. "Thank you for letting me know. I wonder if I should notify her niece."

"Oh, that's right. I forgot her niece is in town. By the way, how was the gallery showing? I forgot you went tonight. Did it live up to the expectations of the newspaper article?"

"It was actually better. You should go while she's here, Bill. Her work is really something. I studied art a bit in college, and what I saw tonight was extraordinary."

Bill tapped his forehead with his finger. "I'll have to remember to do that. When I ran into her at the church, she told me she'd be in town for several months. And she was so pleasant. Not to mention she's a former student here."

Bill obviously had had a different experience with Haven than I had. But then again, he wasn't the one who sent her home to live with her abusive uncle. So she probably was pleasant to Bill, unlike her caustic attitude toward me. "I'll try to contact her in the morning. I'm off to bed then."

As I turned to leave, Bill reminded me that I was on call that night. We took turns for call when the rectory office was closed. The office phone would automatically be diverted to our individual cell phones.

As I made my way to my room, I recalled I didn't have Haven's number. She only had mine. However, I had the number of the gallery where her art was displayed. I would call there in the morning.

Bill headed toward his room, leaving me to my troubled thoughts. Not only did I have to come up with something to tell Haven about that day I sent her away, I had to inform her of her aunt's failing health. Not knowing how close they were, the idea of telling her troubled me.

Sleep eluded me, as it often did. My knees ached after hours of praying, and each tiny movement brought burning pain on my back, reminding me of the welts from my self-inflicted atonement. I still couldn't calm my thoughts. The idea that I'd caused harm to someone else stirred ugly emotions in me. If I hadn't been so selfish with my own needs, a young girl might have gotten the help she needed.

I prayed to the patron saint of chastity, rape victims, poverty, purity and forgiveness, Saint Maria Goretti, who had more strength of forgiveness than I thought I would ever possess. Her story was somewhat similar to my own. I knew if I were a better man, I could achieve what she had.

It was still dark when I put on running clothes and shoes. I needed the punishment and the stress relief that a run would provide. I took to the streets and wound my way through the neighborhoods nearby, moving at a pace that made my lungs and legs burn with a need for more oxygen. But I refused to slow down.

This was the castigation my body craved. I kept up my rhythm until the sky began to lighten and my chaotic thoughts were quelled. I achieved freedom—freedom from pain—and it allowed me to break through my prison of the memories that controlled my life. The screams I kept contained inside of my head were released through running and it was my sanity check. Sometimes I was that bird I envied, flying free without anything to stop me.

All too soon, I found myself back in front of the rectory and it was time to prepare for Mass. I turned the shower to ice cold and soon the bird I'd become outside had clipped wings once again. Sagging against the wall, I shuddered against the icy spray as I thought about how much I could tell Haven. It wasn't possible to tell her what I'd gone through. The truth of that night wouldn't ever leave my lips. Never would I have the courage to speak those words. The only thing I could do was pray that if she asked for an explanation, I could give her one.

I dressed and walked to the church to prepare for Mass. As I celebrated it, I thought of Haven and prayed to the Lord for guidance, as I often did. Afterward, I was changing out of the vestments when my phone rang. I was shocked to see who was calling.

Eleven

HAVEN

Canaan's card burned a hole in my pocket and on my palm as I carried it home that night. My curiosity about what he had to tell me made me want to call him right away, but I hid that desire from Macie. She said I should call him, and I told her I would when I felt like it. The truth was, it took all I had not to pick up my phone all night and punch in his numbers. What did he want to tell me that was so important?

By the time the sun rose, I had barely slept at all. I did my best to make myself busy, but that only lasted so long. Enough was enough, so I decided to make the call. It was either that or go through the day and accomplish nothing.

Before I lost my nerve, I grabbed the card and stabbed my phone until I heard it ringing.

"Canaan Sullivan."

His voice was gruff. Had I woken him up?

"Canaan?" I cleared my throat. I should have probably called him *Father*, but I hadn't quite gotten there on the respect scale yet. "This is Haven. You said there were things I needed to know. Well, here's your opportunity to fill me in." My tone was brusque so he couldn't mistake this for a fun social call.

"Haven. I was going to call you this morning, but didn't have your number. I was waiting until the gallery opened. I have news, and I'm afraid it isn't good."

"News?"

"Yes. It's regarding your aunt."

"Aunt Kathy?"

"Yes. I'm afraid she's in the hospital."

"Oh, no." Even though I hadn't seen her since I'd been back, it wasn't because I hadn't tried. "What happened?"

"You know she's been ill?"

"I know she hasn't been well. My friend's mother mentioned something about that."

I could hear him sigh. "It's a little more than that. Can you come to the rectory? Or I could pick you up if you'd like."

If he wants me to go to the rectory, it must be pretty bad. "Okay, you're scaring me. You have to tell me."

"I didn't mean to upset you," he said.

"Upset? You just told me my aunt is sick and then you ask me to come to the rectory. What did you expect? A Funfetti cake?"

"Please, hear me out. I can't seem to say the right things. She's not in critical condition. The reason I asked you to come to the rectory was so I could explain things before we went to the hospital."

"Why would you go to the hospital? Is she dying?"

He blew out his breath into the phone. "Haven, I'm making a mess of things. I'm going to the hospital because Kathy asked for a priest to visit. We could go together?"

"We? Since when did *we* go anywhere together?"

"I'm sorry. I thought since you didn't know, you might want to go see her. Since I'm headed that way, I just...I shouldn't have made that assumption."

Jesus, Haven, quit being such a bitch to him. He's only trying to be nice.

"No, I'm the one who should be sorry. It's just that it's a shock is all. I didn't expect to hear this news when I called you."

"I understand. I can give you a ride if you'd like?"

As I thought about it, that sounded reasonable. At least I wouldn't have to face that fuckface Kent without reinforcement. "How about this? Why don't I just meet you somewhere and save you the trip? That's a long way to drive."

"I don't mind and that will give me some time to tell you what I know about your aunt's illness. And it's not that far."

For some reason that I couldn't explain, it made me uncomfortable to have him pick me up. "How about we compromise. I usually take the L and then transfer to the bus. Why don't you pick me up there?"

He agreed and I told him where and when.

The L was still crammed with morning commuters when I boarded the train. Fear over Aunt Kathy's health overrode my annoyance at the way they pushed and shoved to find a spot to anchor themselves. I never understood why people weren't nicer when they commuted. The way I looked at it was we were all in the same boat, so why not smile? But they never did. The farther away we got from the city, the more the crowd thinned on the train. When it was my time to get off, I was glad because I needed to hear about Aunt Kathy's condition.

I rushed down the stairs into the parking lot in search of Canaan and I finally located him. He was standing next to a car—his, I presumed. He waved when he saw me and I ran to him.

"Thanks for the ride," I said hesitantly.

"No, I'm happy to do this." He opened the door for me.

When he sat behind the wheel, I expected him to start the

car, but he didn't. Instead, he turned in his seat and looked at me.

He opened his mouth to say something, but I blurted out, "So, are we going or not?"

"Oh, yes." He started the car and drove like an old man. I wanted to push him out the door and drive myself. But I bit my tongue and sat on my hands instead.

"Have you ever heard of lupus?" he asked.

I nodded. "Yeah, but I don't know much about it at all."

"That's what Kathy has. It's an autoimmune disease and can be relatively mild, but in your aunt's case, she has the kind that unfortunately has progressed. It's now affecting her lungs and heart. Haven, there is no cure. They can only manage the symptoms."

Aunt Kathy. An incurable disease. This wasn't happening.

"Is she dying?"

"She's not critical if that's what you're asking, but I'm sure the doctors will be able to tell us more. That is, if your aunt will allow them with the HIPPA laws."

"O-okay," I whisper. My mom first and now maybe Aunt Kathy. Even though I didn't spend much time with her over the last few years, she was still the only remaining family I had. If she died, I'd be alone. And that thought left me feeling terribly lonely.

"Haven, I'm so sorry. Are you all right?"

I scoffed, "I guess God was looking out for me after all."

"What do you mean by that?"

Staring at him pointedly, I said, "If Aunt Kathy had died before I was able to move out, I'm pretty sure I'd be dead. I think the only reason the asshole didn't beat me to death was because of her." As soon as those horrible words left my mouth, I realized how true they were.

"You can't mean that."

"But I do. She had it as bad as I did, or maybe worse."

"How's that?"

"She'd lure him away from me with the promise of sex so he'd leave me alone. At least I escaped that side of it. Except I had to hear it at night and the things he said during. It made me sick. And I didn't understand then or now why she wouldn't leave him. I begged her, but she was as afraid as I was. Then I wasn't in any position to help her. Things have changed. God, how I hate him. You don't understand what it's like to hate someone that much. Why couldn't he have been the one to get sick? Sometimes things are so unfair. Aunt Kathy is just like my mom—kind and sweet. Neither of them deserved this. And that's why I don't buy into your God and church and all those fancy teachings of yours."

"They're not my teachings, Haven."

"Whatever. Look, can you drive a little faster? At this rate, we won't get there until the end of the week."

He quickly glanced at me, then back at the road, but didn't speak. The car did speed up somewhat, though.

"I should warn you, I'm not looking forward to seeing my uncle. I can't guarantee I'll be nice to him."

"Try to think of your aunt. She needs you now. Maybe that will help."

"I doubt it."

As we drove, I thought about Aunt Kathy. But then I remembered the reason I had called Canaan in the first place. So I said, "Oh, I called you this morning for a reason, but I got sidetracked when you brought up my aunt. Last night when I ran into you, you said I didn't know everything. What exactly were you talking about?"

He didn't respond, but I noticed how his hands tightened on the steering wheel. It looked like his knuckles were going to pop right through his skin. He was silent and I didn't think he was going to say anything else for the rest of the trip. His rigid posture and ashen complexion indicated whatever it was, it wasn't good.

Twelve

CANAAN

My vision held on to the road ahead as I tried to think of what to say next. A jumble of thoughts climbed the laborious trail to my lips, and bungee jumped out of my mouth.

"Everyone has joyous days and not so joyous days. That day had been not so joyous and I took it out on you. Father O'Brien had left for his quarters, and it wasn't a good thing for you to show up. Especially, since he would have probably been disrobing."

"How would you know that?"

Her words were sharp and accusatory. I couldn't seem to think straight around this woman.

"He'd mentioned something about cleaning up." Which was true. "I protected your virtue. And maybe if I hadn't been in such a foul mood, I wouldn't have scared you away. You could have talked to Father Matthews. And I have to live with my mistake."

"Virtue," she muttered. "I didn't have much of that then, nor do I now."

I quickly glanced over to see her picking at her nails.

"Maybe one day you'll find it in your heart to forgive me."

Her silence was deafening. I continued to ruin the moment. The quiet sank into the air until we arrived at the hospital.

Once we were parked, she jumped out of the car but didn't bolt for the door.

"Haven, I apologize again."

"No, don't. Just drop it. I really don't want to talk about that day."

"What can I do?"

"You can start by being my shield. The last thing I want to do is attempt murder in the hospital."

My lips curved into a rueful smile. "No, that wouldn't be good."

She shook her head. "And not for the reasons you think. In actuality, I don't want him dying in a place where they can revive him."

I wasn't sure if she was serious or not, so I decided not to respond.

"Do you know what room she's in?"

"Yes, on the fifth floor." We found the elevators and rode them up in silence. She kept chewing her nails and rubbing her palms together, indicating how nervous she was.

"It's going to be all right," I tried to ease her mind.

She crossed her arms over her chest and said, "Easy for you to say. That will only be true when I never have to lay eyes on him again."

The doors swooshed open and I waited for her to walk out, but she stood there like a statue.

"Haven? Are you going to get off?"

Her arms wrapped around herself tighter, and she walked out. Clearly this was not going to be easy for her. We located Kathy's room and tapped on the door. A nurse opened it and said it was okay to come in. Kathy was in bed and a doctor was with her. Oxygen tubes were attached to her nose, and her skin was pallid and drawn. I hid my surprise at her appearance. It was only a week since I had seen her, but the effects of the disease had certainly taken a heavy toll on her.

"We can wait outside," Haven said.

"No, it's fine. Dr. Wallace is finishing up and they were just talking," the nurse said.

Haven took hesitant steps through the door, and that's when Kathy spotted her.

"Haven? Is that you?" she asked in a weak and breathless voice.

"Yes, Aunt Kathy."

"Come here right now."

She went to the bedside and the two women hugged for a long time. I glanced around the room and was happy to note Kent wasn't present. I reached out my hand to the doctor and introduced myself.

"I'm Father Canaan Sullivan."

"It's nice to meet you, Father. I'm Dr. Wallace, Mrs. Frederick's pulmonologist. We were just talking about Haven. Mrs. Frederick was telling me about her talent as an artist."

"Yes, I'm not an art connoisseur, but I visited the gallery where her work is displayed and it's captivating."

By that time, the women had stopped hugging, and Dr. Wallace introduced himself to Haven. Then the three of them began discussing Kathy's condition. Haven asked him a series of questions, after Kathy gave him permission to answer.

"Aunt Kathy, you never even told me you were ill," Haven admonished.

"I didn't want to worry you."

"But this is even worse. I need to know these kinds of things." She turned to the doctor. "Dr. Wallace, how long will she be in here?"

"We are testing out some different medications to see if we

can stabilize her pulmonary and cardiac function. As it stands, she will have to be on oxygen, but hopefully we can get it to the lowest concentration possible. She is progressing very well and I'm pleased with her response."

As he was speaking to her, the doctor's gaze swept over Haven in a non-clinical way. I'd been on the receiving end of those looks and knew he found her attractive. And why wouldn't he? She was a beautiful, young woman.

"Doctor, are you saying that her condition is stabilized and her disease progression is halted?" Haven asked.

"Yes and no. But we're getting there. Our goal during this hospitalization is to get her controlled on the new medications we've put her on."

"I see," Haven said.

Their conversation was interrupted by Kent when he entered the room.

"Ah, Mr. Frederick, your wife is doing much better this morning," Dr. Wallace said.

"Good morning, Kent," I said.

He nodded to both of us and then his eyes settled on Haven. "Well, look who's come to pay a visit," he sneered.

The doctor, who was oblivious to the interchange, kept smiling at Haven, even though she had stiffened and her lips pressed into a thin line.

Dr. Wallace's phone buzzed. He pulled it out of his pocket, and read a message. "Duty calls, but Haven, I understand you have an art showing somewhere. Maybe I'll get a chance to come and see it."

She turned, grabbed his arm, and led him out the door. I imagined it was because she didn't want Kent to hear what she had to say.

Kathy said, "Kent, Dr. Wallace believes I may be able to go home in a few more days." It was hard for me to believe because right now she looked terrible.

"Good. That's good." His tone and expression told a different story. He kept a watchful eye on the door.

It was time to do what I came here for. "Kathy, would you like for me to pray now?"

"I would love that, Father."

My prayers were concluding when Haven walked back into the room. Kathy smiled, but Kent didn't. He eyed Haven in a scornful manner while being quiet for a moment before he commented, "So, you decided to return home, huh?"

"No, not permanently."

"How long are you here for?" His lips curled in disgust.

"About six months."

He rubbed his chin, as if he were thinking about that. "You got yourself a fancy gallery showing, do you?"

"That depends on what you would consider fancy."

"I'm surprised anyone would be interested in your stuff. From what I can remember, it wasn't much of anything."

"You can't remember because you destroyed everything I drew," Haven snapped as her nostrils flared.

"Haven...Kent," Kathy pleaded.

Kent ignored his wife. "So what'd you talk to that doctor about? You know Kathy's health information isn't any of your business now with those HIPPA laws."

A tiny muscle in Haven's cheek twitched, but she didn't say anything reactive. "I realize that, but Aunt Kathy gave the doctor permission to speak freely to me."

"Kent, let it go, please," Kathy begged.

It was an awkward position for me and I thought I needed to diffuse it, but what happened next floored me.

"What'd you do with that doctor out there? Were you acting like a slut, just like your mother? Following in her footsteps?"

Haven deflated as her mouth opened and closed several times before she clamped it shut. But then it was as though a fiery ball of anger lit her from inside. She lifted herself up to her fullest height and balled her hands into fists at her sides. If I hadn't been paying close attention, I would've missed the slight tremble in her lips. Then her reaction came right as I attempted to speak.

Between clenched teeth, she gritted, "How dare you speak of my mother that way? What are you going to do next? Pull off that belt and beat me bloody like you used to?" Even though her words dripped with hatred, her eyes couldn't hide the fear she tried so hard to conceal. She reminded me of a hunted animal the way she peered about wild-eyed. As a man of the cloth, even I found it difficult to find fault with what she said, may God forgive me.

Once again I opened my mouth to interject something, but before I could utter a word, Kent stormed out of the room.

"Good riddance," Haven muttered as she rubbed her arms.

"Haven," I whispered. My voice caught her attention and I jerked my head toward the bed. One look at Kathy and she rushed to the bedside. Tears streamed down her aunt's face, and Haven did her best to calm her.

"I'm so sorry you had to witness that, Aunt Kathy. I swore to myself I wouldn't do that, but damn it, look at me. I'm the worst. One minute with that man and there I go mouthing off." Haven blinked her eyes furiously as though she were pushing back tears she didn't want her aunt to see. I could understand why she might be so hurt with the cruel things Kent had said to her.

"It's okay, and how can I blame you? Sometimes I wish I wasn't married to him anymore, but what can I do? If I leave, I don't have health insurance, and with my situation now, I could never afford my medications, much less my hospital and doctor bills. I'm too sick to work." Then she broke down and wept.

Haven held her until her sobs quieted. It was not my place to interfere during this moment. When Kathy was done crying,

Haven said, "Aunt Kathy, I can help you financially."

"You? How can you help?"

"I have money, and you don't have to worry about that. I've wanted you to leave him for years. We can hire an attorney, and maybe he or she can figure out something with the insurance. I don't know about those things. But we can talk about this when you're feeling better."

Kathy shook her head. "I can't. The church."

"What about the church?" Haven asked.

"They don't condone divorce."

It was time for me to offer my assistance. "Kathy, the Catholic church allows divorce. You could go to church and take communion without a problem. Your divorce would become an issue with the church if you ever wanted to remarry," I explained. "In that case, you would have to obtain an annulment. And it wouldn't be a problem if extenuating circumstances existed, such as abuse."

Haven's head jerked around and her deep frown warned me of the impending storm. "What? So let me get this straight—she would have to have some sort of special committee or whatever put their stamp of approval on her divorce and label it an annulment in order for her to remarry? Do I have that correct?" Haven asked.

"I guess you could word it like that if you wanted to, but yes. Once that's done, she can remarry and receive communion," I said.

"That's utterly ridiculous. She's been in an abusive marriage for years. She should be able to get out and remarry and take communion if she wants. See? This is just one more reason I think religion is over-the-top crazy. All those obtuse rules and such. That makes no sense to me whatsoever." Haven's arms flew all over the place as she spoke.

"I can see why you might feel that way, but the church takes marriage very seriously, and that's why they have each couple go through marriage preparation classes. It's a way for them to come to an understanding that marriage isn't an easy path for anyone to take."

Haven huffed, "I find that odd."

"Why?"

"How can an unmarried priest be knowledgeable about marriage?" she asked.

"I can certainly understand why you'd say that, and he's not," I assured her. "But these classes aren't created by priests. They're created by professionals, and priests are only the moderators, if you will. So to get back to your original argument, Holy Matrimony is one of the Seven Sacraments of the Catholic Church, and because of that, it simply can't be voided. That's why it must be annulled by the church. As in divorce, you have to go through a process. Am I making sense here?"

"I suppose so," she said, though it came begrudgingly.

"I guess we're back to the original problem then, aren't we?" I asked.

"Yes. Aunt Kathy, if you want to leave, I'll bend over backward to make it happen."

Kathy fiddled with her blankets and sighed. "I know you will, but let me get through this hurdle first. Okay, honey? I need to build my strength before I do anything."

"You're right. What's wrong with me? I wasn't thinking." Haven hugged her aunt.

Kent walked back into the room. "How long are you planning to stay?" he asked. I didn't know if he was referring to Haven's hospital visit or her stay in Chicago. I decided to keep my mouth shut.

Haven hugged her aunt again and it looked as though she whispered something in her ear. Then to her uncle she said, "I'd stay all day if you weren't going to be here." She leaned down and hugged Kathy again. "I'll call you before I come back again, but let me know if you get out of here first."

"I will and thank you for coming. And thank you too, Father."

"Just call me if you need me, Kathy. I'm always available, and I mean that. You have the parish number and it goes directly to either Father Cernak's or my phone after hours."

"Yes, I know. Thank you."

We headed to the elevators and as soon as the doors closed, Haven said, "The doctor says she's actually doing a lot better and that she looks worse than she is. Her oxygen levels are coming up and the new medication they started her on seems to be doing its job. He was really pleased. He thinks she'll be out of here within the week."

"That's great news. When I saw her I was shocked because last week she looked so much better."

"Yeah, so was I. It's been a while and I almost didn't know what to say. I'm glad the doctor was there. But I need to get her out of that house and I hope I can do it before I kill Kent. What an asshole." She gave me a sideways glance. "Sorry, not sorry."

I could only shake my head at that. "Let's take this one step at a time. We have to make sure it's what Kathy wants after she's feeling better. This may be one of those things she's saying now because she's sick."

"I want her out of there yesterday. Canaan, he's a devil. I know because I lived under that roof for years. If she said she's ready, I need to act. I should start looking for a place for her to live." Her strides were so long and fast I had to hurry to keep up, and I was a tall man.

"Let's think about it a minute. She's still in the hospital. Maybe you should wait for her to get out and then have this talk with her."

She stopped and faced me. "Then what happens if she changes her mind?"

"Then she never wanted to leave him in the first place," I answered.

"What if he hits her when she's ill?" she snapped.

I didn't have a satisfactory answer for that. "Do you think he'd do that?"

"Yes, I do. Matter of fact, I know he would."

"Then I'll talk to him. Priest to parishioner."

"And you think that would solve everything?"

"Not necessarily. But it may set him on the right path."

"Canaan, he's a bully and has always been one. Worse, he's a power hungry cop. He could cause trouble. Your little talk would be like pouring gasoline on a fire."

"He won't cause trouble. Not if I intervene. And it may be that I don't even have to have that conversation."

Her body reminded me of a steel post she was that tense. "You don't know him. I trust Kent only as far as I can throw him. I have to get to work. Thanks for the ride." Her clipped tone told me she didn't have any faith in me or my abilities.

"Where are you going?" I asked.

"To the bus stop."

"Let me take you to the train station. I assume you're headed back downtown?"

"Yes," she said, "but I'm fine."

"It's no trouble at all." I didn't give her the chance to say anything else as I lightly touched her elbow and led her to the car.

After seeing how Kent behaved around her, my guilt over what I had done grew exponentially. Kent wasn't a nice man at all. And I had sent that defenseless young girl right back into his home where he inflicted all kinds of pain on her for years. How would I ever find a way to make amends?

Thirteen

HAVEN

As I rode the L back downtown, I thought about a lot of things, but mostly I thought about Canaan. One thing that kept bouncing around in my head was he seemed different than the picture I had painted of him in my head. He was pleasant and easy to be around. And then it hit me and I almost laughed out loud. Of course he was easy to be around. He was a fucking priest, for Christ's sake, no pun intended. He wasn't a threat. He didn't want anything from me. He wasn't trying to get in my pants. I didn't have to worry about him beating me. Safe. That's what he was. There was a cone of safety around him and with that came comfort.

And unfortunately, that triggered a memory. I dug my hand into my pocket and pulled out a card. Staring at it for a long moment, I read his credentials. They were impressive. I was surprised they could all fit on that tiny white card. Wilson A. Wallace, M.D. He said he wanted to visit the gallery and see my paintings, but my intuitions indicated there was more behind his intentions. We'd see. The way he was talking, I wouldn't be surprised if he showed up in the next day or so.

By the time I got off the train, it was nearly noon and I was starving. Stopping at a deli, I grabbed a take-out lunch and went straight into work. Jonathon stopped me before I could make it to my studio.

"Where've you been? I've been texting you all morning."

"Sorry. I was at the hospital. My aunt. She's pretty sick."

His demeanor instantly changed. "Is she okay?"

"Better. She has lupus." I gave him the details on her condition.

"Haven, I'm sorry. Are you close?"

"Sort of." I didn't want to talk about her with him. So I didn't offer any more information.

"Do they expect her to be in the hospital for long?"

"Hopefully not too much longer. They're trying her out on some new medications and she seems to be responding."

"That's good news then. Well, I have some more good news for you. Your large painting sold."

"My large painting?"

"Yes, the one you recently completed. The really huge one."

"Oh." My brain spun with this news.

"Aren't you going to ask me?" he asked.

"Ask you what?"

He laughed. "You do have your mind on other things. I'm getting ready to change that. Ask me the sale price."

"Okay, how much?"

"You ready for this?"

He gave me the price.

I scratched the side of my head. "You've got to be kidding me."

Jonathon cocked his head. "That's not quite the reaction I expected to see from someone who just sold a painting for that much."

My brows shot up and I was pretty damned sure they almost hit my hairline. "Did you say what I think you said?"

He chuckled. "You bet your sweet ass I did."

A couple of long moments later, Jonathon's finger was pushing on my bottom jaw. "You'd better close your mouth Haven, or you may be catching some bugs."

I snapped my jaws together. Then I frowned. "Who the hell would spend that kind of money on one of my paintings?"

"A very wealthy family, that's who. Apparently the wife was in here yesterday and must've gone home and told her husband she wanted it. So this morning, right after the gallery opened, he called and asked if anyone else had made an offer on it. When I said that there had been a lot of inquiries on it, he offered me top dollar right on the spot and was here an hour later. Don't forget, that's a huge piece of art, not to mention the other one sold for not too much less. In a year or so, something like that of yours will sell for double."

"Jesus Christ."

"My sentiments exactly. And Haven, they are leaving it here for the duration of your stay. They also want to meet you."

"Oh, absolutely. I want to shake the hands of the people who believe in me that much."

Jonathon added, "Didn't I tell you that article was going to work magic? And one other thing. Your inventory is extremely low so you need to get in your studio and paint."

"That's the plan." Wrapping my mind around something this major took more effort than I possessed. I choked down my lunch, which now tasted like sawdust, and I thought about what a fucknut of a day it had been so far.

Pulling out my phone, I called Macie.

"Hey, chica. What up?"

"You know that huge painting I recently completed? The one I showed you? The picture?"

"Oh yeah."

"It sold."

"Woohoo! We'll have to celebrate this weekend. I see a

martini or five in our futures."

"Cool. But guess for how much."

"Haven, you know I suck at this."

I filled my lungs with a cleansing breath and felt my control returning. Then I collected myself and whispered the amount.

"Wait. What? Repeat that." Macie was clearly as shocked as I had been.

So I told her again.

"Jesus criminy jickets. Holy shit on a shingle." Then she laughed. "You mean, like, with that many zeroes."

"Yep, that's what I mean." And I started laughing again. And Macie joined in.

"Oh my God, Haven, I knew it. I just knew you had it in you. You're famous. You're going to be like Picasso."

"Hardly, but I will make a decent living, I think."

"And if anyone deserves it, it's you."

"I wish I could hug you right now, because if it hadn't been for you and your mom, I never would've kept drawing." And that was the honest to God's truth.

Then Macie shouted, "This weekend. Martunis!" That's what she called them sometimes. And it hit me what my next painting would be. Macie—my girl who had helped me in too many ways to count.

The door to my visionary side unlocked and my brain became a Ninja blender, swirling with ideas. People asked me all the time where my inspiration came from and my answer was always the same. They usually popped into my head from something I had been thinking about. I ran to the closet and pulled out the painting clothes I kept in there. They were nothing but an old pair of jeans and a T-shirt. I threw on an apron I wore because I used it for the pockets in the front. They were perfect for stashing my brushes.

My excitement over this painting grew, but I couldn't start until I had the canvas. I scanned my studio, but nothing I had was the perfect size. Before I knew it, I was running down the hall, calling for Jonathon's assistance. Knowing how much he wanted me to produce, it wasn't long before I was set up and working.

My palette in hand and oils mixed, I had pulled and printed some images of Macie off my phone to use. This would be a puzzle of a collage, coming together in the main focus of a central portrait of her. It was a replica of a picture I had taken when she'd visited me in Manhattan. She was standing in front of Tiffany's with a sublime smile on her beautiful face. The other faces would represent different moods—sad, angry, introspective, and I would even add one of her sleeping. I decided I would create each face in the center of a puzzle piece and fit it into the main one, but slightly blur the edges. Some pieces would be darker than the others, giving the painting a diverse border to it.

Working all afternoon and into the evening nonstop, I was getting close to having the background established in a rudimentary fashion. Jonathon had orders not to interrupt me, so when he stuck his head in, I was surprised.

"How goes it?" he asked.

"It goes."

"Ah, she smiles. It must be good."

"I can only hope. What's up?"

"One, it's going on eight."

"Shit!"

"Thought you'd want to know. And two, that priest who was here the other day is back. He's asked for you." Jonathon had that questioning look about him.

"Canaan?" What does he want? I know it can't be my aunt because the hospital would've called since she added me to the list.

"Didn't give a name. Just asked for you."

"Send him back."

"Haven, are you sure?"

"Yeah. It's fine."

He shrugged and left. A moment later Canaan walked through the door.

"Am I interrupting?"

"No. Time to wrap it up anyway. I've been at it since I got back from the hospital."

"Do you mind if I take a look?" he asked.

"Suit yourself." My frosty tone didn't deter him in the slightest.

He walked around the canvas and stood next to me. "How do you figure this stuff out?"

"Figure what out?" I asked as I cleaned my brushes.

"Where to put everything?"

Was he serious? "I'm an artist. It's what I do. How do you figure your church stuff out? It's your thing. This is mine," I snapped.

"You're very talented. It's a blessing from God."

"Back to God, huh? Thought I already told you I don't buy into your God crap and all that Catholic nonsense. Those things I learned in school."

"I'm not here to argue the merits of God and Catholicism, although I am first a priest and a theologian, so it's difficult for me not to weigh in on this. Everyone is entitled to their own opinion. But I have to say this—God sometimes gives us things—certain talents, and He blessed you with your ability to paint wondrous things."

"Hmm. Well, you can tell your God 'Thanks.' He did help me. Because I sketched to escape the fucking Hell I lived in, if the truth be told," I said in the most scathing manner I could muster. "It was the only thing that kept me sane, only I had to hide it from Uncle Kreep." I couldn't even imagine the sneer that was plastered on my face.

He held up his hands like he was under arrest. "Please, let's not argue. I didn't come here for that. You were upset when we left the hospital."

I waved him away. "Kent's a goddamn asshole. There's nothing new there. Why are you here? What did you have to tell me?"

"I went back to visit your aunt late this afternoon and she looked much better. Her color had improved. Her cheeks were actually a bit pink. It's amazing what oxygen, or maybe the lack of, will do to you."

I drooped with relief and words spilled out of me. "I was so worried. That makes me feel much better." Without a thought, I put my hand on his arm and I could've sworn he jerked. He held his arm still, but I could feel his muscles tense beneath my touch.

"There's something else."

"What?" And then it happened. I gawked at the priest. Maybe it was because I was relieved that my aunt was doing better. That simple fact had diffused my anger enough for me to look at him—really look at him. And damn if the man wasn't more beautiful than people claim Michelangelo's David to be.

"Is everything okay?"

Quickly, I averted my gaze, realizing I had been gaping at him. No doubt I wasn't the first.

"No, I'm hungry. I've been painting all day and didn't stop to eat."

"I haven't either. I have something else to talk to you about, but since you've worked late, and so have I, maybe you would you like to grab something to eat and drink with me? We could talk then."

For a second I deliberated. This was my nemesis standing before me, but now he was asking me to break bread. My stomach could definitely do with some fuel since I hadn't eaten. He dangled that damn carrot and before I could put any more thought into it, I blurted, "Okay. Give me a minute to change out of my work clothes."

He nodded. "I'll wait out front."

A short time later, I joined him wearing the same clothes I wore to the hospital. I was glad he was a priest and that I didn't have to worry about impressing him. We left after I told Jonathon I'd see him the next day.

"Do you mind sitting at the bar?" I asked, ending up a few blocks away at a place that had good food.

"No, that's fine."

We snagged two stools in the back and asked for a couple of menus. I recommended the burgers and the fish and chips. We ordered our food and beers. The beers arrived and we clinked bottles.

"Tell me what was so important that you came all the way downtown to talk to me."

What he told me shocked the shit out of me.

"I had a talk with your uncle. I expressed my concern over the way he spoke to you."

"You did what?"

I pressed my hands to my burning cheeks. It always dumbfounded me as to how my face could go from normal to a thousand degrees in half a second. My chin hit my chest so he wouldn't notice my humiliation, but I was sure I was too late.

"Haven, he was so far out of line when he said those terrible things to you and insulted your mother as well. I told him it was a grave sin to do so. He wasn't pleased, as you can imagine, and he told me to keep my nose out of his business. We went back and forth, but in the end, I told him if he couldn't say anything positive about you, then he should keep his sinful words to himself."

For the longest time, I could only stare at Canaan. Any time I tried to speak, the words became locked up tightly in my larynx, as though someone was fisting it and not allowing them to pass through. Never in my life had anyone ever defended me. Aunt Kathy, in her own way, had tried, but her terror had prevented her from standing up and speaking out. This was entirely different. It was the same as Canaan saying he went to war for me. Me, Haven Richardson. Once again my face heated, but this time it wasn't with shame. It was with gratitude. My palm stretched over my heart as I said brokenly, "Thank you for doing that. No one's ever…" My voice cracked as I swallowed the burgeoning thickness in my throat. "No one's ever done anything like that for me before. The day my mom died, I came home from school and was immediately forced to pack all my things. My life with him began then, and until this moment, I've never had anyone stand up for me." I offered him a weak smile.

"After this morning, it didn't sit well with me, so I had to have that discussion with him. Haven, it probably won't do any good, but at least I let him know that type of behavior is not acceptable and is sinful."

I nodded, agreeing. "I still thank you. At least you tried. I wish I could punch him."

"Believe me, I had a moment of wishing for the same thing."

"For real?"

"For real. I'm a priest, but I'm still human. And that guy pushed my buttons."

"And he shows he's like the rest of us." The best I could offer was a watery smile. My eyes, though teary, were filled with gratitude, not sorrow.

"Priests aren't immune to real life problems."

Our eyes connected, and I wondered what he was trying to say. I saw a man who had once been my crush and the attraction I felt hadn't changed. With my anger dulled, it was hard not to notice his kissable lips. So when the bartender placed our food in front of us and Canaan said a blessing, I almost told him to pray for my inappropriate thoughts of him.

And that was weird for me since I'd never done that before. Not wanting to bring attention to that detail, I bowed my head and said nothing while he prayed.

Between bites of his burger, he asked, "How was your afternoon?"

"Good. Well, you saw that I started another painting. By the way, the one I did—you know, the one you're in?" He nodded. "It sold this morning."

"Congratulations! That's great news for you."

I bit my lips to keep from smiling. "Yeah." I was so freaking excited that I blurted out, "And you wouldn't believe what the price point was."

"What?"

Then I stopped and thought about what I was about to say. Why did I do that? It was not okay to announce things like that. It reeked of bragging. And that was the kind of information I did not want to share with most people, even Canaan, since we had only recently struck up a semblance of a friendship.

Before I had the chance to say anything, his perception clued him in. "It's okay, Haven. You don't have to tell me."

My shoulders slumped as I grimaced. "I'm sorry. I should have never brought that up. It was a little boastful."

"No, it wasn't. You're an up and coming artist and you've been discovered, so I think it's something to be proud of. I don't consider that boastful at all. I'd love to share your excitement with you." He picked up his beer bottle. "Here's to many more successful sales and beautiful paintings."

We clinked bottles again and I thanked him.

"I'm actually surprised I caught you. I thought for sure you would be out."

"Me, no, I would have picked up something and made an early night of it."

"Really, I thought you'd be with your friend or someone else special."

My head jerked at his statement. "You mean like Macie or a boyfriend?"

He chuckled. "That's exactly what I mean."

"Um, no. Macie's busy tonight. And I don't do the boyfriend thing." My head quickly shook back and forth. I was pretty sure I looked like a dog shaking water off its body.

He raised a quizzical brow. "And why's that? I would think you'd be chasing them away."

"Yeah, well, I'm not and won't ever be. That doctor, Wallace, you know, Aunt Kathy's doctor? He asked me out this morning. I'm not sure how to handle that. He's going to stop by the gallery this week."

Canaan sat back in his stool and crossed his arms. His perusal of me made me squirm. "Why don't you date? You're young and..." He paused and I could see color rising in his cheeks. "You're young. You should be out dating to find *the one*."

"The one," I scoffed. "Men aren't trustworthy. They, well, they want things I can't give. And I'm not going to put myself in a situation where I'll feel trapped ever again."

His eyes narrowed in confusion. "I don't understand."

My lips pressed together as I remembered all those nights I heard Aunt Kathy. Shuddering, I looked Canaan squarely in the eyes. "I saw what Aunt Kathy went through. I won't put myself in jeopardy of facing that. Her husband is supposed to be this great guy. Everyone thinks he's wonderful. But he's not." I leaned into him and muttered, "The only time she could manage his temper was when they were getting it on. I heard it at night. I would put my pillow over my head to drown out the awful noises. No thanks."

He rested his head on his hand. "Not all men are like that. Surely you know that. There are plenty of good men who would never hurt a woman. Kent isn't good; I'll give you that. And Kathy shouldn't have stayed to suffer like that. But that doesn't mean you would end up with someone like him."

Without looking at him, I whispered, "My experience with men is on my terms."

"Your terms?"

He was a priest. How could he understand that when I needed what a man offered, I picked them up, brought them home or went to their places for one night only? And that was it. I didn't want anything else from them. They were of no use to me. I polished off my first beer and signaled for another.

"Nothing really. I don't do long term, that's all."

"Will you make me a promise?"

The waitress arrived but said nothing as she sat my fresh beer down.

"Depends."

"Are you going to go out with the doctor?"

"I can't say."

"You should go. Give him a chance that you haven't given anyone else. Just one time at least. If you like him, then go again, but please try. He could be that one good guy."

That made me laugh. Hard. "How the hell would you know? You're a priest."

"Just because I'm a priest doesn't make me an idiot."

The warmth of his smile heated me more than it should. Forcing myself to ignore it, I thought about what he said. He was right. He wasn't stupid.

"Well then, tell me about your experience. How many girls did you go out with before you decided that the church would be your bride?"

His spine stiffened to the point I was sure it was made out of rebar. Two spots of scarlet appeared high on his sculpted cheekbones. Hmm. I'd hit on a tender point here. Had he been in love?

"None."

His curt answer debunked my theory. So then why the

reaction?

"None? Never?"

"Never. Zero."

"You never had any interest in girls? Are you gay?"

The scarlet spots turned into a rosy flush that spread down his neck. There had to be something more to this.

"I didn't say I wasn't interested in girls. I only said I never dated or went out with any."

"Okay, then how many girls did you kiss?"

He squirmed in his seat, and the flush faded a bit, but he answered, "None."

"No girls, no dating, no kissing, anyone? What's up here, Canaan?"

"I had a calling." His voice was low and he looked at me oddly. He was so beautiful. I found it hard to believe a girl had never tried to kiss him.

"Calling? You should know that every girl in school crushed on you."

"Every girl?" he asked with one sardonic brow raised.

I took a deep swallow of liquid courage, polishing off my beer before I set it down with a thud.

"Fine, I have a confession to make. Every girl seriously crushed on you, including me. You were the hot altar boy that all the girls wanted. That's why this is so hard to swallow."

We looked at each other, and when I thought he would laugh at what I'd said, he only stared with his lips slightly parted.

"I don't know what to say besides I didn't deserve any of the attention."

"Does it bother you to have all that attention?"

He stared at me for a while. "As I said, I'm no better than anyone else. At that time, there were so many things going on in my head."

I can't say why I pressed this conversation other than the

alcohol was fuel for my empty stomach.

"Do you regret not ever kissing someone?"

"I have a great many regrets."

I knew I was going to hell and probably shouldn't do it. But for some awful reason, I couldn't stop myself. I rose out of my seat and leaned across the distance. I sank my fingers into his arms and pulled him toward me. Shock registered on his face a second before I pressed my lips against his. That's all. It wasn't an invasive kind of kiss, only the chaste kind.

My memory took me back to when I was young and dreamed of how my first kiss would be. I had this notion that my lips would tingle and my stomach would have a swarm of butterflies fluttering their feathery wings inside of me. In actuality, my first kiss was nothing but a gross, slobbery mess. This, however, was what my first kiss should have been.

In the short time our lips were fused together, my heart skipped, my belly danced as though it were filled with hummingbirds, and my skin buzzed as a current of fire zipped through me. When I dragged my mouth away from his, stunned could best describe how I felt.

My hand covered my mouth because I was certain I was mistaken. I couldn't possibly have felt those things. Those were the things of fairy tales and romance novels, things I surely didn't believe in, for I knew of life's harsh realities. But when I opened my eyes, his forest green ones stared back at me with a potency that couldn't be denied. One, two, and three blinks later convinced me my feelings were real and not the imaginary sort.

Finally, I spoke. "I'm sorry."

"Don't," he whispered. He pulled out his wallet and grabbed some bills out. Laying them on the bar, he said, "Do you have a way home?"

I nodded.

"I'm sorry, Haven. But it's best if I go."

Fourteen

CANAAN

My concentration over the past week had been a hope-less mess of scattered pieces. Bill must have thought I'd lost my mind, and maybe I had. My homilies at the Sunday Masses were disjointed and difficult to follow. The confused expressions on the faces of the parishioners told me far more than I needed to know.

One chaste kiss from a woman I barely knew knocked me for a loop, and I wasn't sure how to pull the bits of my muddled brain together. Every time I tried to refocus, change my aim, all I seemed to recall were the softness of her lips, the lavender scent that surrounded her, and the way her fingers pressed into my flesh. I always *hated* to be touched. But not by *her*. Haven. A name that was so close to heaven.

Acting was my forte, concealing my feelings from the world, forced into it by Father O'Brien. But on Monday, when Bill was called out of town because of an ailing family member, I failed miserably at it. I knew he fretted about leaving everything in my less than capable hands. I assured him, with as much false bravado as I was capable of conjuring, that all would be fine, even though my self-doubts were monumental.

The following morning I made my rounds in the hospital, visiting a few parishioners, including Kathy Frederick. She looked like a completely different person and told me she would be going home the following day. What should've been happy news from her came across as being the opposite.

"Kathy, is everything okay?"

She nodded as she fumbled with her blanket. Not meeting my gaze, she asked, "Father, how should I handle Kent?"

"I'm not sure what you're asking." Her eyes darted around the room, reminding me of a frightened rabbit. "Are you afraid of him?"

"He hasn't hurt me since I've been sick."

"Should I have a word with him?"

Her eyes nearly bugged out of her head. "Good Lord, no. That would surely set him off. If he ever knew I discussed this with you, that would be the end of me."

I assured her I wouldn't say a word. But then I added, "Perhaps you should let Haven know. She would be willing to help. And she will also want to know you're being released."

"Yes, I plan to call her right when I get home."

I had the impression she only wanted a sounding board and nothing else. After I said some prayers for her, I returned to the rectory. Bill called several times to give me updates on his mother, but I was sure it was a cover for the real reason he called. He was convincing himself that everything was fine and I was able to handle things in his absence.

I went into the sanctuary to pray, as was my usual routine, because it offered me a place free from interruptions. Kneeling at the foot of the cross, I begged for forgiveness and to wipe the memory of Haven's kiss from my lips. But the more I pleaded, the more my lips were seared with the branding of hers. Their ghostly impression remained, scorching me with their velvety touch. Worse yet, I wanted more. I wanted to explore the mystery behind them and that was sinful beyond measure. Lust was taking its wicked root in me and spreading its ugly tentacles, bringing forth all of Father O'Brien's vile admonitions. Had he been right after all? Was I the temptation Satan sent? The only way to move forward was to pray—pray for help, for forgiveness, and to beg for God's mercy on my soul.

As I knelt before the cross, my phone buzzed. I reached into my pocket and saw it was a text from our secretary. One of the parishioners was trying to reach either Bill or me. She indicated it was urgent, so I finished my prayers and walked over to the rectory. It was late afternoon, around four-thirty, and the late summer heat reminded me of the way Haven's scent warmed my blood.

Brushing those thoughts away, I opened the office door, and allowed the air conditioning to cool my veins. Mary, our secretary, smiled and handed me a note.

"This gentleman called twice now. He sounds pretty desperate, Father."

"Thank you, Mary. Did he say what he needed?"

"No, only that he needed to speak with either you or Father Cernak."

"Okay, I'll call him right away."

I glanced at the slip of paper and the name sounded a bit familiar. Perhaps I knew him. Greg Clark. I tapped the numbers and waited for him to answer.

"Hello."

"Mr. Clark? This is Father Sullivan. I understand you need to speak to me?"

"Uh, yeah. I do. Are you available now?" a shaky voice responded.

"Yes. Can you come to the rectory?"

"Um, I can be there in about a half hour. Will that work?" he asked.

"That will be fine."

Mary was getting ready to leave for the day, which was usual, so I told her to leave the office door unlocked. Thirty minutes later, Mr. Clark walked in.

After the introductions, he said, "I remember you. I went to Holy Cross. I think we both served as altar boys at one point."

"I'm so sorry, Mr. Clark. I have to admit, I don't remember. I was such a bookworm back then, and so focused on the church that I didn't socialize much. Please forgive me."

He waved a hand. "You were focused on becoming a priest, and I was focused on…other things."

As we spoke, I ushered him to my office. I noted his rather disheveled appearance. His clothes looked like he'd slept in them for days. His hair was rumpled, and he was sporting a few days of unshaven beard. Clearly, the man needed to talk about something important.

Since we were alone, I didn't bother to close the office door. I indicated that he should take a seat, and rather than sit at my desk, I sat in the chair next to him and angled it so we faced each other.

"Now tell me how it is I can help you, Mr. Clark."

"Please, call me Greg." Then he dropped his head in his hands momentarily and rubbed his forehead. When he looked back up, he asked, "This may be a bit unusual, but do you have anything to drink?"

"Oh, sorry. What can I get you? Water, tea?"

"You wouldn't happen to have something a bit stronger? Maybe bourbon or scotch"

He must really have something bad he needed to get off his chest.

"I have both or vodka, if you prefer that."

"Scotch, please."

"Neat or on the rocks?" I asked.

"Neat."

The church didn't condemn drinking as long as it wasn't abused. And Bill kept quite an array of liquor, so I went to grab the scotch. I was more of a beer or vodka guy myself, but if he needed a drink, I wouldn't let him have one alone. I also grabbed some ice for myself, and a couple of glasses. Then I rejoined him and poured us a couple. Handing him one, I nodded. "Go easy on that now."

He took a good swallow and then another.

"So, what brings you here today?"

Without any preamble, he said, "My wife."

"I see. And why is she not with you?"

His hand shook as he picked up his glass before he took another heavy swallow. "I wouldn't let her come. There's something…there's this…thing." He stared holes into the floor for a while, and I gave him all the time he needed. I knew better than to put words into his mind or mouth or nudge him to speak. He finally filled his chest with air and met my eyes. "She said if I didn't come here and speak with you, she was leaving me. That our marriage was…"

It rattled me. It wasn't just that his wife wanted to end their marriage. It was the way he said it. It was the haunted pain in his eyes.

"I see. But I'm going to need a little more than that, Greg."

He snorted out a derisive laugh. "You sound like her."

He wasn't the first husband I'd counseled in my short time.

"Are you having an affair?"

The absolute look of horror on his face answered my question before his words did.

"Oh, God, no! I would never cheat on her. She's my life. But she doesn't believe me."

"Believe what?"

He opened his mouth to say more, but then stopped. I'd learned not to interrupt, so I sat there waiting.

"Believe that I'm being faithful to her."

"Why is that?" I gently prodded.

He downed the glass of scotch and stood, his back toward me. Then he sat back down. "She's pregnant with our second child. She said if I don't get help, she's leaving me."

His response wasn't an answer to my question.

"Okay, so, what is it then? If you're faithful to her, there has to be a reason she's saying this."

He stared into the bottom of his empty glass. "I haven't touched her in…months. Most likely since she got pregnant." He trailed off.

"My understanding is that sexual relations during pregnancy are fine. Did you have this problem with your first child?" He shook his head. "What's different?"

"I've been having nightmares. I don't sleep or eat the way I should. I'm depressed and drinking a lot. Yelling at our son and her. Taking my anger out on them."

"Can you tell me why you're angry?" I asked.

I watched his Adam's apple bob up and down as his face took on a haunted appearance. "We both grew up here, you see, and when she became pregnant four years ago, she wanted to move back. To get closer to our families and all that. I tried to talk her out of it, but you know how women are, right?"

A smile ghosted my lips. "Actually, I don't. But I'll take your word for it."

He looked confused for a moment, but then the corner of his mouth tugged upward. "Well, anyway, she got her way, and that's when it all started—after we moved back here a few months ago."

"You're being relatively cryptic here."

He dropped his head again and clasped his hands together. "The thing that's pulling us apart. That's what started."

"Yes, but what is *that thing*?"

He drained his second glass and got to his feet again. He paced the small room for a few steps, stopped, stared at me, and paced some more. Clearly he was weighing his options.

"I have to be honest here. It's kind of strange talking to you," he said. He noticed my confusion so he rushed to add, "Don't take this personally, but we were altar boys together, and I'm getting ready to spill my guts to you."

Then an idea came to me. "Will it help if we move to the confessional? Whatever you tell me in there, even though it's not a true confession, is sacred, and I cannot, under my vows as a priest, disclose it to anyone else. You would also have privacy in there, you know, behind the screen. So it would afford you the feeling of anonymity. Even though I'll know it's you, it would give the illusion of secrecy. Does that make sense?"

I was met with silence.

Then I had another idea. "How important is your marriage to you?" His stare was fierce, forcing me to believe his next words.

"Let me put it to you this way. I would lay down my life for my wife."

My decision was made. "Then come with me, Greg."

We left my office and I locked up the rectory before we walked over to the church. I told him I would meet him in the confessional. I would wait until either he spoke his piece or let me know he simply couldn't tell me.

"Mind you, Greg, this is not a confession. This is just a safe place for you to talk. What you say to me in there won't go beyond those doors. Understood?"

I was not prepared for what I was about to hear. As I sat waiting, I wasn't sure what he would do.

When the door opened, and he knelt, I slid the partition back. "Are you ready to talk?"

"I think so, Father."

"Whenever you're ready, I'm here to listen and guide."

I heard him take a deep breath and then slow and steady, the words dripped from his lips. If they were painful for him to say, they were like acid as they corroded and ate away at me. "I was sexually molested as a teenager."

I hadn't expected that at all. I knew this unfortunate thing happened to children all over the world. No one expects it to happen to themselves or someone they know.

"And moving back here triggered the memories," I said as calmly as possible. This wasn't about me. It was about someone else.

"Yes. Being here"—he paused—"it happened when I was an altar boy here. It was Father O'Brien. He raped me."

My breath was ripped away like my innocence that long ago day. I had a strong inclination to run. But I was gripped to that chair by invisible bands called guilt and shame.

"Father..."

Somehow I managed to exhale the words, "I'm here."

"I'm telling the truth. I know you may not want to believe me."

Nothing was further from the truth. I wanted to give peace to this poor man. I also felt pulled in two different directions. I wanted to cling to the information that let me know I wasn't alone. I also felt horror for the same reason. But mostly I wanted to know the answer to the question that had haunted me...that still haunted me. But I didn't ask. Couldn't ask. Would never ask because my sin would go to the grave with me. Had he paid the price for my silence?

His own made me realize my duties. I couldn't share my pain. My job was to free him from his own.

"Greg, that was not your burden to bear alone. You were young, I would imagine."

I knew the answers before I asked the questions.

"Yes, fourteen when it first started. You believe me?"

"I don't think you came here to spread lies."

"I didn't. He did this to me."

His choking sobs hid my own shuddering breaths.

"I suppose you feared Father O'Brien. He was quite stern at times." *And more than vicious with his punishments.*

"Yes." His answer was little more than a whisper.

"You had no control over this."

"No."

His meek response was almost childlike.

My hands wrapped around the wooden arms of the chair in which I sat. The way I was gripping them, I wondered if I was going to crush them with my bare fingers. Seething anger simmered inside of me, threatening to gush out, but I contained it.

The ghost of Father O'Brien and his admonishments of my sins floated in my head. What had he told Greg were the reasons for his so-called chastisements?

Unclenching my jaws, I asked in a barely controlled tone, "Did you tell anyone?"

He didn't speak. I looked over through the small window and watched the dark shadow swing his head side to side while rocking himself.

"And now it's affecting your marriage. Is that correct?"

"Coming back here triggered all those old emotions I thought I had finally shed. And then when he died, it was such a r-relief. You wouldn't believe how liberating it was."

Oh, yes, I would.

I could hear him sniff as his sobs subsided. I wanted to weep myself. "I'm sure it was. The man who hurt you so deeply was no longer a threat, and that's nothing to be ashamed of, Greg."

"I'm not ashamed of that. That's not it at all. I wanted him to die. For years, I prayed for it—asked God to take him from this Earth. But now..."

"Now what?" I knew exactly where this was going. My body shook as if he were reciting my own story. And I abhorred listening to it.

"It's like coming back here has awakened this awful spirit or something, and the nightmares keep coming. And my poor wife. I can't tell her. She thought he walked on water. She'll never believe me."

There were times I questioned God and why bad things happened to good people. I didn't believe myself good. Some of what Father O'Brien said to me was true. I was temptation. Haven had proved that. She'd kissed me knowing I'd given myself to God and him alone. But that hadn't stopped her.

"Father, are you there?"

I closed my eyes, remembering what I was supposed to be doing. I would need heavy prayer tonight for my selfish thoughts. This man needed me.

"Greg, listen to me. Your wife pushed you to talk to me because she wants to make this work. When someone loves you that much, she could never hate you. "

"It's one thing to tell your husband to talk to his priest. But it's another to find out he was molested for years."

The flavor of rust made me realize I'd bitten my tongue. It wasn't the pain of the flesh I felt, but the pain of the soul. How many, I wondered? How many boys did he take? How many people did he deem candidates for his punishment? And how much fault did I bear for not speaking out? Could I have saved some like Greg? Had I been the first? But certainly not the last. Guilt poured down upon me like sheets of rain in a summer storm.

"Father Canaan? Did you hear me?"

"I'm sorry, what did you say?"

"She won't want me near her after this. She won't want me to touch her. I'm dirty. I'm a dirty, little boy. That's what he used to say to me."

You're a sinner, Canaan. Your flesh makes even the strongest person weak.

His voice was like an ice pick chiseling a path to my psyche.

As much as this killed me and as much as I had no idea how I'd get through it, I asked, "Do you want me to meet with the two of you?"

"I don't know if I can tell her."

Filling my lungs, though they burned with hatred, I said, "Greg, why did you come to me for help?"

"My wife said she would leave me if I didn't."

"So, if you're not going to open up to her, then what will you tell her?"

"How can I begin to...?"

As much as these words choked me, I knew they needed to be said. "I can be there with you."

"Maybe that would help. Maybe I could tell her with you present. Could you be there?"

"Of course I can." I had no idea how, but I sure would try. The man never deserved what was forced upon him, even if I had. I'd been guilty of temptation but also of weakness. I'd kept quiet and others had suffered. My atonement would be never ending. Nevertheless, I had to somehow try in my own way to undo what pain he'd endured.

"Greg, you understand I'll have to recommend therapy for you and maybe even the both of you."

"Can you do that when she's here?"

"Yes," I said absently. I was giving advice on something I should have done myself years ago.

We arranged to meet the following week. Greg said he needed that time to prepare himself. I didn't think it was a good idea, but he said he couldn't tell her before then. So he compromised and we agreed to meet on Monday evening.

"Father, one last thing before we go. Can you absolve me from my sin?"

"I can, but I want to reassure you, there was no sin on your part, Greg. You did nothing wrong. I absolve you from your *sins* in the name of the Father, Son, and Holy Spirit. Amen." I made the sign of the cross with my hand and blessed him as I said the words. I emphasized the word "sins," so he knew I was absolving all his sins, and not the one that was forced on him.

When he exited the confessional, he appeared less burdened than when he'd come to the rectory. He held out his hand and said, "Thank you, Father."

I clasped it and then we parted ways. As I walked back to the rectory, anger suffocated me again. What would I do to come face to face with Father O'Brien? The church would require I forgive him, as would God and Jesus Christ. I took a step back from those thoughts. What would I have really done? Would I have faced him squarely and told him what I thought? That he should burn in Hell? Or would I have backed off and shied away like the coward I was? I couldn't even face my own thoughts about the man at times, so my bravery surrounding Father O'Brien was nothing but a sham.

My mind was a swirling cesspool of thoughts of Father O'Brien. I knew my only solace would be to strip my mind of him and to kneel once more at the foot of the cross, losing myself in prayer. Hours later, my stomach cried out for food, forcing me to my feet.

If not for my duty, I might have skipped the meal. Instead, I returned to the rectory to make a quick dinner. It was long past the time I should have eaten. It was after eleven when I went to do a final check of the church and lock up for the night.

As I pushed the door of the sanctuary open, a small form was huddled in one of the pews near the back. That was odd, considering how late it was. The church was dark with only the vigil lights and a few dim overhead lanterns casting their glow inside. I would have to ask the lone figure to leave, since it was time to lock the doors, but as my feet carried me closer, the color of her hair set off a warning bell in my head. Why would she be here at such a late hour?

"Haven, what are you doing here?" My voice carried throughout the cavernous space.

"I…I had nowhere else to go."

Something wasn't right. Her voice was off. Tremulous. And she stared off into the distance.

Folding myself in the pew next to her, I asked, "What's happened?"

"He won. Like he always has. I was wrong. I'm not strong. I'll never be that person."

Her words seemed like an echo of my own thoughts this night, which clearly wasn't the Haven I knew. "I'm confused. Explain."

She didn't say a word but rotated in her seat. Even though the light was dim, it was still bright enough to see her face, and her left cheek was swollen and bruised. Her lip was also swollen and cut.

My hands balled into fists a second before I realized it. I relaxed them, trying to hold on to my composure.

"Who did this to you? Kent?" The set of her mouth and the droop of her eyes gave me my answer.

I gritted my teeth and took a few breaths to calm the angry words in my head that wanted out. I was mad at Kent, but I was madder at myself. I'd sent her back to that madman with a few careless words when she was only a child. The fact that she'd kissed me no longer mattered. I owed her for the childhood's worth of pain she endured. Another soul had paid the price for my sins. I pushed that thought aside. Her wounds needed treating, and I couldn't do it here.

When she raised her head, the light caught the glint of where her tears had left their mark. But it wasn't what she said that worried me. It was everything she didn't say in that moment.

"Come with me." I stood and held out my hand.

His question sent me tumbling back in my mind to how it happened.

Seeing my aunt in the hospital reminded me of losing my mother and the fragility of life. When I got the call from Aunt Kathy that she was being released, relief freed my mind. My work had suffered. Her illness had been that thorn in my paw that I hadn't been able to tug out for the last week. Call it guilt, worry, or whatever, but I was happy she was feeling better. Then when she called to tell me she wanted to talk about leaving Kent, my spirits soared.

"Can you come tonight?" When I hesitated, she rushed to add, "Your uncle is playing poker with the boys and will be gone until late."

"Sure. Consider me there. What time?"

"He'll leave around seven so come after that."

"I'll be there by seven thirty. Do you want me to bring you dinner?"

"No, just bring you."

I ended the call and glanced up to see Macie. "What are you

up to tonight? A date with that hot priest?" she asked.

"You are seriously demented. You do know that priests don't date."

"Uh huh. But something's going on with you and him."

"Is not," I said without much force, and I saw the glint in my friend's eye. "That was my aunt on the phone. She's out of the hospital."

Macie's face lit up. "Oh, that's awesome." Quickly, her eyes narrowed. "But you aren't getting out of this easy. You've been hiding from me all week. I know you're hiding something."

I slouched onto a bar stool and rested my head in my hand. "I've been worried about Aunt Kathy. And now she's at home, but she says she wants to talk to me about leaving the dickface."

The ear-splitting screech she emitted had me bolting out of my seat. "What the hell is wrong with you? You about gave me a heart attack!"

"That is so awesome!"

My hand was pressed to my chest, hoping my ticker wasn't going to pop out and hit the floor running. "Jeez, Mace, don't do that again. You scared the crap out of me."

"But this is what you've been dreaming of for years, right?"

"Yeah, but now I'm worried he's going to beat the crap out of her."

She tapped her finger to her temple. "I know. Let me work on finding her a place. In the meantime, go and see her. Make sure she's still on board with this. Maybe you can get your priest to help."

"Canaan? And he's not my priest."

"Yeah. But he's so hot. He wouldn't be bad to have to hang around. And I think your Aunt Kathy might like having him around too."

"You're evil, you know that?"

She sat up and put her hands on her hips. "You know I'm

teasing, right? He's so off-limits no matter how hot he is. But he would be good for Aunt Kathy."

That part was true. What I hadn't told her was I kissed him and I couldn't get the feel of him off my mind. As she went into the kitchen to get ice cream for both of us, I pondered whether to tell her about it. I had agonized over that for the past week. Kisses had never been my thing. Most of the men I'd been with weren't allowed to kiss me. I always believed it was too intimate, too sensual. For me, sex was just a means to get off—to get from point A to point B. Kissing made it something different altogether. It became exploratory, affectionate, *tender*—things I avoided at all costs. But Canaan's kiss catapulted me into a realm I'd never been. It made me *want* those things. Spending more time with him was *not* a good idea.

By the time I made it to my aunt's house, I was a bundle of nerves. Canaan was so close; a blush covered me as I kept thinking about the fullness of his lips against mine. It hadn't been such a bright idea to kiss him. In fact, it had been a huge mistake.

My aunt opened the door looking better than she had in days. We hugged, and I felt the strength in her as her arms squeezed me in return. It was a good sign and something I hadn't felt during her stay in the hospital.

"Wow! You look great, Aunt Kathy."

"I feel better than I have in weeks. I guess I didn't realize how much I'd declined."

I took her hand as we walked toward the couch. "I guess when it happens over a period of time, you tend not to notice. So tell me, you're really ready?"

The smile on her face told me more than her words. "I never thought this day would come. I don't even care that I'm sick. But if you want to know the truth, that's what pushed me to decide. Life's too short. What little of it I have left, I want to be happy. Even if it means being alone."

Putting my arm around her and drawing her close to me, I told her, "Don't talk like that. You're going to be around a long time. And you won't be alone. If you move, I'll come see you. A lot. I haven't visited you because he was always here." And I told her about the time I came and his car was in the driveway so I didn't stop. "Macie said she'd start looking for a place and she'll even help with finding an attorney. She's bound to know someone. You know Macie. She seems to have her fingers into everything."

Aunt Kathy laughed, agreeing. It was so great to hear how happy she was, I found myself laughing right along with her. You might have said we were giddy with excitement, so we never heard Kent walk in the house. There was no telling how long he'd eavesdropped, but when he made his presence known, it wasn't pretty.

"So, how long have you two been scheming this little arrangement of yours?" Kent stood in the entrance of the room in a combative stance, legs spread wide. He rolled his shoulders and then moved his neck from side to side. I heard it crack and knew then we'd made a costly error. As we sat planning Kathy's future, he'd listened and seethed.

I stood, intending to defend Kathy and myself. I was worried he would strike her, and she was in no condition to suffer any of his blows. But that was never his intention. His anger wasn't directed at her. Stabbing a finger in my direction, he said, "You. You waltz in here like you own the world. Well, let me tell you something. You don't. You own nothing. And you have no business poking your nose where it doesn't belong."

"I..."

He moved deliberately toward me. The muscles in his neck bulged as they strained when he cut me off. "Shut up! You don't say a goddamn word. You think you're all high and mighty, some fancy rich artist now. You're nothing to me. Except someone who owes me. Yeah, you owe me for all the damn money I spent sending you to that fancy school over there." His arm shot out in the direction of Holy Cross.

But when he brought up owing him money, I got pissed, because how could I possibly owe *him*?

I loaded my spine with iron and rose up to my fullest height. Over the years I had learned not to fear him any longer. There was power inside of me, and I understood how to project it. Pulling it forth, I shouted, "What the fuck do I owe you for? All the years you abused me? Beat the shit out of me? Did that make you feel like a bigger man?"

His nostrils flared for one tiny second before his arm shot out and backhanded me across the face. But he didn't stop. He was so fast he repeated his action, only this time he closed his other fist and whacked me, landing the jab on my cheekbone, adding the whipped cream to his dessert.

In one instant, all that strength, all the substance I had foolishly believed I had developed over the years was ripped away. Then he launched into a diatribe of some sort, but I heard none of it. Frozen into a pile of unrecognizable mush, I was unable to formulate a coherent sentence.

The need to get out of there, a basic survival instinct, overrode everything else, and I stumbled out of the house. I was that kid again, the abused child, blindly running from my abuser. Without any deliberation or introspection, my feet carried me to the doors of Holy Cross Catholic Church. Winded, tearful, bruised, and bleeding, I yanked on the door until it creaked open. When I went into the vestibule, it was dark and empty. The entryway to the church stood open and welcoming. For the first time I ever recalled, I yearned to be inside the church. For some inexplicable reason, it had become a place of safety for me. I didn't question why, and it didn't matter that God and the church weren't exactly high on my list of important things, I only knew Kent couldn't hurt me within this sanctuary. Finding a pew toward the back, I fell into the seat and stared at the cross.

The day my mom died was my turning point. If I tried hard enough, I still heard her laughter and saw her radiant smile. In my darkest moments and only on the rarest of times did I allow it to creep into my heart—my heart that lost it's ability to love—and let it warm me. I was careful of those times, because when I did, it gave me a false sense of hope, the sense that somewhere out there, someone might care about me. But I knew that wasn't the case. There was no one. I never knew my father. Mom told grand tales about him, but I was sure they were all lies. In all likelihood, I was the result of some kind of fling. In any case, it didn't matter. The only family I had was my aunt and uncle, and I wished they didn't exist. The cruelty that existed under this roof was worse than being alone. Now I understood why my mom didn't like to be around Uncle Kent. And Aunt Kathy, well, she was too afraid of him to do anything because he beat her all the time.

Aunt Kathy was right. I should've paid more attention to what she'd said, but I'd grown careless throughout the year. Besides, it was only art. How mad could he really get over one or two sketches?

As I sat on my bed, like I did most days when I wasn't at school, I sketched a picture of Mom. She sat on her favorite chair smiling, looking like a burst of sunshine to me. Just one more to add to my growing collection of her. It was from memory, because I had no real pictures. They had all vanished or been thrown away with the rest of her things.

Suddenly, my door flew open and Uncle Kent stood there. I had been so engrossed in sketching, I hadn't paid attention to the sound of his footsteps like I normally did.

"What do you have there?"

"It's nothing." I shoved the pad under the covers.

"It's something, or you wouldn't have tried to hide it. Hand it over." His huge paw extended, waiting for me to give him my sketchpad.

Since I had no choice, I pulled it from beneath my blanket where I'd hastily hidden it and handed it to him.

He looked at it and asked, "Where'd you get these?"

"They're mine. I drew them."

"No, you didn't. Don't lie. You stole these."

"No! I would never do that."

"Don't you back talk me, girl."

"I didn't. I'm telling you the truth. Those are my drawings. See? It's Mom."

"Yeah, well, that's your take. This is mine."

"No! Don't do that! Please!" I begged him to stop over and over.

Only he didn't. And I stood there and watched as he tore each sketch up into tiny fragments, leaving them scattered all over the floor. The tiny pieces were like shattered memories of Mom I could never get back.

"Look at this mess. I told you to keep this room clean. I'm gonna have to punish you. Get up."

Slowly, I stood as my arms and legs trembled. His lips were pressed together forming a thin line, but it was his eyes that were the scariest. They were dark and angry. I knew whatever he had planned couldn't be good.

"Turn around and pull your pants down."

"No!" I said, horrified. "I won't!" I tried to run from the room, but his thick arm wrapped around me in no time flat. That cop training of his must have given him fast reflexes or something.

"You can't get away from me, Haven. Now drop your pants for your punishment. You know I hate when you hide things from me."

The sound of his belt coming off brought bile burning up to my throat. I tried to escape from the room. But he was so huge, tall, and stout, there wasn't a chance in a million I could get away. My dead heart hammered in terror as he grabbed my hair and yanked. I screamed as I fell backward into his arms. And then he worked so fast I could barely track. My pajama bottoms came down as I was tossed on my bed when I heard the hiss of the belt. He didn't beat me with the leather end. He used the end with the buckle. My scream jammed in my trachea because another blow landed immediately after the first, and the second, and the third. I soon lost count because the belt hit me all over my back, shoulders, butt, and thighs, and I was sure I even took a few on the back of the head.

Uncle Kent made sure I paid for my mess that morning. I wasn't sure how many times he hit me because I lost count after seven. Afterward, I lay curled in my bed, whimpering.

Eventually, I heard his car leave the driveway. I closed my eyes in relief, knowing he must've gone to work. Even though it was Sunday that meant he'd be gone all day because he was a cop.

My aunt didn't come to check on me. Then again, she could have been nursing her own wounds. I dragged my beaten body out of bed and down the hall into the tiny shower. I held hope it would help me feel better. Only it didn't. Fighting him had only made it worse. And seeing thin rivulets of blood flow down the drain confirmed my fears. But it was the first of many times to come.

Hours later, a hand touched my shoulder, and I glanced up to see his beautiful eyes. I muttered a few answers to his questions before I just admitted the truth. Then he guided me to the rectory, back to his home.

"I don't remember much about walking here, to be honest." My voice was barely above a whisper.

Canaan dabbed at my cheek and lip with a damp cloth. He

didn't say a word or interrupt as I spoke about what had happened. I supposed he was as shocked as I was. He didn't have to tell me how angry he was. His steely posture explained it all to me.

"When Kent hit me, it was like all those years between then and now disintegrated. And I was that scared kid again. Powerless." My shoulders curled inward, like they used to, as I folded my arms around myself.

"You're not powerless, Haven. You're an adult and you have options here. Do you want me to call the police?" His teeth clenched and it wasn't hard to see he was trying to control his anger.

I let out a laugh that bordered on hysteria. "Kent *is* the police. Aunt Kathy was right all those years ago. He'd use his connections to make this go away. And it would be my word against his and who would they believe?"

"A priest."

"Canaan, you weren't there. What help would you be?"

"I could use his display of bad temper at the hospital as an example."

He handed me a baggie filled with ice, and I pressed it to my cheek. "It would never work. Trust me."

He reached out his finger and touched my lip. "He hurt you, Haven. That's wrong." The tiny muscles on both sides of his jaws twitched.

"I've been around one severely angry man tonight. Please don't be angry, too."

The thousand different hues of green in his irises became flinty.

"It's difficult to see you in this condition and *not* be angry."

Without thinking, because looking into his eyes made it difficult *to* think, I placed my palm on his cheek. "You can't worry about me."

"How can I not?" Then he placed his hand over mine and

removed it from his face. The expression he wore could have best been described as tragic.

"What?"

"I'm responsible for this."

My brows furrowed. "Why...?"

His skin puckered around his eyes as he pounded his chest using the tips of his fingers. "I sent you back there. It's all my fault."

This was so fucked up. I almost didn't know where to begin. "So, I know I blamed you for so much. But realistically, even if I had spoken with Father O'Brien, who's to say he would've believed me? It's anybody's guess. You can't shoulder the blame, and as for tonight, Aunt Kathy and I were careless. We shouldn't have been talking so freely."

"He shouldn't have hit you. That's domestic violence, and it's a crime," he said through gritted teeth.

This whole night had exhausted me to the point where I was hardly able to stay on my feet. I must've swayed, because Canaan grabbed my arm.

"You need to sit."

"I'm sorry. I'm really tired."

"Here," he said, walking me to a couch in a small den. "Can I get you a drink?"

"Do you have any liquor?"

"We do. What would you like?"

"Anything strong. My face is on fire."

He left and came back with some amber liquid in a glass, two ibuprofen, water, and some more ice in a baggie. I accepted all, but took a huge gulp of the liquor first.

"Whiskey?" I asked.

"Bourbon. Bill enjoys it. I'm more of a vodka guy."

"Same here. That and beer."

He chuckled. "It seems we share identical tastes in spirits."

I wondered what else we shared. It was disturbing being

this close to him but not to be able to touch him. Why did he have to be a fucking priest?

"Why the frown?"

My eyes burned from fatigue and I rubbed them, but in the process inadvertently hit my cheek and flinched.

"What is it?"

That error saved me from having to answer. I couldn't very well tell him I was pissed at him for being a priest. "I accidentally hit my cheek. It's a bit sore."

"You're lucky he missed your eye. What will you tell them at the gallery?"

"Oh, fuck. I hadn't thought about that." Then I realized what I said. My hand covered my mouth.

"Haven, it's not like I haven't heard it before. Just because I'm a priest and don't speak those words or let anyone say it in the house of our Lord doesn't mean my ears are unsullied."

My mouth curved, or I should've said the half that wasn't swollen and cut did. "I just have this idea in my head that you're so good. You know, immaculate."

It was weird because it looked like the blood drained from the capillaries in his cheeks. His flesh paled, turning him anemic-like.

"I'm miles from that, believe me. So, work?"

Downing more bourbon, I said, "Yeah. I have no idea. I guess I'll say I fell. I can't tell them the truth. I know it's lying, but to tell what really happened would—"

"Be the best thing for you and Kathy," he cut in, "not to mention Kent. He has to be stopped. And now, will Kathy want to go on with her plans?"

"Oh, God! I hadn't thought of that. I was in such paralysis after he struck me, I scarcely remember how I got out of there. I'm surprised he didn't chase me down." I tossed back the remains of my drink. The liquor had gone to my head since all I'd had for dinner was ice cream. It was late and I was drowsy.

I leaned my head on the back of the couch with the intention of closing my eyes for a minute. What would Kathy do? I hoped he hadn't hit her after I left. The rat-faced dick.

Stretching, I rolled on my side and was disoriented. My hair was a tangled nest, sprigs shooting out of the knotted bun I'd had it in. I pulled it free of the elastic and tried my best to sort it out. But it was still dark, and when I became accustomed to the light—or lack of it, I didn't recognize the bed, or the room I was in. My hands massaged my forehead and brushed across my cheek when pain exploded, reminding me of what happened last night. Then I remembered being in the rectory, and Canaan and I talking. But whose bed was this? I sat up and looked around. There was a bathroom on the other side of the room, so I went to use it. I noticed men's items, such as shaving things. Was this Canaan's room? Did he put me to bed? I glanced down and I was fully dressed.

I washed my face as gently as I could stand it and used my finger to brush my teeth, borrowing his toothpaste. Then I walked out of the room, tiptoeing down the hall. I found my way into the den, where Canaan had contorted himself to fit on the couch. He was far too large to be sleeping there, but he gave up his bed for me. No doubt I must've conked out last night. It was only a little after five in the morning. I needed to get out of here. It would not do for anyone to see a woman leaving the rectory at this hour.

His face during sleep was even more perfect than while he was awake. Full lips, sculpted cheeks, high cheekbones—why did I have to find a man I wanted to touch my lips to over and over, only for him to be chaste and unable to be talked out of that decision because he was a priest to boot? I allowed myself the pleasure of staring at his innocent perfection for a few more minutes before waking him. He wore a short-sleeved T-shirt, and I'd never realized how muscular he was. I knew it was wrong, but I wanted to touch him, to slowly walk my fingers over his smooth flesh. His usually neat dark hair was tousled, out of place, making me want to smooth some order back into it.

Tapping his arm, I whispered, "Canaan."

"Hmm." He rose gracefully.

"You should've woken me up last night."

He blinked, but I wasn't sure if it was to shove the sleep away or to think. "You were weary. I didn't want to."

For a moment that was far too longer than it should've been, I swam in the forest green of his irises. It was only when he cleared his throat did I pull my gaze away from them.

"I have to go. It would not be good for someone to see me leaving."

"Yes. Let me drive you."

"No. I've been enough of an imposition."

He slanted his head. "Why ever would you think that?"

"I should have never come here." And I shouldn't have. Canaan evoked too many things that were out of reach for me.

"I'm glad you did." He bent to put on his shoes. "Come, I'll take you home."

I followed him out, knowing it was wrong. But I didn't exactly feel safe going to the bus station alone at this time of early morning.

"I'll let you take me to the L and that's it. You have duties and I won't take you from them. Don't you have an early morning Mass to say?"

"Yes, I do."

"Then the L."

He didn't argue. When we arrived, I sat for a second. "Thank you. Again." But when he pinned me with his gaze, something came over me, and I reached for him. I meant to kiss his cheek in a chaste thank you. But the closer I got, the more pull I felt. And as if he felt it too, he turned in time for my lips to press to his. Foolishly, I wanted that contact again.

Again, he was the one to pull back, breaking that connection I felt. Hurriedly, he said, "Haven, we can't. I can't. I have…I'm married…"

He tripped over his words much like my heart skipped several beats.

"To the church. I know. I'm sorry. It won't happen again."

I put my hand to my lips as I hurried away from his car. Why did it seem like his kiss burned a path straight to my soul? The rejection burned even though I knew a million reasons why he could never reciprocate. Even worse, he was the only man who ever made me feel good anyway. And not sexually either. He made me feel worthy of his tenderness and not like some harlot. I had taken advantage of him.

When I got home, the sun was poking its rays into our apartment. I put on a pot of coffee and waited for it to brew. What was wrong with me? Men had never been something I'd spent more than a fleeting thought on. Why now? Why Canaan? As I agonized over it, a hand landed on my shoulder and I screamed. Then Macie screamed.

"What the hell are you doing?" I asked.

"Nothing! I thought you heard me."

"Well, I didn't."

"Jaysus, what the hell has you so jumpy?"

I had to tell her. It was something that needed to be discussed and I had to get it off of my chest.

But before I could say anything, she yelped, "What the fuck happened to you? Your cheek and lip?"

So I rolled it all out. "Kent nailed me last night. But that's only part of it."

"What?"

I gave her all the dirty details, up to where I ended up at Holy Cross Church.

"Holy Cross? Why'd you go there?"

I grabbed my head. "No idea other than that's where I went

that one time. I don't even remember walking there. Or running." And then I told her about the part with Canaan.

"So let me get this straight." She ticked off the details, finishing with, "And you woke up in his bed. Do I have it about right?"

"Yep. You've got it right."

"Criminy jickets. You slept in hot priest's bed?"

I squeezed my eyes shut. "There's a little more."

She grabbed my arms. "What?"

"Don't get your hopes up. It's not that lewd. But I kissed him."

"Holy Mary, mother of God!"

Her eyes nearly popped out of her head.

"Where's the holy water?"

"Exactly."

"You actually kissed a Roman Catholic priest?" she asked while fanning herself.

"Yes. But it wasn't the first time."

"What the fuck? What do you mean there was a second time?"

"The first time happened when I was a little drunk and he said he'd never been kissed before."

"Hold up! Why were you talking about kissing to him?" She sat and matched my pose and angled her head in her hand so we looked each other squarely in the eye.

"I don't even know."

"Okay, okay. Now back to the kiss. Was there tongue?"

"No tongue. He practically ran out of the bar."

"Wait a minute! You were on a date?"

"No!" Finally, I spilled my guts, telling her everything that happened with the first kiss.

"You know you're going to hell, right? Where's your rosary? We should start praying now," she declared.

"I know," I whined.

"You're like a Jezebel or something."

"Thanks, Mace. Thanks for your support. It's not like I meant it. I shouldn't have done it. I don't know what's wrong with me."

She stared at me for a long while. "It was a drunken mistake. Maybe you should apologize. Then you can see him again. If he gets flustered, you know he's interested."

"You are so not helping."

She sat up and put her hands on her hips. "You know I'm teasing, right? He's so off-limits no matter how hot he is."

"It's too late for the apology, because I kissed him again, remember?"

"Oh shit. You did say that. Haven! What the exact fuck are you doing here?"

"I don't know." I dropped my head in my hands. It didn't stay there for long because Macie pulled it up by the unrecognizable excuse of a bun I had going on back there.

"Look at me."

I did.

"Now give me the entire scoop from beginning to end." And I did, including all the bits and pieces of how utterly beautiful he was and how pissed off he was at Kent.

She scratched her chin. "He likes you too. But you two are star-crossed. There is no way on this Earth should you ever see him again."

"I know. He's the only man I've ever wanted to kiss."

"You need to go out with another man and get this Canaan out of your system."

"There is the doctor."

Her eyes went wide. "Doctor?"

I filled her in on that part of the story.

"Deffo call him ASAP. Oh my God, a doctor." She clobbered my shoulder. "That's exactly what I mean."

"Ouch." I rubbed the sore spot.

She pointed a finger at my face and circled it around. "Now what are you going to do about *that*?"

"Hope no one notices?"

"Okay, and how do think that'll work for you?"

"It's not that bad," I huffed. Of course it was terrible. "A day or two of ice and some makeup will do the trick. I'll call Jonathon today and tell him I have a migraine."

The height of Macie's eyebrows told me all I needed to know. But it was going to have to do for now. And what about my aunt? What had happened to her after I left? Was she safe? Had Kent hurt her? Anxiety over her had my belly swimming with sharks. But my worst problem was my heart. Even though I told myself I was being silly, I couldn't stop thinking about Canaan. And why the hell did I allow that to happen?

Sixteen

CANAAN

My heart thumped wildly, giving me the sensation of suffocating. It was something I hadn't felt since the day I entered the sacristy when I returned to Holy Cross. But this time it was for a very different reason—*Haven*. She was the last thing that should be on my mind. I had no business thinking of her this way. I was a priest, married to the church, sworn to live a life of celibacy. *Pull yourself together, Canaan.*

How could I do my priestly duties—celebrate Mass, pray for people, administer the sacraments, counsel others—when I was in such turmoil and committing these grave sins by my unholy thoughts? Perspiration dripped down my forehead and cheeks in rivulets, stinging my eyes, and I blinked repeatedly, attempting to clear my vision. When I got home, I was dismayed to see I didn't have time for a punishing run. I would have to suffer the pain of the belt and hope it would suffice for now. Since Bill was gone, I was sure to make the blows count in their strength and ferocity.

During Mass, I was reminded of my self-abasement each

time I moved. The burn the leather left behind was a reminder of my repentance and a plea for mercy to ask Jesus to cleanse my soul from the sins that sullied it.

Instead, the evocation of Haven's memory and how her lips felt—how soft they were against my own—burned hotter than Hell's fire within me. Her scent, the soothing properties of lavender, was counterproductive. They flooded my being with agitated excitement when she elicited the nefarious kiss, tormenting me with the need to inhale every tiny bit of her. I didn't know how I found the strength to push her away. Only if I hadn't, I would've thrust my tongue into her mouth, because that was all I thought about. Was there a way to make this stop?

I pushed through the Mass, and afterward, with no discernment of how I'd done it. The whole undertaking was a blur. Even entering the sacristy hadn't had time to weigh on me. Taking off the vestments, I sat down heavy-hearted.

The answer came swift and true. I could see I wouldn't be able to have any contact with Haven again. The temptation was far too strong for my weak spirit. As though my brain were detached from my body, I stumbled to the prayer station and fell to my knees. Awareness clutched at me when I understood that Father O'Brien had been right all along. I was that sinner. My soul was tarnished. I was the embodiment of temptation. And ultimately, I was hurting Haven by being near her.

As the day wore on, I knew what had to be done.

Bill would be home later that day, and I'd promised Haven I would check up on Kathy. So I placed a call to her to see how she fared.

"Hello."

"Kathy, this is Father Sullivan. I wanted to see how you were doing?"

She paused for a long moment and said, "I'm doing okay, I

guess."

Her voice held a cautious wariness I understood too well.

"Are you feeling well?"

"Yes, I'm fine."

"Would you mind if I came to see you?"

"Uh, I suppose that would be okay. Can you come before my husband gets home from work?"

"I can. When will that be?"

"He usually gets home around four thirty."

We decided right away would be best. When I arrived, she opened the door, and it shocked me to see how far she'd regressed. In that moment, we were twin spirits, her haunted eyes mirrors of my own from long ago. Only one who's been defeated would recognize the truth they held. She took a seat on the couch and huddled there like a woman twice her age. Concern for her safety pushed me to speak.

"Kathy, I need to ask you something. Did Kent hit you last night?"

She slumped forward and stared straight into her lap, remaining as still as a statue. I refused to break the silence, giving her the time she needed to compose her thoughts.

"He hit my niece last night. Twice. It was terrible. She ran out of here, and I've been so worried about her I've been unable to sleep at all. I didn't dare call her because he was here, watching my every move. He took my phone from me and didn't give it back until he went to work. And now I'm too ashamed to call her."

I understood her more than I could admit.

"Did he hurt you?"

Her head moved back and forth. "No. But I would've rather he hit me than Haven. She stood up to him. I think she was afraid he would hit me. He overheard us talking about me leaving. We didn't hear him come in. I'll never be able to leave him now. He knows. He told me if I tried to leave, he would hurt Haven."

I sighed. "Kathy, this is very serious. We need to file an order of protection with the police."

"Father, you don't understand. If we do that, he would make it go away. It would be my word against his."

I wasn't sure if she was right or not, but she was convinced of it. I couldn't act without her wanting me to. My hands were tied. And I didn't want to push her because if, on the outside chance that something did happen, I would have to live with the burden of it.

"Okay, promise me if anything happens where you need help, you'll call the authorities and me."

"Yes, I will."

We prayed together before I left. I continued to pray for Kathy's safety and health the entire journey home. It seemed it was raining bad news from all angles.

When I returned to the rectory, I hadn't been there for more than five minutes when the police arrived. The first thing that came to mind was Kent Frederick. But that wasn't why they were here.

"Hi, we're detectives with the Berwyn PD. I'm John Hernandez, and this is Scott Collins. We're here to discuss the death of Father O'Brien."

I remembered Bill telling me the police had been around asking questions.

"It's nice to meet you. I'm Father Canaan Sullivan, and you'll probably need to talk to Father Bill Cernak. Unfortunately, he's out of town at the moment. I'm new and wasn't here when Father O'Brien passed away."

They glanced at each other for a second, then John Hernandez said, "That's fine. Can we have a minute of your time anyway? This shouldn't take long."

"Sure, but I doubt I can be of any help to you." I ushered them into my tiny office and we sat.

Detective Hernandez did all the talking. "When we came out after Father O'Brien died, we did so because the death looked like it had the potential to have some foul play involved. But after we had a good look at the autopsy, it appears that Father O'Brien died of natural causes, specifically a heart attack. He must've fallen after he died and hit his head. So there was nothing suspicious about his death. We wanted to give you the news in person."

I wasn't sure how to feel. As much as I shouldn't want it, the idea that he'd died in terror wasn't all that offensive to my sinful mind. There would be much prayer for me tonight for even thinking that way.

"Thank you for stopping by and telling me. I'll certainly pass this information on to Father Cernak. Does Father O'Brien's family know?"

Did they know what kind of man he really was?

"Yes, we've informed them."

"Well, thank you. Is there anything else?"

"No, the case is officially closed."

I stood and held out my hand. Both men shook it, and I walked them out. I held my tongue the entire time. I wanted to ask them about Kent—whether or not they knew him, and if so, did they know he was abusive to his wife and niece. But I didn't. I figured it would open a door I would deeply regret.

After I let them out, I returned to my office and made my decision. I hit the numbers and when she answered, I almost backed out. But I didn't. I hung in there, sticking to my plan.

"Canaan? What's up?"

Her voice, the way she spoke my name, was a salve to my wounded soul. "I saw Kathy today."

"How'd she look? I talked to her this morning. She was all I could think of and I worried about her after the way I left last night."

"She looks a little worse for wear. But her spirits are good.

Although I think she's more afraid than the brave face she puts on."

She huffed out a groan, "Aren't we all?"

I didn't tell her that I wasn't and that I could probably take him down without a problem. I kept my mouth shut on that subject. Violence wasn't my normal course of action.

"Haven, I...we can't see each other anymore. It's...well, to be perfectly honest, it's too unsettling for me. And for you, I believe."

There was a brief pause, and I had no idea what to expect when she spoke again.

"Okay, that's fine. I understand." Her choppy words sounded unusually distant. "Besides, I took your suggestion. You'll be happy to hear I've got a date with that new doctor."

The word *good* that left my lips sounded as though someone else had said it. Her comment and the way she was so casual about it hit me like a battering ram. It punched my solar plexus and I wasn't prepared for it. Had I not been seated, I would've been knocked off my feet.

It took me so long to respond, she said, "Canaan, are you still there?"

"Yeah," I wheezed. "I'm really very sorry. I didn't mean for this to get out of hand."

"Hey, you're making a bigger deal out of it than it is."

Again, her flippant attitude took me aback. I thought she felt what I'd felt. Maybe I'd been a fool for believing it. It was impossible to respond.

Her indifference was further punctuated when she added, "Well, look, I've gotta run. I'm pretty busy here. Talk to you later. Or, not at all, as it seems. Have a great life."

She ended the call. I sat at my desk feeling lots of things, but none of them relief. In fact, I reeled with loss. What kind of priest did that make me?

My head was buried in my hands when I heard a knock on

my door.

"Anyone in there?" It was Bill. I was not in the least ready to talk to him. He was too perceptive and would see something was wrong.

"Yeah. Come on in."

One look and he said, "Are you ill?"

"Only a headache. I'm fine otherwise."

"Stress. I should've come home yesterday."

Waving my hand, I said, "Don't be ridiculous. I don't think it's stress. It could be my sinuses from the weather." A stretch of the truth, although they had bothered me lately. "How's your mother?"

"Better, thank you. She's going to be fine. Gallbladders these days are nothing like they used to be."

"Except extremely painful," I managed half-heartedly.

"Too true. She told me to thank you for letting her priest son come and pray for her."

"I have a feeling your mother is a grand lady. And a firecracker."

"Why would you say that?"

In our downtime, he'd shared stories with me.

"From what you've told me. And from you. You have this all-encompassing personality and you had to inherit it from somewhere."

"Canaan, she is more like a stick of dynamite than a firecracker. She was ordering the doctor and nurses around to the point I felt sorry for them. She's one huge kick wrapped up in this tiny package, let me tell you."

"Well, I'm thankful to our Lord Jesus Christ that she's going to be fine."

He smiled and patted my back. I cringed because the welts on my back were especially tender. And that, in turn, reminded me of Haven.

"So, is there anything you need to fill me in on?"

I told him about Kathy Frederick being released, but held back on her situation with Kent. I wasn't sure if she would be willing for me to share that piece of information. Then I ticked off the list of parishioners who were in the hospital and nursing home, and we reviewed the other bits of church-related items, but it didn't amount to much.

"Oh, and two police detectives stopped by to let us know it's been determined that Father O'Brien died of natural causes. It was a heart attack after all."

Bill sighed. "Well, that's good to know. Not that he died, of course, but that foul play didn't have a hand in it."

I found myself agreeing, though I wasn't sure I really did. May God forgive me, but that man would've deserved it. Those black thoughts made me think of Greg Clark and his poor wife and what they will face because of Father O'Brien.

"Why the frown?"

Rapidly shaking my head, I answered honestly. "I had a parishioner show up here and he faces some real tough times ahead. I'm not at liberty to discuss it at this point, but my heart hurts for him."

He clasped my shoulder, saying, "It pleases me to see your heart's in the right place, Canaan. Although it's not always easy to help parishioners, the fact that you empathize with this man means you'll do all you can for him. Well, I'm off to unpack and get some work done."

I nodded, hoping he was right, and went back to thinking about Haven. I wished there was someone I could talk to about her, but it was ridiculous to think of it. The best thing for me was to expunge her from my system. The only way to do that was more penance.

Only later I found that all the atonement in the world wouldn't help me because nothing could erase the scent of Haven from my sheets. When I drew them back, lavender wafted up, inundating me.

At that moment, I wanted to get in my car, drive to her, and see if she was okay. An overwhelming urge gripped me with the need to examine the bruises on her face, to see if she was still hurting. Further, I wanted to place my fingers on her lips, trace the outline of them, and commit to memory each iniquitous curve. I craved to feel her hands upon me, to identify their touch once more, but I knew my wicked thoughts would never come to fruition.

Priests weren't allowed to have these lustful thoughts after all. We were vessels of strength and piety. Our job was to pray for others, and for peace, in the name of the Holy Father and his merciful Son, Jesus Christ. Falling to my knees next to my bed, I begged the Holy Spirit to come into my heart and soul as I repented for my sinful thoughts. When I rested my head on my sheets in prayer, Haven's scent washed over me once more. I knew then I was truly a condemned man.

His news blasted every bit of air out of me and I don't know how I was able to respond to him. After last night in his bed, all I did was smell his clean scent every time I inhaled. And now he wanted to cut things off. And what the hell was I thinking? How could it be any different? He was a priest, for Christ's sake.

The brush in my hand shook as I contemplated his words. This was a distraction I didn't need. Macie's face stared back at me from the canvas, saying, "I told you so, you little tramp." To free her words from my mind, I was an inch away from drawing a mustache on her face, but then I stopped. Crazy laughter burst out of me, and I covered my mouth with my arm, since both of my hands were in use. What was wrong with me? I was losing it. Going abso-fucknut batty. Setting my palette and brushes down, I went to the little bathroom and splashed water on my face. Too late I remembered the cover up job I'd done on my bruises. "Fuck. Godammit!" My fingers tore through my hair and instantly got tangled up in my twisty bun. "Double fuck." There was no winning for me today. Now

I looked like a bruised up porcupine.

"Fuck it all. I don't even give a shit anymore." Hands up in the air, I walked out of the bathroom, and Jonathon was standing in front of my painting.

He turned in my direction and the expression of horror on his face was priceless. "What the hell?"

"Don't ask."

"Um, you have paint all over your hair."

"Tell me something I don't know," my grumpy self said.

"Your next painting has already sold."

What was he talking about? "But it's not finished."

"You have a wait list, Haven. You are getting requests for certain scenes and portraits too."

"Oh, God, no." An artist's nightmare, or at least this artist's, were portraits.

He held up his hand, saying, "I already explained that you don't do anything traditional, and they don't want trad."

That was a relief.

"What I did tell them was if they furnished you with a picture or pictures that you would have free rein to do what you wanted. And they agreed."

"I can work with that."

Jonathon laughed. "Good, because your list is already growing."

"How long?"

"Don't ask."

"What does that mean?"

He made a noise like cha-ching. "Dollar signs for you and me, baby. No more money problems for you, if you play your cards right. You'll need an investment broker."

"I'll take that into consideration." That was something I'd never thought of before, but he could be right. The money that would be coming in would be much more than I'd ever imagined.

Aunt Kathy and I had only texted a few times, and I worried about her. But she claimed she was fine and that Uncle Kent hadn't touched her, in a bad way at least. I stared in the mirror at the face reflected back at me. The little makeup I'd applied hadn't taken the worry lines away.

"Did you fall in the toilet?" Macie called through the door.

I opened it to let her get a gander of the outfit I wore.

"Well, that doctor is going to get more than an eyeful."

I shrugged. This was my go-out outfit. I'd planned to try something different with him, but I needed a good fuck to get Canaan out of my head.

"Turn around." Macie twirled her finger in the air.

It was an easy enough request, and I'd missed her sisterly like advice while living in New York.

"He's totally going to swallow his tongue when he sees you."

"That's the idea."

A knock came at the door. Macie's eyes sparkled with delight. "Spare no details when you get home."

I nodded and she took that as her cue to race to the door. I stepped into the living room as they traded pleasantries.

When Wilson glanced at me, the heat of his gaze warmed me. Every inch of his attention was centered on me.

"Haven, you're..." His pause was a confirmation that I should be pleased he'd noticed. Only my fingers pressed my lips, remembering another man's against mine. "Simply beautiful."

I dropped my hand because I was damned if I thought I could have what I wanted.

"Thank you."

His proffered hand was an invitation. And though I didn't

want to accept it, I did. Macie, however, noticed all as discerning eyes narrowed on me as I passed by.

"Later," I said, feigning a grin.

She didn't smile back.

And the truth was, the handsome man before me wasn't enough to change the course of my heart. My childish crush fulfilled in a stupid kiss bulldozed over my beliefs that I would never want a man for more than a quick one-night stand.

The evening was spent with my attention pinballing whenever a man with the slightest resemblance to Canaan crossed my path.

The good doctor either didn't notice or he chose to ignore it. I should have invited him in for a night of pleasure that would surely have cleansed my spirit. Instead, I found myself on a train and bus to stand in front of the rectory. We couldn't be together, that was clear. But what was even more frightening was I found myself headed down a path that led to the impossible...a bridge to nowhere. Because if Canaan felt the same way I did, we wouldn't want to be apart either. The idea was as far-fetched as it was ridiculous.

The door to his office was halfway open. The blinds weren't closed, so I spied on him like a peeping Tom through his window. His head was bent over a book as he examined it with a single-minded purpose. The man was beautiful and I was royally fucked for thinking so. I took a quick look around and made a hasty decision. It was dark, but I turned the flashlight in my phone on and found a few pebbles. I threw one at his window. The damn man was so engrossed in his book, he didn't notice. The next one I tossed a bit harder, hoping it wouldn't crack the glass. That one grabbed his attention. When he finally opened the window, I was able to speak.

"Unlock the office door."

"What?" Clearly he was nonplussed. I was actually shocked when he left the room.

Walking to the office entrance, I met him there and grabbed his arm, not stopping until we reached his office. I shoved the door open and barged into his personal study, dragging him behind me.

Then I let him go. "I know you said we couldn't see each other."

His head jerked and his eyes widened as if he saw the anti-Christ himself. And maybe that's what I was. Because this shit was crazy as hell. I knew better, but Satan himself couldn't stop me from my path.

"Haven—"

I cut him off because he'd said his piece. It was my turn.

"I spent the entire night unable to enjoy my date because everywhere I looked I saw you. And I get it. So don't get on your high horse and spout off all the reasons this is wrong because I know."

His eyes darted to the open door.

"Please," he began.

I shut the door and lowered my voice.

"I'm not here to strip the cloth from you, Father. But I am here to tell you I'm not going anywhere. There is no reason we can't be friends."

"And where did friendship get us?"

His voice was wrapped in despair and sealed with a bow of regret.

"We weren't friends. We were more like a bad ending to a Lifetime movie."

I almost laughed at his confusion. "Basically, I'm saying I never tried to be your friend. You were my broken childhood crush turned enemy and then you were a step toward forgiveness. And I let the confusion between the two turn your kindness into desire."

The seconds ticked by as he studied my face, and I tried my damnedest not to investigate his mouth.

"You are not alone. We are sinners on some level. And as much as I would like to be your friend, it would be counterproductive. I can only serve you under the strict formalities of the priesthood. And as you've made it clear you are no longer an active member of this parish, there is nothing I can offer you."

"Is that a challenge?" I asked, getting to my feet.

"It is simply the truth."

I walked to the door, but before I left I added one more thing, "Well, then, I guess I'll see you at Church next Sunday."

The hint of a smile on his lips lightened my steps as I vacated the office. I saw our potential friendship as the only way to quiet the lust-filled thoughts I had about Father Sullivan.

Eighteen

CANAAN

Friday afternoon, I dodged traffic on the expressway leading into town. Frustration with the sluggish flow of cars had me asking God for patience. The L would have been a better choice, but hindsight was always clearest. Locating my destination, it took me another twenty minutes to find parking. One more reason I should've taken the L. Once my car was situated, I had to jog to make it on time. The late summer day was hot and humid, as can sometimes be the case in early September in Chicago. With dismay, I noticed the sweat marks on my T-shirt. Too late to worry about it now. At least I wasn't wearing my collar. It would've been worse. I opened the doors and the dark coolness was a welcome change to the outside heat. I walked with a solid purpose, as I knew I had no choice, opened the next door, and knelt. Words poured from my mouth. The dam had burst.

"Bless me, Father, for I have sinned. My last confession was six days ago." I heard the priest say a few words and then I launched into my disclosure. "I have committed a grave transgression in the eyes of our Lord God, Jesus Christ. I have had lustful thoughts about a woman. And these thoughts have plagued me for days and nights, interfering with my duties and obligations."

"My son," the priest began, "it is not uncommon for a man to have thoughts such as yours."

"Father, these thoughts are wrong, and to take them further, I kissed this woman."

"Have you had sex with her outside of marriage?"

"No, Father. But you don't understand. That would never be possible because I have received the Sacrament of Holy Orders. I am an ordained priest."

Dead silence greeted me, so I assumed the poor man was reduced to speechlessness. I couldn't imagine how I would feel.

"Father, I don't know what to do. I have begged God for mercy, asked Jesus for help, pleaded with the Holy Spirit for faith to overcome this affliction, to no avail. I am at a loss."

"You must say your penance, my son, and not commit these transgressions again. Am I to assume you have not broken your vow of celibacy?"

"Besides kissing her, I have not."

"God sends us many obstacles and Satan sends us many temptations. Just remember that God is very forgiving." He doled out my penance and said his prayers of reconciliation, absolving me of my sins, while I recited the Act of Contrition. I left the confessional not feeling the tiniest bit better.

Saturday, it was my rotation to celebrate Mass. I was fully prepared and my soul was anxious to be spiritually fed. As I entered the sacristy, the expected sense of dread filled me. It was the scent of incense that triggered my harshest memories. I'd tried desensitizing myself over the years, to no avail. My body knew. It knew what to expect when the odor was near me. Sweat trickled down my forehead and chest, and I shuddered. Kneeling at the prayer station, I continued to ask God for assistance, though I knew it was fruitless. I knew all the appeals to God would go unanswered. Wasn't I the ultimate sinner? Hadn't I been told that all those years ago?

Many deep breaths later I put my vestments on and one of the altar servers stuck her head in and told me it was time.

I joined the small group in the vestibule, and on cue, the music began playing as we marched up the aisle. Celebrating Mass was a balm to my broken and dirty soul. I begged God's forgiveness that he deemed me worthy as a celebrant.

As I walked to the podium to begin my homily, I glanced out among the church members, smiling, as I normally did. Only this time my vision stumbled upon a blonde-haired beauty seated in the front row. *Haven.* She'd made good on her promise. I wasn't sure if she'd been serious, but now I knew.

My message for today was based on the Gospel of the Lord, and looking at her, smiling at me, had my hands shaking and my tongue tripping all over my words, as though it were my first speech in college.

My face heated as though the air conditioning in the church was broken. I sped through my lesson, ending it, unsure if it made any sense whatsoever. And at the end, I could've sworn she winked at me. My relief must've been written all over my face as I turned away from the congregation to move on to the Eucharist and consecration portion of the Mass. When I finally announced, "Mass is ended. Go in peace," I wanted to kick my heels in the air. I nearly ran down the aisle to the exterior of the church.

Mostly young people attended this Mass. A few elderly parishioners were there, and I greeted them a bit overly enthusiastically. There was a good chance they thought I was high on drugs. At least I didn't reek of alcohol. The younger members floated out and chatted a bit, but I knew she was hanging back. She was waiting for a time to talk without being seen by anyone. When I was the last man standing, I went inside, and there she sat, in the last pew, closest to the sacristy. Great.

"Nice threads. You're looking rather priestly."

"That's what I am. A priest, you know." Nervously, I glanced around to ensure we were alone. "Haven. A little warning would've been nice."

"I thought I did warn you when I saw you last."

"Hmm. If I recall correctly, you said, 'See you Sunday.' Today is Saturday."

She waved her hand. "Oh, that minor detail. I figured I'd come today. Getting here on a Sunday morning might be problematic."

"Why's that?"

She had an impish look in her eye. "I like to sleep late."

I pressed my lips together, trying to look stern, but failing, I was sure. "In other words, God is less important than sleep?"

Her lips formed a perfect little O, which didn't help me in my predicament of wanting to kiss them. "That doesn't sound very Catholic, does it?"

"Not very," I grimaced.

"So, Father, about your homily."

My face went from ninety-eight point six to a thousand degrees in a half second flat. "What about it?"

"Am I embarrassing you?"

"I think flustering me would be more apt," I explained. "You must know how things are for me."

Her chin dropped to her chest as she folded her arms. Her mutters were so quiet, I had to strain to hear. "Yes, I do. And no matter how hard I try, I can't stop thinking about you. I want to, Canaan, I do. But my brain is on overdrive. There's one question that keeps repeating itself in my head."

"What's that?" And I knew when the question left my mouth I never should've asked it.

"Why is it that the only man I've ever been interested in has to be one I can't ever have?" Then she stood and without a backward glance, left me sitting there alone.

For the first time ever, I felt lonely in the house of the Lord.

The day I'd been dreading arrived. And how appropriate that it came with thunderstorms and rain. My appointment with Greg Clark and his wife was in thirty minutes and my panic was mounting. I had to calm myself before this got out of hand. Employing deep breathing exercises was all I had time for and that did very little for me.

They arrived and I ushered them both into my office. Celia Clark was very pregnant, and I could tell by the lines around her mouth and bruise-like moons under her eyes that she had been under a great deal of stress. My heart ached for this couple.

"May I get you something to drink? Water, coffee?" I asked.

They both declined.

Greg endlessly rubbed his hands on his pants and then together. I kept thinking he was going to run out of here. But then he'd look at his wife, and I knew he wanted to get this over with.

"So, both of you came today to work on some marital issues. Celia, Greg came to me last week and shared with me something that happened to him while he was a teenager...something you aren't aware of. But before we get started here, I'd like for us to pray together. So if we could bow our heads." And I said a prayer for them as a couple that their marriage could endure what Greg was about to disclose. When I finished, I said, "Celia, some of this may be difficult to believe, to even understand. But you must listen with an open mind and an open heart."

Her bewilderment grew as I spoke, but it wasn't my place to tell her the truth. Only Greg could do that. I nodded to him and that was his cue.

Greg ran a hand across his face and began. "Celia, you wanted to know why I've been acting strange. It has to do with moving back here. You've probably tied the two together." He glanced at me and I nodded. "You see, when I was a teenager, I was an altar boy here at the church."

Celia said, "I remember that."

I had to commend Greg because now his voice was calm. "What you don't know is that Father O'Brien r-r-raped me. He molested me."

"What? How can that be?" she exclaimed.

Greg's voice shifted from calm to dead. "Like I said, I was an altar boy, and the first time it happened after Saturday Mass."

"Wasn't anyone around?" Celia wanted to know.

"No," Greg said. "We were alone in the sacristy. I had changed my clothes and then collected all the items from the altar and took them back to the sacristy, like we usually did. When I got there he asked me if all the people were gone. They were and I told him that. Then he told me to lock the door. At first I was surprised because he'd never asked me to do that. But it was Father O'Brien, so I always did what he asked. Only I should've run away. As fast and as hard as my legs could've carried me. It was awful. The first time. I never knew something could be so…"

My vision spun as I was sucked back in time. Fear and pain swirled into one as his words mirrored my memories. Father O'Brien had given different reasons for his transgressions, but his doled out punishment remained the same.

"Wait," Celia said. "Why didn't you tell anyone?"

Many reasons, I thought to myself, feeling the crushing weight of guilt from her question.

"More than anything, shame," Greg said.

"I don't understand. How could you let him do that to you and not say anything?"

Greg lost all color from his face, and I had to intervene. The words clawed at my throat, but I managed to get them out.

"Celia, this isn't a place of judgement. We aren't here to question Greg about something he can't change. We're here to offer him support and a safe place so he can share this with you. He loves you and wanted you to understand why he's been acting the way he has lately."

Her eyes filled, so I handed her a tissue.

"And it happened here in this church?" she asked.

He nodded while she looked all around.

"You're so very brave," Celia whispered.

She had no idea.

Greg needed more help than I could possibly offer. So I suggested they seek out a family therapist while offering to continue to counsel them if they wanted additional support.

After they left, time came to a paralyzing halt. I found myself in my room as the memories assaulted me with a one-two punch. Celia's questions had been some of my own. I'd thought I'd protected myself, making sure I wouldn't be alone with Father O'Brien after the first time. Yet somehow he'd caught me unawares again. Positively frozen in fear, his touch sent me to another place where I retreated and pretended I was anywhere else in the world.

But it was his voice in my ear that would constantly bring me back as if he knew what I'd tried to do. His heated breath against my neck made me ill as he grunted words like sinner, temptation, and lust into my ear. Most of all, his reasons for doing the things to me had always been my fault. And weren't they? I'd been a magnet for unwanted attention all my life. Only he'd been the only one to act on that desire.

I woke in the middle of the night gasping for air. The feeling of his hand on my back pressing my face forward into the table crawled over my skin. I quickly stripped my shirt and reached for the leather belt that was never far from my bed. Whipping it over my shoulder quickly masked the remembered feel of his skin against mine. The burn of the belt was better than the burn I'd experienced years ago.

My eyes seared with the disgrace from Celia's questions to her husband, which were a reflection of my own. I'd kept my ordeal to myself and others had suffered. Maybe I had been ground zero, but there had been more. The real question was—how many more? Father O'Brien led me to believe I was the only one. But that wasn't true at all.

Bile rose to my throat and sent me to my small bathroom to empty the contents of my stomach. What was worse, over time during his possession of me, I'd lost control of my own body. It would react even as my hate for the monster behind me consumed my soul.

I stood in the mirror and splashed water on my face as I pondered for the millionth time what my body's reaction had meant? It was a question I never thought would be answered until she came into my life.

Haven.

My small bed dipped under my weight. As I breathed in her scent that still seared my sheets, I knew Father O'Brien had been right about me all along. I was a sinner because she was all I could ever want and never have.

Nineteen

HAVEN

Why was I so flirty with him? Why did I have to make him so uncomfortable during what should've been his peaceful time? But in all fairness, I did tell him. Well, maybe not. Like he said, he thought I was coming on Sunday, not tonight. I really needed to scrub these smutty thoughts of Father Canaan Sullivan from my mind. Why did he have to be a fucking priest? Or an *un*-fucking priest as it were? I laughed at my little joke.

Macie was just about to take a giant bite of pizza when I walked into the apartment. "Can you possibly fit any more of that in your mouth?" I teased.

Her cheeks bulged as she tried to answer but then gave up, laughing as she held her index finger in the air. I motioned to the box of pizza, asking for permission, and she nodded. Glad to see she'd ordered it, I eagerly grabbed a piece and took a bite, though not one nearly as large as hers.

"Sorry. I was starved. I hadn't eaten all day," she admitted.

I swallowed my bite. "From the looks of it, it could've been all month."

She threw her napkin at me. "Shut up. So where have you

been?"

Around my bite, I managed to say, "I went to church."

"Church? Where?"

"Holy Cross."

"What? Why'd you do that? You never go to…oh my God. Or should I say priest?"

"Staaaaap!"

"I will not. Spill. All of it."

After my pizza was sitting comfortably in my stomach, I said, "I went to see him the other night. I was tired of messing around."

"Messing around?"

"Macie, I swear when I went out with Wilson the other night, all I saw was Canaan. Everywhere I looked I thought I saw him. It was crazy. I'm crazy."

"Yes, you are. Canaan's off limits. You can't have him. I know I teased you about him. But he's untouchable. Get over it, okay?"

I fell back against the couch, grabbed a pillow, and cuddled it against me. "I know that. But it's not helping me. He told me we couldn't see each other. After the second kiss. But it was driving me batshit crazy. That's why I went. And he reiterated it so I told him I would become a church member. If that's the only way to be his friend, then that's what I'll do."

She gawked at me in disbelief. "You don't honestly expect me to believe that, do you?"

"Believe what?"

"That you only want to be his friend?"

"But I do," I insisted. Only I wasn't sure if I was trying to convince her or me. "He's like a drug. If I try to stop cold turkey, he'll constantly be on my mind. This way, I can ease my way out of my crazy thoughts."

"Come on, Haven, this is me, Macie, your bestie you're talking to."

"Ugh!" I buried my head in my hands. "I don't know what I want. I don't know him very well, but I want him more than I've wanted any other man." My hand flew to my mouth, covering it. I hadn't meant to say that. And even that wasn't the entire truth. I wanted more with Canaan than I had with other men.

"I knew it! I just knew it. You want to fuck the priest!"

"Oh, Jesus, Mary, and Joseph, what am I gonna do?"

"Well, you can't fuck him. He's off limits, you ho. You're gonna have to take out your sexual frustrations somewhere else. Another guy or your silicone rabbit."

"Don't you think I know that?" I got up and took my empty plate into the kitchen. She followed me.

"Maybe you need a change of scenery. Why don't we head to the beach in the morning? You've been working your ass off and this is a great time to be at the beach."

I stalled. I hated bathing suits. She knew why.

Macie jumped in to halt my train of thought from getting too far down the tracks to Hell. "That's why I said this is a great time to be at the beach. It won't be blistering hot and you can leave your shirt on. No one will think a thing of it. Wear a one-piece with extra coverage, too."

"That's all I have, you dork."

"Right. Well, you in?"

"I guess."

"Coolsies. Let's leave around ten."

I agreed and headed to my room. When I got there, an image of Canaan celebrating Mass struck me. I couldn't get the many faces of him out of my head. I always kept a canvas ready to go set up on an easel just for these inspiring moments. Sometimes they turned out to be nothing more than pieces of junk I trashed. But I wasn't sleepy, so I grabbed a palette, my spare brushes, and paints, and started mixing.

The first image of him was the way he looked after I kissed

him the first time. Startled eyes the color of a forest at dusk, lips slightly parted, and dark hair that wasn't perfectly in place but not exactly messy either. Anyone looking at the picture wouldn't call him sexy, but to me he was sinfully so. His beauty radiated off the canvas in such a way, I found it difficult to get oxygen past my scorched throat. Once I completed the central image, I stared at it long into the night. If I had to say, it was probably my best work yet. It far surpassed anything I'd ever done. Was it because I had feelings for him? I didn't have an appropriate answer, but I had to finish this piece quickly. I would work on it every night until it was completed.

The next morning, Macie knocked and woke me up. "Are you ready?"

I grumbled something to her about oversleeping. That was a mistake because she walked in and there was no hiding the painting.

"Holy fucking priests. You did all that last night?"

"Uh, yeah." I still was in bed.

"Jaysus, Have. I've never seen anything like it. Are you done?"

"No, I've only started. I'm doing the many faces of Canaan."

"Look at me. Right here." She made a V of her two fingers and directed them at her eyes. "What's going on in that head of yours?"

"What'd'ya mean?"

She pinched her lower lip. "Uh, you don't do shit like that for the hell of it."

"Oh, I couldn't sleep."

"Okay. Usually when you can't sleep, you watch Netflix or read."

She stood there, waiting for an answer. She was right. But I didn't know what to tell her. Taking a seat on the bed, she grabbed my hand. "You have to give it up. He's out of reach. What, is he going to leave the priesthood for you so you guys can live happily ever after? Is that what this is all about?"

"No," I said, snatching my hand away.

"You swear?"

"Yes, I swear."

"God, I hope so. I don't want you to get hurt. You've guarded your heart for all these years, the last thing I want is for you to fall for someone who is completely off the grid."

"I know. Me too."

Her eyes were so sympathetic, I wanted to cry. Instead, I said, "How about we blow this joint and go to the beach?"

"You sure?"

"Yep, I'm sure."

We both went to change and then met up in the kitchen as she grabbed some drinks out of the fridge. Then she asked, "Which beach?"

"You choose."

"Either Oak Street or Hollywood."

"Hollywood?" I asked, puzzled.

She laughed. "That's what everyone calls Osterman Beach these days. It's because of all the hot sweaty men who play beach volleyball there. At least that's what they say."

"Osterman gets my vote, hands down. I need that kind of distraction."

Macie agreed. "Yes, you abso-fucking-lutely do. And it's less crowded too."

"Bonus!" I yelled as we fist bumped. We left the apartment and went to the train station. We took the L and when we arrived, I was surprised to see a new beach facility there that contained restrooms, concessions, and even a lifeguard station.

"Wow! This is all new," I commented.

"Yeah, this place has it all," Macie said.

We situated ourselves fairly close to the volleyball nets and plopped out on our towels for a day in the sun. I put in my earbuds and listened to music. Not long after, a group of guys started playing volleyball, like Macie predicted. I watched in fascination as the muscles in their arms, chests, and backs undulated as they moved. Was that how Canaan would look if he took off his shirt? *Stop it, Haven. Get your mind off him.* Bringing my concentration back to the male specimens in front of me, I thought how nice it would be to feel some of that tightly wound brawn react beneath the tips of my fingers. Who knew, maybe I would get lucky tonight. It had been a while since I had gotten any and I totally needed something to get my mind out of the unholy gutter it kept falling in.

When was the last time I'd had sex? Then I remembered it was the fiasco with the guy who believed slapping my ass was okay. Well, fuck me, no wonder I couldn't get my mind off hot Canaan. That had been forever ago. It was high time for another stab at a one-nighter. Macie may not approve, but I wouldn't let anyone get close after all I witnessed during those years of living with Aunt Kathy and Uncle Kreep. No man would ever have that kind of control over me. That would never happen. Ever. And I admit, right now I needed—no, craved—a man's hands on me, as long as it was in the right way.

A pile of sand came spraying my face as the volleyball skipped past me and landed on the other side of my head. A sweaty face appeared over me. "Sorry 'bout that. Did it get you too bad?"

Brushing the sand out of my eyes and off my face, I said, "I think I'll survive."

"Good. I wouldn't want to hurt anything as pretty as you." I spit out some grit, and he said, "Do you need some water? We have a lot of water over there. Can I get you some?"

Once I finished getting the sand out of my mouth, I sat up and grabbed my water bottle to show him. His smile plummeted.

"Are you sure you have enough?"

Macie watched this whole exchange with great interest.

"Yeah, really. But if I need any, I'll definitely let you know."

"Okay. Fine. What about a beer instead? We have plenty of that too."

I finally gave in and laughed. "Do you want me to go over there with you or something?"

"Or something? No. I mean, if you want to, then yeah."

I shaded my eyes with my hand because even with my sunglasses on, the bright sun was blinding. Turning my head, I lifted up a hand to block the sun and checked out the other guys. I found them all watching the exchange between us.

"I think your friends may be waiting on you."

He was very cute with short blond hair, great physique, and a crooked smile that turned his friendliness into something very endearing.

"Okay, to be honest, we all wanted to meet both of you. We sort of sent the ball flying over here on purpose."

Macie and I busted out laughing. Then Macie said, "This is the absolute best pick-up strategy ever."

"Really?" volleyball guy asked.

"Yes," she said. "But you left out one very important thing."

His smile vanished. "What's that?"

"Your name."

"Ah! I'm David."

"David, I'm Haven and that's Macie."

He stuck out his hand and we all shook. Then the other volleyball guys started yelling and cheering. We both got off our towels and walked over to meet them. They were overly friendly, which made me slightly suspicious of their motives. Then again, as they were all pretty hot in their board shorts and flashing us sexy grins, my intentions were pretty much in the slut house. Which considering how long it had been since I'd had sex was understandable.

They handed us beers and asked us to stay. It wasn't a hardship to agree to watch them play. The day turned out to be more fun than I'd expected.

"Where are you two headed now?"

Macie shrugged. "Probably home."

David smiled. "Why don't you hang with us tonight?"

"Where?" Macie wanted to know.

"A friend of ours plays in a band, so we'll be headed to a place called Night Owls. It's in Lincoln Park."

Macie looked at me and I shrugged. "Let me have someone's number so we can text you."

All the guys reached in their pockets at the same time.

"Only one," Macie said. A chorus of groans went out.

David ended up being the lucky guy. I pulled on my shorts during this exchange. When Macie finished, we walked to the L and chatted about our new friends.

"Do you want to meet them tonight? I think I've heard of this Night Owl place. It's a club with the hipster types, but it supposedly has good food. Being in Lincoln Park is a bonus."

"Maybe it's even close enough to walk," I said, since Macie's apartment being in Lincoln Park made that a real possibility.

"So how's this? If it's close enough to walk, we go. If not, we don't."

Laughing at her logic, I said, "Deal." I pulled out my phone and checked out Night Owl, and it was definitely close enough to walk. Six blocks away made the decision for us.

On the ride home, we started laughing about the volleyball guys. There were women all over the place and they only wanted to talk to us.

"We must be special, Have."

"Maybe so."

By this time, we'd gotten off the train and were close to home. We hurried in to shower and change. Macie and I checked each other out for our stamps of approval. We laughed though, because we both wore dark jeans and platform sandals, but I had on a black silk blouse and she wore a flowered tank top.

Night Owl wasn't crowded yet, so we were able to get a table and order some food. "I'm starved," Macie said.

"Same. We should be. We haven't eaten since breakfast."

As the waitress brought our food, we spied David and the gang enter. They waved and came up to our table.

"You beat us here. Mind if we pull up some chairs?" he asked.

"Not a bit," Macie answered. David and two of his friends sat down. The other two wandered off toward the back where the band would set up.

I scooted my chair over to give the guys more room. "Have you eaten?"

"Yeah, we grabbed something at home. We were too hungry to wait," David answered.

The lights dimmed and the band started warming up. David leaned over to me and said, "You're going to love this band."

He was right. They were awesome. Before long, David and I were out on the dance floor, twirling and dipping to the music. He was a great dancer and I hoped I was keeping in step with him. I'd had a couple too many so I was a tad wobbly on my toes. But he was good-natured and only laughed when I missed the beat.

As the night wore on, David's soft brown eyes and crooked smile had me imagining what it would be like to feel him inside of me. But then his face would morph into Canaan's, and I'd grow angry with myself.

"Hey, what's the frown for?" he asked.

"Frown?"

"Yeah, you were just frowning." He reached out and smoothed his thumb over my brow. "There, that's much better." His smile was disarming. Or was it the alcohol?

However, it didn't affect me like it should. But I wanted it to push aside the memories of Canaan so badly, I flashed him my most brilliant grin and grabbed his hand to pull him close.

This was going to be a fun night, no matter what I had to do. I swayed against him and his hands tightened on my hips. He dipped his head for a kiss and I allowed it. My lips molded to his and it wasn't bad, it just wasn't Canaan. I surprised myself, though. I wound my arms around his neck, proving to myself that I could do this.

He broke away and his half-hooded eyes told me everything I needed to know. He wanted me. But was I willing to go through with it?

"You're so sexy, Haven." Then his mouth grazed mine again.

Being brazen, I pulled on his hand, leading him off the dance floor, and down the hallway toward the back where the restrooms were. There were people scattered about and I hunted a place with a little more privacy, when he said, "Follow me."

I can do this.

He opened a door that appeared to be a supply closet. He flicked the light off and it was so dark I freaked a bit.

"Too dark?"

"Yeah."

"How's this?" he asked. There was another switch he flipped that cast the room in a dimmer light. It hit me that he must've been in here before, but I didn't care. I was testing myself more than anything.

"Better."

His index finger touched the hollow in my neck and went to the first button on my blouse where it stopped. Then he unbuttoned it and his mouth followed his finger. He unbuttoned another one and kept going. I couldn't lie. It was heating me up somewhat. Until...until his hand reached into my bra to free my breast. All I could imagine was Canaan's accusatory glare.

"David. Stop. I…I can't do this. I'm so sorry."

A confused expression met mine, and I only shook my head.

"You were the one who initiated this," he said.

"I…I know, and I'm sorry." I tugged my bra over my boob and buttoned my blouse up. "There's someone else." It was all I could come up with, and even though it wasn't quite true, it also wasn't a lie either.

He rubbed his hand over his face and nodded. Not saying another word, he whirled around and left me alone in the closet. I could understand why he was pissed. I had led him on and it wasn't right. Damn Canaan for giving me a guilty conscience.

Macie was sitting at the table when I got there, so I mentioned to her I was ready to leave. She gave me the thumbs up after getting her friend's number. David was nowhere in sight so we left.

"That was fun, yeah?" Macie asked.

"Yeah. You seemed to hit it off with your guy."

"He was cool. He said he wanted to go out again. We'll see. What about David? He was totally into you."

"It was a disaster," I explained, but left out the part about Canaan and my guilt.

"Damn, Haven, he's cute and super sweet. I don't understand you."

Shaking my head, I said, "I don't know. I thought he was nice and all, but I just couldn't get into him."

She stopped and grabbed my arm, forcing me to look at her. "It's him, isn't it?"

"Him who?"

"Don't play dumb with me."

"Macie, it's nobody. I just wasn't into him."

"Okay, it was Wilson, the doctor, and now David. How many are you going to go through before you admit it?"

I shook her hand off my arm and walked toward home again.

"Haven?"

I stuck my hand in the air. "Listen, this is my cross to bear and I'll deal with it."

"Nice choice of words," she snickered.

When I realized what I'd said, I busted out laughing. We walked the rest of the way home talking about the music. We decided to get some snacks and nibbled a bit before heading to bed.

Twenty

HAVEN

After Macie went to bed, I disappeared into my room and found I wasn't tired enough for sleep. My encounter with David flustered me more than I cared to admit to Macie or myself. The antidote for that was staring me in the face, the cause of my agitation, so I fell into my painting once more. The next image I painted was one of Canaan in his priestly vestments as he said Mass. He was posed in prayer over the altar and his face was a mixture of many things—joy, sorrow, peace, consternation, but as I dug deep, the thing that stood out the most was conflict. Could he possibly be as conflicted as I was?

It was well past two when I finished and I was very pleased. Canaan the priest was completed, and I was on to Canaan ministering to the sick. I pulled from my memory how he looked at Aunt Kathy's bedside, praying. Black shirt with his white collar, head bowed, holding my aunt's hand and it was then I realized how much love this man shared with others. He was no ordinary human being. God had gifted him with so much spirituality that he was compelled to offer it up to others.

When I finally crawled into my bed, I thought how fortunate he was, that God had blessed him with such gifts. Those were my last thoughts as sleep took me away.

It was a funny thing, but Canaan's painting inspired me to finish Macie's painting. The following day in my studio was frenzied. I painted like my brushes were running on electricity. By day's end, the piece was near completion. Jonathon was amazed.

"This is stunning," he said. My first thought was, *He should see what I'm working on at home.* But no one would ever see that. It would never leave there, and never be for sale.

"Yeah. I love it. And Macie will too."

"Does she know?"

"Sort of. I've hinted, but this is her dedication as my best friend ever piece."

Jonathon stared at me. "I take it you have her permission to sell it."

"I haven't asked."

"Haven, it's sold already."

I shrugged. I wasn't as worried about it as he was. If Macie wanted it, I'd figure something out with the buyer.

He bumped into my thoughts. "You're not worried about this, are you?"

"Nope. I can give them something else."

"Haven, they want this."

"They haven't even seen this."

He shifted about and glanced away, which alerted me immediately. "What aren't you telling me?" I asked.

"They have seen it." He actually had the grace to flush.

"When? It's been in my studio the whole time. I thought we had an agreement. All work in my studio was off-limits."

"Yeah, well, about that. It was a high-paying client and they asked. I broke the rule. I apologize. I should've told you about that."

"Yes, you should've. You have a lot to explain to them, then. If Macie gives her approval, fine. If not, it's a no go. I'll be happy to paint them something else."

"Come on, Haven. You've got to help me out here."

"I'm sorry, Jonathon. You should've told me about this. I'll talk to Macie, but I can't make any promises. Macie is her own person."

"Tell her she can have my commission."

I laughed. "Do you think I was going to take the money I earned off this? I planned on giving it to her anyway."

I got a huge kick out of watching his jaw drop. I had lived on very little for so long, giving up the money from one painting wouldn't hurt me at all.

"Now if you'll excuse me, I have work to do." I went back to painting. But he'd destroyed my concentration, so after a half hour, I decided to call it a day.

I unlocked my door, walked into the apartment, and went directly to my room. When I looked at the painting, it conjured up a memory of Canaan from long ago—as an altar boy. And it wasn't long before that piece of the puzzle was on its way to being completed.

The next evening, when Macie came home, I told her about my confrontation with Jonathon. "This is the second time he's fucked with my shit."

"What are you going to do?"

I looked at her pointedly. "It's not up to me."

"What do you mean?"

"Were you not listening to me? This is your painting, so basically you hold all the rights to it. If you don't want to sell, we don't sell. My idea was to give you the option and if you decided to, then the money was yours."

She laughed. Crazy laughed. "I want the money. You can always paint me again."

"Listen to me first. I won't be able to paint exactly that. And if I become super famous, that painting could be worth triple that someday."

Macie laughed, "You're my friend. I can get another one. I'll sell."

"Don't you want to see it first?"

"No, because then I might change my mind. Oh, and I will not take all the money. We'll do a fifty-fifty split."

"I'll let Jonathon know, but I'm going to tell him he owes you his commission because I had to beg you to sell." I winked at her.

"Oh, Haven, that's the best. He doesn't deserve to make a cent on this one." Then we high-fived.

When I told Jonathon about Macie's decision the following day, it was like I'd handed him the world. He grabbed and hugged me. This was one of the rare times he ever did this.

"Thank you, Haven. I'm not sure what I would've done if she had said no."

"It took a ton of begging and you won't make a dime on this one."

His smile didn't waver. "It's worth it to keep that client pleased."

"Whoa. This must be some client for you to say that."

"It is. You'll see when you meet him."

"If you say so." In reality, I was grateful that I had admirers such as these. But Jonathon's behavior still pissed me off.

When the weekend hit, Macie gave me hell on Saturday. "You're not going to church for the right reasons. In fact, it's quite the opposite. You're going for all the wrong reasons."

"No, I'm not," I argued. "I want to go and I want to get to know him as a priest. I can't do either if I don't go to church, right?"

Her raised brow only emphasized her skepticism. "You can try to convince yourself all you want, but this chica isn't stupid." She pounded herself in the chest with her thumb. Then she stomped away in a huff.

I checked the time and knew I had to get a move on if I was going to make it in time. So I hurried over to the train station and impatiently waited for the L. By the time I got to the church, I'd barely made it to the pew when the music started playing. I wasn't going to lie to myself—seeing him walk down the aisle made my heart beat faster, and I hoped I didn't look like a lovesick idiot because that was exactly how I felt.

Twenty-One

CANAAN

Mass was finally ended and pangs of remorse hit me. Instead of my soul being filled with the Body and Blood of our Lord Jesus Christ, all I thought of was Haven as she occupied one of the seats in the front pew. Afterward, I was brief with each of the parishioners as they spoke to me. At all the other services with Haven not in attendance, I engaged in conversation with as many of them as I could in order to expand my knowledge of them. Not today. The Clarks approached me, and in good conscience, I couldn't avoid them.

"Father Canaan, we wanted to let you know that the therapist you recommended is excellent. We've had one session and will continue to see him," Greg said. The absolute terror he'd worn on his face the first time I saw him had lessened. His wife nodded and gave me a tight smile. They would have a long road of recovery, but I was relieved by this piece of information. A small weight had been lifted off my shoulders. They left and others approached me.

Haven's stare bore into me. Or that was the excuse I gave

myself when I found I was more rushed and a bit short in my conversation with those who waited to speak to me. Finishing up with those duties, I entered the church and saw her seated a few rows up, but one of the altar servers stopped me. In my haste, I almost didn't notice him.

"Father Canaan, I've brought everything from the altar into the sacristy. The only things left are the consecrated hosts, and you have to do that."

I chuckled. This boy was always a bit overeager to please. "Thank you, Joey. I'll take care of that. You're free to leave."

"Okay, Father. See you Monday at school. My dad's taking me to the Cubs game tomorrow. Have you ever been?"

"Yes, I have, but it's been a while. I hope you have a great time. Let me know how you like it."

His big eyes lit up, reminding me of spotlights, and I had to stop myself from chuckling.

"I will, Father. Well, see ya." With a wave, he was out the door.

My attention back on Haven, I saw her head slant and her body shook with silent laughter. She must've overheard Joey talking to me. I slid into the pew next to her.

"He sounds excited," she said.

"Yeah. But he's always that way."

"So, how was your week?"

It was strange to hear her ask me that. No one but my parents ever wanted to know. "It was good. Routine."

"Routine." Her face beamed like I was the most fascinating person in the entire world. "Tell me, what's a day in the life of a priest like?"

I smiled at her question. "I begin with Mass, then depending on how many of our parishioners are in need of our ministering, Father Cernak and I tend to divide that up between us. I visit the hospitals and nursing homes. I teach catechism classes here at the school." And she stopped me there.

"Aw, I bet those little ones are the cutest things ever."

"Yeah, they are. Bill and I rotate through all the grades, but I do love the lower grades the best. They really are funny too, trying to grasp everything. One little girl wanted to know if we died and went to Heaven, how we would all fit on one cloud. She had it in her mind that Heaven was one cloud, and no matter what I told her, that was it."

We both chuckled, but Haven asked, "How did you get her over to your way of thinking?"

"I said that what only appeared to *look* like a cloud was in actuality a vast universe that would fit every person and then some. You should've seen her eyes." I glanced over at Haven and the grin on her face made my heart trip.

"I bet all those little girls have wicked mad crushes on you, Father Canaan."

My cheeks heated and I wanted them to cool off before she noticed. "Why would you say that?"

"Because I did when I was young. And now you're the priest that I'm positive all the girls think is hot. Trust me. I'm a girl. I know these things."

The topic needed changing, so I asked, "So what about your week?"

Her smile instantly drooped. "Jonathon, my sponsor, pissed me off again." Her hand covered her mouth and she grimaced. "Sorry."

"Go on."

"He sold one of my paintings, and it's the second time he's pulled this crap on me."

"What happened?" I prodded.

She reminded me of how he'd sold her mom's painting. "The thing was, it hurt for a couple of reasons. One, it was my *mom*. Douche-face Kent destroyed everything I had of hers, all my sketches I did when she was still alive, so I'd had to go from memory. And that one I did when I was a lot younger. And you know how your memory dims things? When he sold it, it almost felt like my mom died all over again. And then the second part was that he never asked me."

Her words put a dent in my heart. My mother was still with me. I couldn't imagine growing up without her. Haven didn't have either of her parents and then this person she worked for took the last remaining item, the final tether she had to her mother and callously sold it to someone who didn't even care. How selfish of him. All I could offer her were a few words. "I feel terrible for you, Haven. That's not very professional of him not to have consulted you first."

"It was in my contract, actually," she explained.

"Hmm. Fine print stuff?"

"Yep."

"That's terrible. Did you try to get it back from the buyer?"

"I did and it was a no go. I even offered to paint a similar one and he said no. So I'm out. It gutted me for a while. I was..." She waved her hand in front of her face, as if she were trying to stop her tears. "Sorry, it's just a bit too emotional for me."

"It's okay. You have every right to be emotional about something like that. I feel terrible for you."

"Thanks. But then he did it again today. He sold a picture I painted of my best friend, Macie, without telling me. He's an all-about-the-money kind of guy. He crossed all kinds of boundaries on this one."

"It sounds like he overstepped his authority, too."

"Oh, he did, and he knows it. Nevertheless, I still have to deal with it." She waved a hand like she had everything under control. "So tell me something nice. Like what's a nice priest like you doing on a beautiful day like today?"

If she knew the truth of how mundane my days could be sometimes, she wouldn't have asked that. I laughed, because her life was so much more exciting than mine. I noticed she rubbed her arms and couldn't help but see the goosebumps that rose as she shivered.

"Are you cold?" I asked.

"No," she whispered. She was quiet for a minute before shifting topics again. I listened, feeling she needed to get something off her chest. "In New York, I volunteered at a children's shelter. There were all kinds of kids there from places I could relate to. You know, kids who had lost something that meant everything to them—maybe a parent or sibling. I liked helping them out, even if it was just spending an hour or so, telling stories, reading books, because I didn't have that after I lost my mom."

"Yeah, I understand. Listen, not that this will help with you losing your painting or anything, but I volunteer at the local children's shelter here. They're always in need of some extra hands. If you ever want to go, let me know. I'm sure they'd love to have an art teacher show up on a Saturday."

"You seem to gravitate toward kids. Is it because you'd like to be more lighthearted or because you're really one at heart?"

I thought about it for a second. "Probably both."

"Ah, serious Canaan wants to kick up his heels a bit."

"You think I'm too serious?"

"Your picture is next to the word in Merriam and Webster." Then she spit out laughing. "You should see your face. Don't tell me you didn't know."

"Well, I guess I have my moments. But all the time?"

She nodded very slowly.

"Goodness . I'm a grump."

She chuckled. "No, you're not. You're just serious. There's a big difference between the two. But, Canaan, when you smile, the room lights up." The way she said it, the way her voice tripped over the words made me feel like I wanted to spike a football. I turned in my seat and grinned. I couldn't stop had I tried.

She swiveled to look at me.

My heart stammered again as our eyes locked. Her blond hair gleamed, even in the dim light of the church, and her eyes were large—the brightest of blues as they searched mine. My heart skipped over the unspoken need in her eyes. But it was something I couldn't give.

I watched her throat work as she swallowed, and then she said, "Canaan, I..."

"It might be best if you don't say anything."

She nodded, then stood. "I'll see you next week," she mumbled as she scooted past me. When she brushed my knees, my body jerked—not in revulsion, as I usually did when touched by someone unexpectedly, but in response to her. I wasn't sure how long I sat in the church. I only knew when I left the sun had long set.

When I entered the rectory, Bill sat in the small den with a glass of whiskey in his hand. This was strange, for though he liked a drink every now and then, he wasn't one to drink alone.

"Bill? Is everything okay? Are your parents okay?"

He nodded and waved a hand. "Yeah. All's well there. But something else happened."

I took a seat in the chair closest to him. "What's up?"

He leaned forward and put his elbows on his knees, cupping his glass in both hands. "I had a very disturbing phone call earlier today. With someone needing to talk."

Bill's behavior was odd. He was terribly troubled. Usually he was upbeat and positive, and not introspective like this.

"And?"

He blew out a long breath. "The thing is, I've been asked not to discuss it, so I'm not able to tell you much. But Canaan, this is weighing heavily on my mind."

"How can I help?"

Bill tossed back the rest of his whiskey, got up, and refilled his glass. "A parishioner gave me some disturbing news and

I'm not sure what to make of it."

"Can you share some of it without breaking their confidence?"

He thought about that for a second.

"This goes back to something Father O'Brien has been accused of."

As soon as I heard those words, a fine buzzing began in my ears and my heart raced. I followed Bill in that I filled a glass with liquid numbing agent. I briefly reflected on how I'd managed over the years not to become an alcoholic.

Bill's words floated to me over my dimmed thoughts.

"This could be an issue if someone else makes the same accusations."

Deep in my soul, I knew I had erred in keeping my silence. Now there were three of us. Had I spoken out, I could've saved two others from this pain I had endured.

"I'm not quite sure how to counsel this person."

"Maybe he needs to see a therapist."

Bill's head jerked toward me. "I didn't say it was a *he*."

"I know. I just assumed. Maybe you need to talk to the bishop about this if it's bothering you this much. You don't have to disclose anything. He may be able to guide you better than I can."

The truth was, I needed to get away from this conversation and seek repentance, because now my sins had deepened even further.

"Maybe you're right. This is serious enough that I should consult him. Thank you, Canaan. If for anything, thank you for listening."

"Isn't that what we have each other for?"

I said good night and escaped any more conversation. But when I entered my room, the scent of Haven was there, still lingering on my sheets. And it was my fault, my wrongdoing. Because I refused to launder my sheets, refused to wash her scent from my bed. Now my sins were so many, I feared God could never forgive me.

Twenty-Two

HAVEN

The weather was turning cooler as fall was in the air. The mornings were crisp, but the days were warm and sunny. It was my favorite time of year. My determination to finish my painting of Canaan was in full gear. When I left the church on Saturday, I had the final two images planned out. One was of Canaan the teacher, and the other was of Canaan, shirtless, in the prayer pose. I'd imagined him kneeling in this position before he went to bed at night. Though it was shameless of me, I would paint it nevertheless.

By Wednesday, it was complete, and all I had to do was put on the final touches. I planned on doing it when I got home from work that night.

I was just about to walk out of my room when Macie knocked.

"Yeah?"

She walked in. "Did you ever call that doctor back?"

I plopped my ass on the bed with a huff. "No. I don't think it would be fair to go out with him. The more I think about it, the more I know it's a waste of both of our time. He needs to go out with someone who has at least half an interest in him."

She scowled. "Okay, I might give you a pass on him. What about David? Has he called?"

"He's not going to call after what happened between us."

Her scowl deepened. "Maybe you should call him?"

"No. Now will you get off my back?"

"Then call the doctor."

I rolled my eyes at her. "I'm not going to do that either. You're the worst, you know?"

She sat down next to me and threw her arm around me. "No, I just worry about you. That's all." Then she hugged me and as she was leaving, she caught sight of the painting. "Holy fucking priest." She swallowed and gawked at it for a full minute. Then her penetrating gaze landed on me. "Oh, honey, you're wrecked, aren't you?"

"Huh? Nooo! I'm not wrecked." Of course, I was in complete and absolute denial. I was crushed to smithereens, beyond hope of ever returning into my pre-Canaan Haven.

Her head oscillated. She never uttered another word, but left my room.

Work was going great. Jonathon was like a woman who'd just purchased a new pair of Christian Louboutins, bouncing all over the place, grinning. My painting of Macie was on display, earning the gallery more interest than ever.

"Haven, be prepared for an onslaught of orders. You may need to consider moving to Chicago."

"What?" Why did he say that? My life was in New York.

"Think about it. You've garnered a lot of business here and it's only growing. If you stay, it will continue. And down the road, you could even open up your own gallery."

My head spun. The possibility of something this major had never crossed my mind.

He chuckled. "I can see by your eyes you're shocked. But the reality is you're a fabulous artist. And now in high demand.

You won't be able to keep up with your requests and soon you'll stop taking them and paint for yourself. You'll establish a price point on things that people will pay, no matter what. Being in Chicago will only help you. Just give it some thought."

Maybe he was right. I never wanted to come back here because of my past. Kreepy Kent had destroyed any love for this area. But to be perfectly honest, when I was downtown in the apartment I shared with Macie, I rarely thought about him. It was similar to living in New York. He knew I was here and yet he hadn't come back trying to harass me. Perhaps it could work out and be my dream come true—my own gallery and studio.

I did what any normal girl would do. I picked up my phone and called my bestie.

"Hey, chica. What up?" Macie answered her phone.

"You won't believe it."

"Don't keep me in suspense."

"Jonathon wants me to move to Chicago."

"Wait. You mean you might be my roomie permanently?" she squealed.

"Maybe not permanently but for longer than a few months."

"Woohoo!" she screamed, nearly rupturing my eardrums.

"Ow, that hurt my ears."

She only laughed in response. "That's what you get for telling me such amazaboobs good news."

"Amazaboobs is not a word," I tsked her.

"It is, too. I hear it all over the place."

I wasn't going to argue this point. "So, I've gotta paint, but we can chat when I get home."

"Let's go out and grab dinner tonight."

"Good suggestion. Why don't we meet at your favorite watering hole?" It was actually both of our favorites, but she'd get the idea.

"Yes! How about six thirty? I'll work a little late and that will give you extra time to paint."

"Perfect. See you then."

It didn't take long for me to get going on my next piece. It was a landscape of Tuscany that someone had commissioned. I conceptualized it to my taste, adding some textures using painting knives that pulled out the scenery a bit. It would take a little time because I wanted it to be unique in that I was blending the knife and brush. It was considerably smaller than Macie's painting and that of Canaan, but I wanted it to be different than anything I'd ever done.

By the time I left the studio for the night, I had my ideas firmly cemented on how it would look as the end product. I was sure the owners would love it.

Macie was waiting for me, already seated, when I arrived. She'd ordered us drinks and the sushi menus waited for us.

"I'm starved," I said, pulling my chair in.

"Same. I was so busy today I only had time for a bite or two at lunch. Look."

She passed me a folder and I was curious. I opened it up and inside was a list of ten three-bedroom apartments for rent in our neighborhood.

"What's this?"

"I asked my boss to run this."

Macie worked for a realtor who specialized in downtown listings for residential and commercial properties.

"It's a listing of available apartments. I figured we should start looking. You need an art studio, so we'd need a three-bedroom."

I sighed. "Mace, this isn't a done deal yet."

"You should move. I've thought about this all afternoon. It makes so much sense. Even down to the fact that your aunt is sick. And don't glare at me like that. You know if she gets worse, you'll be feeling guilty as all hell that you're not here.

I'm only trying to point this out to you now."

She was one hundred percent right. "I know. But maybe you're jumping the gun. I think Jonathon was thinking down the road a ways. Like next summer or next fall."

"I can understand that, but why not now?"

I shrugged, because I didn't know. The waitress came up asking for our order and saved me from Macie's interrogation. But when she left, Macie was back to being that dog hunting a bone.

"So?"

"Okay, one, I don't know yet because I have to talk to Jonathon. Two, I still have my lease to consider in New York. Three, my head is spinning with all this. I need to slow it down a minute."

She grinned. "Understood. But will you at least look at these?"

"Yeah." And when I did, I was surprised to see they were all great, and the rent was so much cheaper than in New York. I was beginning to be swayed.

"Nice, huh?"

"Very nice."

We toasted and our food arrived. After we finished, we discussed it more and it would be a great idea to move, but I stuck to my plans. I wanted to see how it all panned out first.

As I walked into my room, Canaan's face stared right through me. The painting only needed a few touches and it was ready. I decided I would give it to him. When I thought I would be leaving in several weeks, I knew I couldn't keep this. Every time I looked at it, it would only remind me of his scent, his touch, his voice. But if I stayed, it simply wasn't possible to keep it. Having his face to look at every day with him being so close would be absolute torture.

On Friday evening, I wrapped it up and requested an Uber. A train and a bus ride were out of the question carrying a painting of this size. When my ride arrived, Macie only shook her head as I left. It was quite a struggle getting the damn thing in the car, but we did it, and off we went to Holy Cross rectory. My driver dropped me off and I was glad to see Canaan's car parked in front. I hadn't thought to text him to see if he'd be there.

I knocked on the residential part of the building, since I knew the office was closed, hoping Father Cernak didn't answer the door. When Canaan opened it, I smiled.

"Haven, what are you doing here?"

Self-consciousness invaded every pore. Part of me wanted to hide in the bushes next to the porch and the other wanted to play like I had this under control. I didn't at all. My stomach was an army of worker bees buzzing around the hive. "I...I brought you something. Is it okay if I come in or...?" I let my words trail off.

"No, it's fine. Father Cernak is gone. His parents are elderly and he went home to visit them. He won't be back until late tonight."

"Ah. Okay." I bent down to lift up the painting.

He opened the door wide so I could pass through. "Here, let me get that," he said as he saw me trying to lug the monstrosity through the door.

"Be very careful with it, please."

When we got in the den, I told him to unwrap it. "It's for you." Another wave of shyness washed over me and I was suddenly afraid my work wasn't good enough for him.

He gently tore the brown paper off the painting, and when it was fully revealed he only stared, silent.

When the silence became unbearable, I blurted out, "If you don't like it, you can give it away. Maybe to your parents, although they may not like it either. And it's okay if you don't like it. I won't be offended or anything like that. Everyone has different tastes. Art is one of those things—"

He stopped me from vomiting any more words and further embarrassment. "Haven, you painted this for me?" His voice was so low and quiet I had to lean toward him to hear. He glanced between the painting and me several times before placing it on the couch so he could get a better look at it. He went around and turned on every light in the room and then went down on his knees to inspect it. And I mean he scrutinized it to the point where he lovingly touched each image, every brush stroke, and eventually looked up at me from where he knelt on the floor.

When he lifted his face to mine, I covered my lips with my hand. I'd never seen an expression of adoration like that until now.

"This is the second most beautiful thing I've ever seen in my life. The work is stunning. I know a bit about art, though I'm no expert, mind you, but you have managed to capture such emotion, I feel as if I am looking into a mirror." A V had formed between his brows and I wanted to massage it away.

"You like it?"

"I'm overwhelmed by it. I don't like it—I love it. And I'm flattered and touched by your generosity that you would go to these extremes and spend the time doing this. Haven, I don't quite know what to say."

My smile must have taken up half of my face. He said exactly what I wanted him to say. "You've said enough. I'm pleased you like it. You wear so many hats, I wanted to capture you in all of them, but I'm pretty sure I missed a few."

He kept touching it, running his fingers over the different images. "Why did you do it?"

"I got the idea one day and my creative juices started to flow. That's the way things transpire for me. The many faces of Canaan kept showing up in my mind, and when that happens, I need to transfer them to canvas."

"Was the painting of your mother like this?"

My smile faded. "No. It was a singular portrait of her. She was a blonde, like me. And I thought she was the most beautiful thing in the world. She would let me brush her long hair, and I sketched her as she'd sat on the chair, her hair gleaming, but I had woven flowers into it and for whatever reason, it worked for the painting. And her eyes, they were blue with hints of silver in them, and in the painting I brought out the hues so she looked very ethereal."

"You still miss her."

"I do. I knew she was sick, even though she never told me. She would lie on the couch watching TV and tell me she was tired. But she never let on that she didn't feel well. And one day I came home from school and BAM! She was gone." It was strange telling him because I never talked about this to anyone, except Macie.

The room filled with silence again and all I wanted to do was precisely what I couldn't. At that moment, it became abundantly clear that I needed to walk away from Canaan Sullivan for good. There was a certain kind of closure to this, me bringing him this painting. What started out as my enormous animosity toward him ironically had morphed into great respect and more. However, Macie was right. Though he was an extraordinary man, he was out of my reach, and by showing up at church, coming around here and trying to see him, I was only prolonging the inevitable. There would never, could never, be anything between us, other than pure friendship.

"Canaan, I'd better be going now. This is my way of saying goodbye. For good." His head slanted as his brows rose, but before he could ask me anything, I went on. "We both know there's more to this than friendship, but I've been foolish to think I could be just 'your friend'." I used my index fingers and squiggled them when I said the words *your friend*.

"It can never be, and it was silly of me to have that young

girl's crush on you again. But if I'm honest with myself, it's more than a crush. You've turned out to be a man—a man I can trust and admire, a man I could love. But I know you could never love me back. I knew cutting you off cold turkey wasn't possible because I kept thinking about you. You were always there. So I figured if I became your friend, it would be a gradual thing, and maybe this ache in my heart would be alleviated."

I placed my hand on my chest and rubbed circles on it, trying to ease the ache. Only it didn't help. Nothing would. I knew that now. "You're constantly on my mind—hence the painting. It's becoming torture for me and quite possibly for you. But you have your life, here at Holy Cross, and it's what you've wanted your entire life. So thank you for being the way you are, and helping me, and my aunt, but I think it's best for me to bow out gracefully, as they say, and carry on with my life. I do have to tell you something though."

Looking up at the ceiling, I gathered my thoughts for a moment. "Because of you, I believe I'm a better person. The other night, I had the opportunity to be with someone and I backed away from it. In the past, I wouldn't have thought twice about that. Maybe you've brought some self-respect into my life." I offered him what I hoped was a full-on smile, but I was pretty sure it was an epic fail.

"Haven, I'd like to tell you things could be different, but we both know they can't."

"I have to ask you. The painting—you said it was the second most beautiful thing you've ever seen. What was the first?" As an artist, I wondered if he'd been to the Vatican and viewed some of the artwork there.

"You. You're the most beautiful thing I've ever seen."

I could only swallow the knot of unshed tears that clogged my throat.

There was a deep sadness in his voice. Did he already feel as bereft as me?

Nodding, I muttered, "Well then, I guess I'll be on my way."

"I should drive you."

"No, you shouldn't. I'm fine. It's not that late and I do this all the time."

I walked up to him, stood on my tiptoes, and placed a chaste kiss on his cheek. But to my surprise, he changed course, catching me off guard. His mouth crash-landed on mine before his tongue timidly traced the seam of my lips. One of his arms circled my waist, drawing me into the frame of his body, and he left me with no choice but to grab on to his shoulders. The sexual side of me wanted to latch onto him with everything I had, responding with flaming intensity as blood scorched my veins and heat flushed through me. But reason won out and I gently pried myself away.

We were both panting as we stood together, his arm still imprisoning me. The warmth of his flesh radiated from him, making me want to run my hands over his skin, through his hair. But I didn't. I fell into the forest green of his eyes as he stared, wanting to stay like this for eternity.

"I...please forgive me. I'm so sorry. I don't know...I didn't mean..." he stumbled on his words awkwardly.

"Canaan, it's fine." But it wasn't, because it showed me how good it could be and what I was truly missing. He'd driven that nail home and now I knew what I would never have. Disengaging myself, I took one step backward and licked my lips, still tasting him there. I clenched my eyes shut for a second before I pasted on a smile.

"You're an amazing man, Canaan, and you're going to bring an abundance of joy to many people as a priest. Have a happy life. You deserve it." Without another word, I hurried away before I lost my composure.

It was a long ride home, but I was glad for it. I wasn't exactly in the mood to face Macie. I needed to get my shit together first. And I thought I had. Until I walked in the door and she asked how it went. That's when I broke down and told her.

Twenty-Three

CANAAN

When Haven walked out the door, she didn't know how wrong she was. She wasn't the only one who had fallen. The thing was, I hadn't known how far I'd plunged and had no idea how to pick myself back up. My heart felt as if it had been scraped raw as I watched her leave, and I wasn't quite sure how it had all happened. That piece inside of me that gave me life was now so defective, I felt as if she reached inside of my chest and ripped it out of me. It wasn't supposed to be this way. A man of the cloth was forbidden to love a woman. Even with the wall I had attempted to construct, I had failed completely.

With my thoughts on Haven, I carried the precious painting to my room. Setting it on my desk and resting it against the wall, I stared at it, lost in the intricacies of the details it contained. The complexities were mind-boggling and the fact that her small hands created it was proof that God had bestowed a mighty gift upon her. I sat on my bed, and as I did, traces of her lavender scent that still lingered on my pillows wafted up. I had washed my bedding but not the pillowcases. She wasn't the only one with the crush after all—or far beyond a crush, as it were. Once again, the sinner in me reared its ugly head. There wasn't enough penance in the world to make me atone for my transgressions. My daily routine of repenting would be longer and harsher than I had already made it. I now questioned whether I was worthy to even wear the holy cloth. It seemed that it had all been a mistake to grant me such an honor and privilege.

The weekend crept by, and on Sunday, my parents invited Bill and me over for dinner. It was a welcome distraction, moving my mind away from its sinful thoughts. Mom made her usual giant spread. There was enough food for the entire Holy Cross School. After we ate, we sat around and enjoyed an hour of congenial conversation before Bill and I left for home.

If I knew a way to purge thoughts of Haven from me, I would do it. Even though she was gone from my life, I saw her face in everything I did. I was a dying man trying to resurrect myself. Losing one's heart wasn't something I would ever recommend, and I'd never imagined how hopeless and pain-filled it left one feeling.

"Canaan?" Bill's voice cut through my thoughts.

"Yes?"

"I'm expecting a call from the bishop any time. I wanted you to know, in case it came through while I was outside. The call has to do with that issue I spoke to you about several days ago."

"Okay, if he calls and I answer, I'll be sure to let you know."

"Thank you." Bill ducked back into his office. Whatever happened had to have been grave for Bill to get the bishop involved.

I didn't ask Bill about his conversation with the bishop afterward, other than to see if he was okay. He seemed fine with the results, so that was okay by me.

Bill left the following Saturday morning to visit his parents. "I hate to leave you."

"Are you serious? Family is important." I did my best to reassure him.

"I know, but so is God."

I smiled. "It would please God to know you're taking care of your parents." I reminded him about the priest who was stepping in on Sunday morning to say the nine forty-five Mass. "I'll be fine. That leaves me with only two. It's nothing monumental by any means. Now go."

"Thanks. You make me feel better about leaving."

"As you should," I assured him. He got in his car and I watched him drive away.

Saturday was gloomier than usual. The clouds rolled in and rain threatened. I celebrated morning Mass and then later made my rounds at the hospitals and nursing homes. I held confession from two to four in the afternoon, so I brought my Bible and my phone in case there was a lull.

It had been a slow day, as expected. The rain started about noon and it seemed when it rained, people tended to stay home. I checked my phone to see what time it was and saw I only had another five minutes to sit in the small closet-like room. I figured that would be it until I heard the door open and close, and then someone knelt on the other side of the screen. I drew the screen back and gave my blessing to the confessor, and he began to speak.

"Bless me, Father, for I have sinned. My last confession was one month ago."

The voice on the other side was male, perhaps that of a very young teenager. It hadn't quite developed the deep tone of an adult.

"Father, I've done something bad. Real bad."

"What is it? What have you done that needs God's forgiveness?"

He whispered the words. "I killed Father O'Brien."

His confession hung in the small box, then it expanded until it felt as though it echoed and bounced off the walls. How was that possible? The detectives came by stating he'd died of natural causes.

"Did you hear me, Father?"

"Yes, yes, I heard you." I swallowed, not knowing what to say.

"I didn't mean to, but I know I did it." There was definitely an edge of desperation in his tone.

In a voice that was much calmer than I felt, I said, "Go on." This boy was mistaken, but something clued me into the fact that there was something much deeper buried beneath his words, and I wasn't going to like what I heard.

"It was, uh, yeah, well..."

"It's okay, son, you're confessing and whatever you tell me stays between God, you, and me."

His voice trembled as he answered, "O-okay. It happened after Saturday Mass. I stood up to him and told him I wouldn't let him do it anymore, that I wasn't going to take it again. And if he touched me one more time, I was going to tell everyone. Maybe even call the police."

My apprehension worsened with every one of his faltering words.

"He started to say something about being a sinner, like he always did, but when his hand reached out for me, I was so mad that I didn't think, and I just pushed him. I pushed him, Father, and he fell. I didn't think I pushed him that hard, but I guess I did. And that's what happened. I ran out of there as fast as I could because I didn't want him to get up and chase me. I didn't know I killed him until later." The sounds of his anguished sobs penetrated the thin screen that separated us. My heart ached for this young boy because he had thought all this time he was responsible for the evil priest's death.

Absolute guilt surged through me as my emotions choked me. If only I had spoken out, how many lives could I have saved from this same pain? One, five, a dozen? There was no telling. And here was this boy, kneeling before God, confessing to a sin he didn't commit. I bore the liability for that as well. What a tangled web I had woven. The sin of omission had certainly come home to roost upon my shoulders, and its burden was heavy indeed.

"Take a deep breath, son, and let me show you the way through this." *Lord Jesus Christ, please give me the strength to guide this young man and set him on the path of righteousness to Your door.* I could hear him breathing on the other side of the screen as his sobs lessened. When it was apparent he was more in control, I continued.

"I need to share information with you, but first you must understand something. Did Father O'Brien touch you inappropriately?"

"Yes, Father."

"That was wrong of him. You must know that first off. When you pushed him away from you, that wasn't wrong. Do you understand?"

"Yes, Father."

"Good. Second, the police investigated Father O'Brien's death. They wanted to rule out anything that might be suspicious. They found that he died of a heart attack. When he fell, he did hit his head, but he was already dead. Do you understand what I'm telling you? You weren't in any way responsible for his death." I was as emphatic as I could possibly be here. It was imperative this child believe me. The thought did cross my mind that what the young man said to the molester may have precipitated his heart attack, but I didn't share that with him. Could the fright of being discovered scare the priest into cardiac arrest? Who knew? Only God, and Father O'Brien had to face Him for all his atrocities on the day he died.

"I– I wasn't?"

"Not at all. You did not kill him."

I heard a long, slow sigh come from him.

"Being in the confessional grants you anonymity, but as your priest, I would like to ask a favor of you. Would you talk to someone about what happened to you with Father O'Brien? And I'm not talking about you pushing him. I'm talking about the other thing."

When he said nothing, I added, "I know it's difficult and that you may feel ashamed. But you shouldn't. Even if you don't tell your parents, would you at least come and talk to me about it later, and I could set you up with someone else, someone who could help you?"

"Help me?" he asked in a small voice. "He's dead now, so I don't have to worry about him anymore."

"That's true, but it would help you deal with the other stuff. Like the nightmares you don't tell anyone about."

"How...?"

"I just...know. So will you think about it at least?" I would pray that he did so it wouldn't ruin him for relationships later in life.

"Okay. And thanks for telling me. About his heart attack and all."

"You're welcome. And now I'm going to bless you and pray for you." I said my usual prayers but added extras because he needed it. I saw myself in him—the way I was back then—and guilt and remorse suffocated me.

It was almost five forty-five when I got back to the rectory. I was saying Mass this evening because Bill was at his parents'. What I really wanted to do was to take a long stiff drink to erase what had just occurred. If it kept happening—boys and men confessing their interactions with Father O'Brien—I wasn't sure what I'd do. A man could only take so much. And right now, I needed penance to help me deal with this. Forty-five minutes later, it was time to return to the church. The sacristy loomed before me and now my uneasiness overwhelmed me; all the strides I had made in the past months seemed to have fled. As I entered the room I hated so much, my body shook and I almost threw up on the threshold as the scent assaulted me. I fought it with every cell in my body, and when it was time to leave to say Mass, I was drenched in sweat.

I stood with my back to the wall. The air in my lungs had become solid, making it impossible to inhale or exhale.

"Father, are you okay? You don't look so good." It was Shelby.

Her jovial presence thawed the brick of ice in my chest. "I'm fine. Just a bit hot. Are you ready?"

She nodded, and I questioned whether I'd make it through Mass. My reasoning told me I'd been through much worse, so I figured this would be easy. I wasn't sure how to feel when it was clear Haven had made good on her words. She wasn't there. So I focused and lost myself in prayer. It was like riding a wave until it hit the shore. Celebrating Mass and the Liturgy had that effect on me. Afterward, though, thoughts of that young man and how he'd been suffering rushed into me again. I finished greeting the parishioners and luckily it had started pouring rain so nobody lingered.

Upon returning to the rectory, I walked straight to the cabinet where Bill kept the liquor and poured myself a Scotch. No ice. Straight up. It wasn't my usual style, but I needed the burn of the numbing agent to ease the burn in my heart.

How many? The question kept tumbling in my head like a roll of the dice. If only I had a time machine. But I didn't. Three drinks later and I felt no better. Why do they say alcohol numbs the pain? It wasn't working on me. How much of the stuff would I have to drink before it did anything? My decision was made. I would drink until nothing mattered tonight. For one single night, I wanted to feel the absence of everything.

Standing, I poured myself one more when my phone rang. Reaching in my pocket, my heart came to a halt when I saw who was calling me. It was only yesterday when she said goodbye.

Twenty-Four

HAVEN

Saturday night I decided to pay a visit to Aunt Kathy. It had been a couple of weeks and it was nagging at me that I'd been a negligent niece. Now that my evening was free, I could do the right thing for once.

"You're going without calling first?" Macie, my fierce protector, asked me.

"It's fine. I'm sure he won't be there. He doesn't just hang around the house anyway, especially on a Saturday night."

"How would you know? You haven't lived there for years."

She had somewhat of a point. But she didn't know him like I did. When you lived with a man who beat you the way he had beaten me, you memorized his every move. "You're right, I haven't, but when I did, he never stayed home on Saturday nights and he certainly never took my aunt out. A man like Kent wouldn't start staying home now. If I were to bet, I'd say he'd be spending more time away these days."

"I don't know, Haven. I don't think it's a good idea for you to go alone. I would go with you, but I'm afraid my mouth would land us both in more trouble."

"You can't go. You have a date with your hottie tonight. Don't worry. I'm fine." I didn't give her any more chances to object because I ran out the door. I heard her telling me to be careful as I went.

When I got to Aunt Kathy's, I wasn't going to lie to myself—it was a relief not to see my uncle's car parked out front. I rang the doorbell and there was no answer, so after what I thought was a reasonable amount of time, I rang it again. Maybe Kent had taken her out after all. But out of the corner of my eye, I saw the curtain move, so she was home. I fully expected the door to open, but when it didn't, I began to get scared.

"Aunt Kathy, can you hear me? Are you okay in there?" I pounded on the door. When she didn't answer, I was about to go to get the key hidden out back, but I heard the lock turn, and the door opened a crack.

"Haven, go away."

"Aunt Kathy, what's wrong?"

Her voice sounded off. Not exactly weak, but not herself either.

"Just go home. You can come back another time."

"Are you sick?"

"No, I'm fine." She definitely did not sound fine.

"Please, let me in. I'm worried about you."

"No, just leave, please."

"I don't understand." I peeked in the crack and it was so dark inside. She had all the curtains drawn and it looked like she didn't have any lights on. "Aunt Kathy, if you're not feeling well, I can at least call the doctor for you." I think I still had Wilson's card. It might be a little awkward, but I didn't care. This was my aunt that was ill.

"I'm not sick." Her voice was low, but when I thought it through, she didn't sound ill. She wasn't short of breath and wheezing like she did when she was in bad shape.

"Then what is it?" And suddenly I knew. I just knew. "Aunt

Kathy, open this door. Now. Or I'm pushing it down. I mean it."

She opened it wide enough for me to enter. It was so dark that I couldn't see her, so I hit the light switch on the wall and the room brightened. When I got my first glimpse of her, I saw red. Fury built in me to the point I almost screamed.

"When? When did he do this?"

"It doesn't matter. I'm fine."

"Bullshit. This matters and you are clearly not fine. You can barely speak. Your face is so swollen, I..." My hands went up in the air. I'd had it with him. He was a monster and could not keep getting away with hitting women. I pulled my phone out and started snapping pictures.

"What are you doing?"

"Building an evidence file to use against him. He is such an asshole."

Aunt Kathy could barely walk to the sofa. He must've done a number on her. I gave her time to sit and collect herself.

"Will you tell me?"

"He came home from being out with the guys. He doesn't like the fact that I'm sick. And it escalated from there."

What a piece of shit. He takes his anger out on a sick woman? I paced the room as she sat. My anger was front and center, obliterating any words of comfort that I should've been offering her. Mumbling several choice curse words and every nasty thing I could call him, I decided it was time to call a spade a spade. This bullying of his had gone on long enough.

I dropped to my knees in front of Kathy. "I care about you too much to see you hurt like this. I have a question for you. Have you been to the doctor since this happened?"

She shook her head. I didn't think she'd go. "I'm taking you Monday. You're not as strong as you once were, even though you're feeling much better. I know you're going to balk at this, but you need to get checked out. I'll see that you do."

When I stood up, she asked, "Where are you going?"

"To find him. Where did he go?"

"Out with the guys, I'm sure."

"Does he still go to the same hangouts he used to?"

"Haven, I don't know because I don't care. But don't you go chasing after him. It'll only anger him more."

"He's always angry at something, but he shouldn't be taking it out on you." I kissed her cheek and left.

His favorite hangout, or at least what I hoped was still his number one place to go, was only a few blocks away, so I hoofed it over there. With each step, I got more pissed off at him. What a prick he was to beat my aunt in her condition. Who did shit like that?

When I opened the doors, the place was almost empty and dim. The room was long and narrow, and in the back were a pool table and several dart boards. A group of guys were shooting pool. I imagined they were friends of Kent, so I steered clear. Instead, I sat down at the front near the door so I could make a hasty exit after I spoke my piece. My angry piece, that was.

Needing some liquid courage to face the devil, I ordered up a shot of Absolut. When the bartender delivered my goods, I tossed it back and let the liquor warm my guts. Thrumming my fingers on the wooden bar, edginess seeped into each of my nerve endings, making me jittery. As soon as the bartender turned my way, I held up a finger and ordered another shot. The bravado I'd felt in front of Aunt Kathy was leaking away, and I needed to plug the hole before I lost my nerve completely. The man handed me my second shot and it landed where the first one had gone. Patience wasn't in the cards, so I found myself ordering a third. If this shit didn't kick in soon, my ass would be scooting out the door before I did anything with the bully Uncle Kreep. After my third shot, I began to calm down, but when my nerves fled, so did my courage. I second-guessed my motives and realized that if I confronted Kent, he may very well take it out on Kathy. The last thing Kathy needed was another beating.

My decision made, I needed to hightail out of Kentland. I was settling up my tab when the door opened and in walked the demon himself.

"What the hell are you doing here? You trying to pick up some of my guys, whoring around my bar?" His sneer derailed me as I was just finishing up closing out my bill.

"What? No!"

"Yeah, right. You're just like your mom. Always acting like she was a goody two shoes when she was putting out all over the place. Like mother, like daughter. Two slutty peas in a pod."

The anger that had fled instantly returned. "How dare you talk about me? Why don't you tell everyone here what you did to your wife?"

His eyes darkened and his sneer only grew.

"What are you going to do? Spout drunken lies?"

Meaty fingers clamped around my arm and he dragged me further into the bar. And worse, no one stopped him. I managed to dig in my heels before he took me down the secluded hallway ahead.

"Is this how you treat women?"

"Not women, only drunken little lying sluts like you."

A voice rang out behind him. "What's going on here?"

I sighed, finding faith that maybe he wouldn't get away with his treatment of me.

"Kent, does she need a little time in the drunk tank?"

My eyes opened as wide as my jaw dropped. His grin only widened.

I pulled free from his grasp, slapping his hands away as he tried to get a hold of me again.

"That appears to be assaulting a police officer to me," another man behind him said.

They were going to arrest me. I took off for the hall and found a bathroom. I turned the lock on the door as Uncle Kent laughed on the other side.

"You have to come out sometime."

More laughter rang out. I slid my back down to the dirty floor, knowing if he wanted in, he would kick in the door. He'd proved that to me before. With shaky hands, I made the call and begged Canaan to come get me.

Twenty-Five

CANAAN

The alcohol rang through my veins like liquid flame. My heart pounded in my chest when I pushed through the doors of the bar, a man on fire.

Faces, too many, stared at me as I glared back until I found the one I sought. Dressed in his uniform, I was glad I still wore my collar. We would see which was mightier.

I barreled forward and stood toe to toe with the monster who dared to smile.

"Father Canaan, I wonder what brings you here," he smirked.

My hands curled in fists, and for a second, the desire to show him what it was like to be struck consumed me. But a quick inner prayer for strength of character held me back.

"Where is she?"

He laughed. "A priest. I should have guessed."

I shouldn't have played into his hands.

"Guessed what?" I snapped.

"Guessed like her mother she whores her way into making

a man want her, even supposedly the best of men." He downed the contents of his glass.

"I can't begin to untwist your mind. Just tell me where she is."

He tipped his head back and laughed. "Or what?"

His words slithered off his tongue like the beast of hell and they'd found their match. "Or I shall bring you down with God's wrath," I hissed, not caring who heard, but not yelling the words either.

He leaned in and whispered, "God's wrath?" He chuckled. "Bring it on. You're in a cop bar and I'm a cop. You may be a man of the cloth, Father," he scoffed and gestured to the room. "But I am their brother in arms."

With all eyes on us in our quiet standoff, his hand moved to the weapon on his hip.

Words left my lips like a prayer or maybe a promise. "You don't scare me, Kent. You may like scaring your wife and your niece with your bullying tactics, but I have God on my side. And no weapon formed against me shall prosper."

In the silence around me, I heard a door open. I glanced up to see Heaven. I blinked, because it was Haven. I moved around Kent as she plowed into my chest. Her body shook with sobs.

"Come on, let's go."

I tucked her against my side where she fit snug to me. We marched for the door and I dared any man to cross my path in that moment. There was no way God would condemn me if I had to defend myself or the woman on my arm. We'd almost made it out the door, but he had to have the last word.

"This isn't over, Haven. Not by a long shot."

She tried to tug out of my arm, but I kept her close and headed outside.

HAVEN

The fresh air was a welcome reprieve, but I still wanted to yell and scream at the men and women who'd stayed quiet while my uncle terrorized me. They had to see it wasn't right. Yet, they'd done nothing to help.

We'd made it a block away when Canaan stopped and faced me.

"Why would you go there?"

I'd never seen him angry, so I stopped, stunned by the rage displayed on his body. Eyes that had turned the color of a stormy sea were even more pronounced by muscles that stood so rigid I feared they would rupture. The set of his mouth alone was enough to frighten me, and the only thing comforting me was I knew I was safe because it was Canaan. I rubbed my arms feeling small and stupid for what I'd done.

He closed his eyes and turned toward the store we were in front of. His fist hit the stone with so much force, I grabbed his hand knowing what I'd find.

"Your knuckles—they're bleeding."

Green eyes churned with deep emotion. My mouth hung open, faced with it. I pulled my shirt free to use the end of it to dab at his wounded hand.

"We should get you home. I'm in no condition to drive you. Can you call a cab?" he asked.

I nodded, fumbling in my purse for my phone when the skies opened up. Rain poured down in sheets without a second's warning. A warm hand found mine and then we were racing through the streets. We ended up down the path behind the church that led to the rectory.

Soon we were inside and the sudden chill in the air caused shivers to overtake me.

"Let's get you dry."

I followed him into a familiar room and stopped short. I didn't remember being brought into Canaan's room before. I'd only woken up in it. It was such a simple place with a small bed and chest of drawers. As I tried to recall distant memories, a towel was draped over my shoulders. Canaan moved to the chest as I clasped it around me and stood as if I were naked. And I did feel naked, especially when Canaan, with his back to me, pulled off his shirt.

"Father Cernak?"

It was all I could muster as I saw his back. I felt choked seeing his was marked with scars much like my own. I couldn't breathe and I knew it wasn't proper for me to be here. And I didn't want Canaan in trouble.

He turned, and God damned me because he was a study of perfection, even more so than I had dreamed. Every muscle of his was defined down to the V that dipped past the waistband of his pants.

"He's out for the night."

A shirt covered him far too soon for my liking as he sensed my penetrating stare. Then he reached in the drawer and pulled out other things. He stood before me, hands filled with articles of clothing, and I couldn't think beyond the lust and questions that saturated my brain.

"You should change out of your wet clothes. These will be too big for you, but they are all I have." That was an understatement as he towered over me and handed me some clothes. "I'll be in my office."

He practically ran out of the room, leaving me to watch his retreat. But I'd seen his eyes on my lips and felt his struggle as much as my own against the attraction we had for each other.

CANAAN

With shaky hands, I poured myself a double. My bloody knuckles were a reminder that I needed to get Haven out of here. At the same time, she was someone in need. I could overcome the overwhelming desire to touch her and counsel her on her unwise choice to confront her uncle. No doubt the little spitfire had done exactly that. But why? And why had she gone there alone?

The movement of fabric warned me of her presence as she came into the room. I grabbed another glass and poured her a drink.

Turning, I was struck by seeing her in my clothes. They swallowed her, hanging off her smaller frame awkwardly. Only it made me want to know what was underneath that much more. I'd seen pictures of unclothed women, paintings of the human form when I'd studied art and in museums. But I'd never seen it in the flesh. And I hadn't known how much I wanted to until she'd innocently rammed her way into my life.

"Canaan."

She said my name so softly, yet it was what I needed to jerk me out of my untoward thoughts. She had the towel in her hand and pressed it to my knuckles as we stood gazing at each other. I had to break the spell.

"Here," I said, handing her the glass of amber liquid.

She took it, leaving the towel behind. I watched her cradle the glass in her hand like it was a steaming cup of coffee. I closed my eyes, knowing that's probably what she needed to ward off the cold, not alcohol. Before I could offer something else, she moved the glass to her lips, forcing me to swallow hot air down my parched lungs.

I cleared my throat. "So tell me why you went there, Haven?"

HAVEN

I wasn't ready to answer. Instead, I asked, "What is this?" holding up the glass.

"Jack." I watched him pour one for himself too. Then he said, "Now, will you tell me what happened?"

I unloaded on him like a dump truck. "I went to see my aunt," I began and didn't leave out any of the details. Over the course of the few months I had known Canaan, I'd found out one very vital piece of information. I could not lie to him. And he wasn't pleased in the least with my foolish actions. He let me know how reckless I'd been. Canaan was right. Kent could've taken it out on my aunt. It was selfish of me. I needed to do a better job of controlling my anger.

"You need to contact the authorities." I shook my head violently in opposition to his words. "I understand he's a cop. But there has to be someone you can tell. You can't continue to live in fear of this man."

"You don't understand."

"I do. More than you know," he said quietly.

"No, you don't," I retorted.

Out of the blue he hit me with, "Then why me?"

"What do you mean?"

"You could've called Macie. Why did you call me?"

"I trust you."

"How could you trust me? You obviously don't want my help. And let's face it; if not for me and my secrets, you wouldn't have been in that situation. You would have gotten away from Kent."

"Secrets?"

It was his turn to gesture *No* with his head. "Never mind. It doesn't matter anymore. You need to stay away from him...and me. I have enough guilt. If something happened to you..."

His words trailed off and I was left to my restless thoughts. I wanted to ask more but was afraid he'd send me away.

After three shots and on my fourth drink, I fell into the pond of his penetrating green eyes. I swam in their countless hues, drowning in their endless beauty, and tried to think of something to say that wouldn't sound stupid. But the only words that floated around in my head were inappropriate for a priest's ears, so all I did was stare and kept my thoughts to myself.

CANAAN

Her eyes pinned me with hope and longing, dislodging my own feelings I thought I'd tucked away in a small corner of my heart.

"You shouldn't trust me either. I think you should go," I said.

I took the glass from her hand after putting down my own and placed hers next to it. Cupping her elbow, I led her out of the confines of my office. The four walls were too private and my thoughts were spiraling out of control.

"What's wrong, Canaan? Why are we going to the church?" she asked after we were almost to the doors of the sanctuary.

She stopped in the middle of the walkway, and it was only then I looked up in surprise as to where we were. The rain had stopped, but there was still a damp chill in the air. I hadn't meant to drag her here and end up right in front of the place where it all started.

"I'm a cancer, a poison to the soul. I don't deserve your forgiveness."

My statements hung between us like a flimsy rope bridge in the middle of nowhere.

"What's going on? I don't understand. And you were drinking before you came to get me, weren't you? What happened to you?"

Unable to answer, I turned toward the room where all my dreams had turned into nightmares.

Twenty-Six

HAVEN

He stared at the door to the side of us with troubled eyes.

"Don't you see? I'm failing at this. I should be counseling you, not the other way around." Pain echoed around each of his words.

He was holding back and I latched on to something he'd said before. *Secret.* Whatever that secret was, I had a feeling it had to do with that night long ago. Wasn't that what he was hinting at?

"What happened here that day? My painting. I didn't see it then, but I painted you with haunted eyes the same as I'd felt at the time."

His mouth clamped shut, and I saw the lock turning in his head.

"Don't do this. I deserve to know."

"Haven, please."

I charged forward and turned the knob. The door was unlocked and I stepped inside the sacristy. It was as I'd remembered it. Everything was put away in cabinets. The main piece in the room was the large table that boldly sat in the center.

When I turned back, Canaan stood stricken with distress on the other side of the door as if he couldn't bring himself to step over the threshold.

The pieces of the puzzle were scattered in my brain, but I took a chance.

"Was it here?"

He paled to the color of chalk and sounded as though gravel was lodged in his throat when he spoke. "Was what here?"

I moved further into the room and hopped up on the large table. When I glanced up, he looked as though he might faint. So I was getting close to whatever the secret was.

"Is this where you got your scars?"

His shock wore off and his jaw gritted tight as he said, "You shouldn't be here."

And that was all it took to bring me back to that night. Tears welled in my eyes. I slid down to stand in front of the table. "That's what you said to me that night." I turned my back to him and removed his borrowed shirt. "And this is the result of your words."

The air he sucked in his lungs blew out as he said my name with so much remorse. "Oh, Haven."

I didn't hear him move, only felt his hand touch my back and trace my scars. The contact was lightning in my blood and it struck me square in my heart.

"I deserve to know what made you say those words to me." I turned to face him, cradling the shirt to cover my breasts for his modesty's sake, not my own. "I once thought you'd sent me away because I wasn't worthy, or at best, you were an awful person. But now I know better. Something happened to you that day. Something made you cold. I need to know. I have to understand."

"Please, Haven. I can't. Some secrets should remain buried."

CANAAN

Stepping forward, she dared me to admit the truth, "No, some secrets bury you. Whatever happened that day haunts us both. And your scars match my own."

She was right about everything. But I couldn't uncap the cork I'd placed on the memories that threatened to expose my shame.

"I saw your back. Someone hit you like my uncle hit me. You must know if anyone could understand it's me. Did your father beat you?"

My mouth dropped. "No, never. My father…" I shuddered to think she would tie the punishments at the hand of a monster to my dad. "He would never touch me. He's a good man."

"Then who was it? And what does it have to do with this room?"

"Haven, we've both had too much to drink. Let's call a cab and get you home."

"No. Who. Hit. You?"

The words flung out and stung me like a slap.

"I did," I shouted back.

I stepped back as her abhorrence covered her face.

"What?" she cried out.

Her confusion made me keep my eyes closed.

"Why would you do that?"

The question was a legitimate one. I opened my eyes and faced her. Maybe it was the alcohol. Maybe it was my conscience. But the confession flew from my tongue, unburdening my soul.

"I'm guilty. And he was right all along. And I deserve to be punished for all my sins."

"Punished? Who was right? And why would you need to

punish yourself?"

Her eyes were soft, but I didn't deserve their warmth. She clutched my shirt to her breasts as she stood before me with the scars of her torment. I had been the cause for sending her straight into the hands of her demon.

"Because I am temptation. Because I am tempted. Because I kept the truth to myself and others paid the price for my silence, including you."

It wasn't enough. She was full of questions I didn't want to answer.

"What could possibly be so bad that you would punish yourself? What made you send me back to the house of the devil? What has you so spooked you look like you fear this room?"

The weight of guilt pressed on me. I walked over to the table and gripped the sides. I longed for the strength of Samson so I could flip the damned thing over on it sides for all the horror it held. But I didn't have it.

Her hands landed on my back and she pushed the fabric of my shirt up, revealing my penance to her scrutiny. I shivered as her cool hands began to trace my scars much as I had hers moments before. I waited for the revulsion to hit me. Her standing behind me should force the memories of him to the foreground.

I spun around as a wave of a different need crept over me. I stilled her hands as her eyes widened in surprise.

"Haven, I am too weak. You have to go."

She stepped closer, backing me into the table. "I'll leave when you tell me the truth."

"I can't."

Her eyes narrowed and her lips trembled. "Well, how about this truth? After you sent me home that day, Uncle Kent tossed me in the basement. Made me strip."

"No." The thought that he touched her the way Father

O'Brien touched me caused bile to explode to the back of my throat.

Her story was different though.

"He beat me until I thought I would die. I told him I'd gone to church, and he didn't believe me. Or maybe he did. Maybe he realized I'd planned to rat him out. So he hit me within an inch of my life or so it felt. So you tell me. What made you send me back to him?"

Her confession guilted me into telling her the truth.

"I couldn't let you see Father O'Brien. I sent you away for your protection."

Her voice rose as understanding hadn't hit her yet. "You said that before, and I still don't understand."

The words burst from my mouth before I could stop them. "I didn't want him to touch you like he touched me. I didn't know then that he only liked boys."

She stepped back and covered her mouth with her hands. "Oh my God, Canaan."

"Don't." I gestured for her to stop as silent tears streamed down my face. "I don't deserve your pity," I said through clenched teeth. I clasped my hands in front of me to avoid striking that very table—the symbol of so much pain for so many years.

"It's not pity." She wiped at tears on her own face. "I can't believe I hated you, and you were only trying to protect me."

"And I failed."

She reached out and unclasped my hands. Her touch was such a balm to my soul, so I allowed her the simple act. She threaded her fingers through my own as she stared me down with a conviction I didn't feel. "You didn't fail. He failed you."

"But I did. I sent you away from one monster and into the hands of another."

Her sobs choked her words. "But you didn't know. You had no idea, and I held my silence too."

"You don't know the truth. He was right about everything. That time was the first of many of his lessons. And had I told someone, then maybe there would have only been the one time. Maybe no one else would have been used by him."

"You were just a child."

"So were you," I countered back. But the dam had been broken, and I couldn't hold back the words I'd hidden for so long. "The truth of it was I said nothing, not because of fear, but shame. How could I have explained to my parents that I'd found release by his hands during that nightmare? His touch shouldn't have made my body betray me and my faith. But it did. And he laughed and told me I wanted it as much as he had. And I believed him."

Disgusted with me, she pulled back, releasing our hands. And I knew the truth would be the hammer that smashed the bonds between us. My heart ached as it was shattered by the same blow.

HAVEN

Tears fell from my eyes in torrents, mimicking the rain that had resumed its downpour outside. My heart was battered, much like Kent had done to my body, for the man before me. He'd been broken and demoralized by his tormentor, someone who was supposed to have been a man of God, and I'd thought I was the only one who suffered by the devil's hands.

"It wasn't your fault," I said softly.

"How wasn't it?" he snapped.

The guilt that formed his expression broke whatever morals I should have had. I strode to stand before him and did the unthinkable to a priest. I cupped his dick and felt him react to my touch. Our eyes locked and I breathed my next words. "You see, you are a good man, Canaan, a good priest. But you respond to me despite the conviction I know you have for your vows."

He didn't remove my hand. I blamed shock and the revelation of a secret for his lack of brush off.

"That's the thing, Haven. For the longest time, I assumed I was gay. But I can tell you right now the thoughts that I have for you are not those of a gay man. All I want in this moment is to at least kiss you."

I was surely going to hell. "Then kiss me."

His hands moved to either side of my face and he leaned in. The press of his lips against mine was like a bomb going off. Reason fled and desire won out. More than anything, I wanted to erase the memories of his horror while erasing my own. I thrust my tongue into his virgin mouth and tasted the whiskey there. We were drunk on Jack, but more so on each other.

He may have been new to kissing, but he found his own as his tongue stroked against mine. I gripped his cock, but wanted more. I let go of the shirt that covered my breasts and reached for the waistband of his pants. I pushed at them, letting gravity take hold, springing his cock free. I hadn't seen it yet because our kiss continued on, but I began to stroke him, needing him to understand two bodies didn't care what their profession was or their gender.

I used my free hand to remove one of his from my face. I placed it on my breast and was surprised by his gentle touch. I moaned in his mouth as his fingertips grazed over my nipple so tentatively until my strokes sped up. He was on the verge. I could tell when his grip grew bruising. I dropped to my knees, freeing myself from his capture. I wanted to taste him as he went over the edge. There was no time for rational thought. I just acted.

His skin smelled of soap, but he tasted all man. He let out a shuddering gasp as I went as far as I could, sucking him until he reached the back of my throat. His fingers wound in my hair as I pulled back. It took only a few strokes before jets of cum squirted into my mouth. I took it all before releasing him.

The rod of steel was still rigid and showed no signs of deflating.

"Haven."

His eyes were husky and full of need.

"Canaan, it's your choice. I won't take that away from you like he did."

Yes, I'd just sucked him off. But was he ready for the whole of it? And my body ached for his. I took a step back, giving him space to find his own answer.

CANAAN

She stood bare from the waist up as my pants pooled at my feet and my shirt had been tossed somewhere behind us. The beauty that emitted from her was as deadly as it was glorious. Her breasts were as round and bountiful as they'd felt under my touch. And even though she'd done something to me I had abhorred the thought of before, she looked shy, almost afraid of how I would answer.

I knew in the back of my mind what just happened had been wrong. And going further was one of the gravest sins. Only that voice was but a mere whisper to the other shouts in my head. Many things had been stolen from me in this room—my innocence, my courage, my faith, and my manhood. Most of all, my choice had been taken from me. I wanted it back. I wanted to know this act with this woman by my own choosing.

I deserved to know something different other than feeling helpless to the whims of that man.

"Yes, I want to."

Her thumbs hooked into the sides of my pants she wore. I sucked in a ragged breath as she slowly revealed herself to me. She was smooth and hairless down below. All the paintings I'd seen had a woman hidden behind a palm full of curls. But nothing hid her to me. I saw and wanted to touch, but had no idea what to do. She must have sensed my ineptitude because her quiet words rang out.

"Lie back."

The table I'd been forced to hold was now at my back and not my stomach. She climbed up and straddled me, leaving me confused as to where to look. Her center or her breasts, then again, I wanted to see her face to understand if she wanted this as much as me.

She took me in her hand, and I thought I might erupt again. Her mouth had felt so amazing, I couldn't imagine what being inside her was like. Something was building beneath her hold. It drew me tight as a bow and made me stupid with want. When she lifted onto her knees with her legs on either side of me, I watched as she positioned herself above. I didn't understand. I could see no opening until she pushed the tip of me between her parted lips below. Then slowly those lower lips swallowed my length in their warm silky depths.

My vision blurred and I lost sight of her. The feeling was cataclysmic. There was no pain, no anger, no fear. As she sank on me, I was lost, only this time it was in hope and desire. When she rose up, I just knew my eyes would get stuck as they rolled in the back of my head. I closed them to revel in the moment, wanting to remember every movement, every touch.

"Canaan, look at me."

I blinked, clearing my sight, wondering if the sin of pleasure had caused me to go blind. Finally, I saw. She moved like a siren calling me to shore; I was lost under her ministrations.

She began to move up and down with more speed, more pleasing friction. I was getting to the climax of things quickly and I wasn't ready for it to end. I reached out and gripped the sides of her hips. In response, she tossed her head back as I held her still.

HAVEN

I would have been a blind woman not to have absorbed the beauty of Canaan as he lay beneath me naked. His sculpted muscles tensed with his want and there wasn't a single part of him that wasn't molded to perfection. Eyes wild with the same desperation I felt, he held me in place as his large fingers dug into the flesh of my hips. I craved his touch more than I cared to think about. Leaning down, my breast was a mere breath away from his mouth. And he didn't disappoint. His wet tongue flicked out before one hand left my hip to draw me closer. His full lips wrapped around my nipple and he didn't need any instruction on what to do next.

The suction of his mouth propelled my hips in motion, and I rubbed my clit against his firm length as I restarted our movements. His mouth left my breast and he cupped the back of my head. Our lips collided as his tongue sought out mine. He tasted every corner of me as if he were looking to discover all my hidden secrets. I moaned in his mouth as awareness struck me—this was what every kiss should be. Then he started thrusting up, meeting me in the middle as we found our rhythm. He was reacting on instinct as he moved his hips up and inside me. My body wrapped around his like a tailor-made glove. Every nerve ending inside sparked as friction did its job.

I wanted time to suspend, but it didn't. My orgasm struck me on a scream as my inner walls spasmed all around him.

His hand left my hair and returned to my hip as he thrust harder upward, groaning as he found his own release. A few more grunts between us and we lay spent on the table, panting.

As sweat cooled on our skin, I realized something so very important, yet mortifying. I had fallen for him hard. There was no turning back…until I looked into his eyes. My smile faltered. The bright light that filled the room as we became one had now dimmed.

Regret drew unhappy lines around his lips. The walls of my heart fell, much like Jericho's, as the room and what we'd done spun all around me. Shame covered me. I'd spoiled the virginal priest much as Father O'Brien had. I was the harlot who tempted him into breaking his vow of celibacy. What had I done? I scrambled off him, gathering the clothes he'd given me and darted out of the room. My conscience and heart couldn't endure the look of utter despair on his face.

CANAAN

There were no words for what I was—sham, charlatan didn't come close. Yet I had the gall to parade around in priest's clothing. I'd allowed the whispered words of a serpent to lure a woman into committing an act that defiled what should have been a sacred room. And instead of apologizing, my mouth stayed glued as I cowardly allowed her to flee from the room where I'd sinned in the most depraved way.

Alcohol and bad memories had destroyed what goodness was in me. It was late. I needed to get her home. Quickly, I got dressed and searched for her. But she was nowhere to be found. I headed out into the night, where I jogged toward the street too late to stop her as she got in a car and drove away.

I shoved a hand in my hair, not sure how I should react. I'd broken my vow, but for some reason, I didn't feel dirty. I felt well loved, which was crazy. She wasn't my wife and couldn't be. I'd cheated on the church and my heart broke for that, whereas the other part of my heart had been healed from our joining. I stayed there, halfway between the church and the street, not knowing where I belonged.

Rain fell down on me as if the heavens wept for my transgressions. With nowhere to go, not yet at least, I headed back inside. I cleaned the floor and the table, wiping away the sins committed in the sacristy before heading back to the rectory.

Once in my room, I pulled out the belt and stared at it a long time before tossing it unused on the bed. I climbed in the shower and hung my head. I prayed for Haven and myself while making plans. I couldn't stay much longer and didn't know of a way out. I needed to talk to someone. Maybe when Bill came back, I would think about requesting a leave to go see my mentor. He might be able to help untangle the mess I'd created.

Twenty-Seven

HAVEN

What in God's name had I done? Sex with Canaan? I couldn't bear to think about it. Yet, that's all I saw when I closed my eyes. The ride home was interminable. When the Uber driver finally reached Macie's building, I hurried away from the car. I was sure it was way more than enough. My brain and guts churned with the guilt of what I'd done as I pushed open the door to our apartment, only I stopped short. Macie was on the couch with her date.

Shit, shit, shit! I was still dressed in Canaan's oversized sweats and T-shirt, soaked from standing in the rain.

"Haven, holy crap, are you okay?"

"I'm fine," I muttered, hurrying past them into my room.

Voices exchanged phrases behind me, but I didn't pay attention to them. Only one thing occupied my attention and he wasn't in this apartment.

Macie barged into my room without so much as a knock. "Did he hurt you? Did that fucker hurt you?"

"Why would you think that?"

"Because he used to beat the shit out of you and now you

come home looking like this."

I was so lost in thoughts of Canaan, I immediately thought that's who she was referring to. "Oh, that." My body was wracked with shivers from the wet clothing. "I need to get out of these."

Her narrowed gaze told me I was in for the interrogation of my life. "Right. But then I need answers."

I didn't bother to respond and headed straight to the bathroom. The shower was both a blessing and a curse. It took the chill away, but it didn't rinse away the guilt that coated me. It also washed Canaan's touch and smell from my body. I would have gladly left it there forever. His perfect blend of innocence and beauty had tunneled inside of me, had pierced the impenetrable walls of my soul, allowing my heart to open up. And what had I done in return? I had twisted that love around and forced a carnal act upon him, and now he had broken his sacred vow of celibacy. What kind of person was I? Uncle Kent had been right after all. I was a slut. Worse than that, I was unscrupulous and licentious. Canaan should've been off limits to me from the very beginning.

With shaking hands, I turned off the water and dried myself. The reflection in the mirror showed me someone I didn't even know anymore. What happened to the girl I used to be?

"Haven, you have to come out of there sometime. It might as well be sooner rather than later. I have some tea made to warm you up."

Wrapping myself in a towel, I walked to my bedroom to throw on my pajamas and then went out to the living room where Macie sat waiting.

"Here." She handed me a cup of tea.

"Thanks."

"So?"

"What happened to your date?

She glared at me. "I sent him home."

"Why did you do that?"

"Because you are more important. Now spill!"

I started at the beginning, from when I got to Aunt Kathy's and ended at the point where I ran out of the sacristy. I left out the part about his molestation. That was Canaan's story and his alone. She'd only interrupted me for clarification every now and then, until now.

"So let me get this straight—you rode the pony, and I'm talking Canaan's pony, on top of the vestment table in the sacristy?"

"Ugh. You make it sound so utterly disgusting. I may be utterly disgusting, but he's not. It just wasn't that way, Mace."

"Can I just explain something to you? You had sex with a Roman Catholic priest. One who received the Sacrament of Holy Orders, which, if you may have forgotten, included a vow of celibacy?"

"Oh, for God's sake, I haven't forgotten. What do you take me for? An idiot?"

"I might. At the moment anyway."

My head hung down with tears gushing down my cheeks like the rain that pounded the sidewalks outside. Macie was instantly by my side, holding me, doing her best to calm me down.

"I didn't mean it. I know you're not an idiot, Have. I do." She hugged and patted my hair and back, but I cried like a baby on her shoulder. It took a while, but I eventually reined the blubbering mess in, enough at least so I could speak.

"I've ruined him. Tarnished his perfect soul, Mace. I've marred that beautiful man and forced him to break his vow and now he won't be able to..."

"Stop this train wreck of thoughts right this instant. You did not force him to have sex. He's an adult. He could've walked away from you at any time."

I wrapped my arms around myself. "No, you don't get it, and I can't explain it either. Canaan is...he's not like anyone I've ever known."

Hands gripped my shoulders and she drilled me with her gaze. Then she squinted and said, "You're in love with him, aren't you?" Not wasting a second, I looked away. "Haven, answer me truthfully."

My head fell back down while my hands plowed a path straight through to the roots of my hair. I nearly pulled it out the way I tugged at it. "Yes, I'm in love with him." Lifting my head, I said the words directly to her. "I tried not to. I did. I avoided him as best I could. Then I attempted the friend thing because going cold turkey was killing me. But look where it got me. I'm that person who is not worthy, Macie. I'm going to Hell for sure. Not because of what I've done to myself, but look at what I've done to him."

Macie threw her hands up in the air. "You're being ridiculous. He had a choice. Everyone has a choice."

"No, they don't. Not when..." My hand fluttered in front of my face, trying to stem the tears. Talking was next to impossible.

"What are you trying to tell me? That you raped him?"

She had gotten under my skin and now I was so completely agitated. I wanted to shake her. "No, I didn't rape him." My head lolled back as I collected my words. How could I adequately explain this to her without spilling the horrors of Canaan's secret? "There's something I can't share with you, and I have to leave it at that. But as we talked and he tried to calm me over the Kent thing, we drank and then one thing led to another. It happened, Macie, but *I* was the instigator. It was my fault. *I* should've stopped it, and I didn't. I pretty much seduced him."

Her mouth gaped open. Mine would've done the same had she shared this piece of information with me.

By now, I paced the floor, wringing my hands.

In a calm and quiet tone, Macie said, "Haven, you've known me how long? Since the first grade?"

Nodding, I walked over to the liquor cabinet and poured a vodka.

"You can't blame this entirely on yourself," she said.

I took a big gulp of my drink. "Yeah, I can. He didn't even know how to kiss me, Mace. How do you think I feel, knowing I'm the one who urged him on? There's a lot to this story I wish I could share, but I can't. And I know you don't understand, but trust me on this—I'm the bad one here and I bear responsibility for it."

Macie stared at me, shaking her head. There was nothing she could say to ease my grief. Nothing in the world could do that. I sat back down next to her and drained my glass. As I did, tears came for Canaan. I cried for the young boy who had been damaged at such an early age and was ashamed and frightened to tell anyone. I cried for the young man who had buried the pain and heartache deep within him all those years. I cried for the priest who had endured the guilt of what he saw as being a sinner when he wasn't. I cried for the adult who had finally released the truth only to be seduced into sinning. And it was just as grave, if not graver, because it was not forced upon him. And lastly, I cried for the man Canaan who was every bit as beautiful inside as he was on the surface.

Twenty-Eight

CANAAN

My lips tingled with the memory of hers, the pressure of them still lingering there. If a heart could ache any worse than mine did, I never wanted to feel it. Lost, hopeless, disoriented were terms that best described me. After I returned to my room, my body hummed with want for her. Sleep was a thing of the past. There were many things I thought of doing, including drinking myself into oblivion, but none of those would erase her from my body and soul. At three, it was time to try to rest, and I did so fitfully. At five, I woke up with my hand in my pants, stroking myself, a vision of Haven on top of me. I jumped out of bed and fell to my knees, begging God's forgiveness. Masturbation wasn't something the church allowed. It was considered a mortal sin that turned us away from God and selfishly toward ourselves.

My hands shuffled the items on my nightstand in search of my rosary, where it usually stayed. Once it was untangled from its place of rest, I launched into prayer, tenderly handling each of the round beads. I recited the Hail Mary—the dominant prayer in the rosary, devoutly. I begged the Virgin Mary for her help, although why she would stoop to help a tainted soul, a fallen priest such as myself, was beyond me. Had I not deemed myself unworthy of one so pure as her? Even so, I continued on, until it was time to prepare for Mass.

Minutes passed like hours, until late afternoon when I was able to lace up my shoes and go for a run. It wasn't until the sun started setting that I headed for home with aching thighs, burning lungs, and a parched throat. The run had clarified something and I knew where I'd be heading the next day.

Since this was my second visit, I took the train because the first time taught me about the traffic and parking. It turned out to be easier and less stressful riding public transportation.

When I entered the church, I had no idea what to expect. Would the priest condemn me for what I had done? It would be deserved if he did.

There was a green light over the confessional, so I entered. "Bless me, Father, for I have sinned. My last confession was one week ago."

He said a prayer for me and then asked, "What is it you wish to confess today?"

"I have committed a mortal sin." Air locked in my lungs, and I was unable to say more.

"And what sin is that?"

"I have been with a woman, sexually. I have broken my vow of celibacy. Father, I am a priest."

There was a long pause. "You were here before? After you kissed the woman?"

"Yes, Father."

"I see." Again, silence. And then, "I am afraid I don't quite know how to advise you. God forgives all sins, even that of your broken vow. Jesus Christ forgave Judas who betrayed him, and God sent his Son to save us sinners. I will absolve you from your transgression, however, I can't offer you advice, and

I suspect that's what you came here for, along with absolution."

"It is, Father."

"I'm terribly sorry to disappoint you. As you are aware, celibacy is a discipline as opposed to a doctrine. Was this woman you had relations with married?"

"No, Father."

"Then you must seek the forgiveness from your bishop and ask for his absolution for your sin. Strictly speaking, you broke your vow when you kissed her and continued your relationship with her. Having sex took it further. My recommendation would be to discuss this openly with your bishop. If you plan to continue your duties as a priest, you must not see her again."

"Yes, I know. I have done penance and prayed, and I never intended to continue this relationship."

"Temptation is all around and we must be aware of it at all times."

"Will you pray with me, Father?"

"Yes."

We went through a series of reconciliation invocations, and then he administered my penance. I left the confessional and went inside the church to pray. A million questions rolled through my head as I gazed as the crucifix. Was I good enough to remain in the role of a priest? Did I deserve the Holy Orders I had received? Never before had I doubted my duties to the church, until meeting Haven, it had become abundantly clear that there was more to me than my dedication to Catholicism. God-fearing that I was and true to my convictions, I never had reason to question myself before. But the priest set my wheels spinning, particular with regard to Haven. She hadn't acted like the temptress, yet the priest had inferred that she was. That wasn't the way it had been at all. What we shared, in my eyes, had been beautiful, even though I wasn't supposed to think of it that way. She had coerced me into confronting my demon, and remorse filled me for staining her character that way. We were both victims of cruel circumstances.

My aching knees told me it was time for me to leave. My obligations at Holy Cross hadn't vanished, so, deep in thought, I found my way back to the L. The early November chill reminded me that the holidays would soon be here bringing many other church commitments. There was one person who could advise me, but it wasn't very likely I could get away this time of year. I had to check with Bill first. A visit to Notre Dame and a talk with Father Tony might be something that could set me to rights.

Twenty-Nine

HAVEN

"Tell me you've decided to move here." Macie had that look. The one that told me if I didn't give her the answer she wanted, she would bug me to death until I did.

Lugging a box filled with art supplies into the apartment, I said, "I haven't made my decision yet. You know I need to go back to New York and figure out things with my lease first."

"What about Kathy?"

The box in my arms almost dropped to the floor. "What about her? Did something happen?" My heart skipped two dozen beats just from that single question.

"Calm down. I was only saying that because we'd started the search for her apartment earlier."

I set the box in my room and flopped down on the couch. "Oh, Macie, I wish she'd give me the go-ahead. But she won't commit. Even after I told her about what that shithead did at the bar."

"Yikes, and that was a couple of weeks ago."

"Yeah." And it was the last time I saw or spoke with Canaan. But I thought about him every single minute of the day. Was he okay? Had he forgiven himself for what happened, because no doubt he would've shouldered the blame? "I'm going to give her a call again and remind her I'm leaving soon and won't be here to help her. Maybe that will spur her into action. She's been hinting about me taking her to church, and I've been quickly changing the subject every time it comes up."

Macie looked at me with pity, which I hated, and I called her on it. "Listen, I can handle just about anything, but don't ever pity me."

"I wasn't—"

I cut her off before she could finish. "Yes, you were. I know you, so don't try to wheedle out of it."

"Okay, but I feel bad for you. I know how hard these last two weeks have been on you."

She got that part right. Some days going into the gallery had only been a blur, I was so out of it. "Fine, I get that, but just tell me. Don't look at me like I'm a puppy getting ready to get hit by a car."

"Okay, okay. I heard you. So, about church, are you still going to go? What are you going to do?"

"I pretty much have to go. What explanation can I give for not going? Especially since I'll be leaving soon?"

In Macie's fashion, she said, "Don't worry. When it happens, I'll be there with you for support."

"Thanks. I can always count on you."

"Which is exactly why you need to move back here."

She was probably right. However, if I did, that would bring me permanently closer to Canaan, and that was the last thing I could handle, him being so close. What I did need was to get as far away from him as possible. Maybe then I could piece back the crumbled bits of my heart. And the worst thing about it was I couldn't turn my hate on him. I only had myself to hold accountable for getting into this mess. He hadn't done a single thing wrong. The whole thing was my fault. I'd made the catastrophic error of falling in love with a Roman Catholic priest.

Unfortunately, as I predicted, when I called my aunt, she requested I take her to church the following Sunday. Macie said she'd accompany us as promised. Since I would be leaving Chicago in another week, there was no way to refuse her.

Early Sunday morning, Macie and I took the L and went to Aunt Kathy's. When we arrived, I was expecting to see my uncle. Macie stood in front of me on the porch in case Kent was there, only he wasn't. My aunt came out and the Uber we took from the train station instead of the bus waited on us. Walking to church wasn't an option for Aunt Kathy yet.

"Aunt Kathy, you look much better than the last time I saw you."

She offered me a timid smile. "I feel better. He left in a huff this morning when I told him you were taking me to church. I'm not sure where he went."

"Would you please consider moving before I go back to New York?" I begged.

She only nodded and by that time we'd gotten to Holy Cross. We went inside and found our seats. One part of me hoped for a glimpse of Canaan, and the other prayed he wasn't here today.

I breathed a bit easier when I saw Father Cernak walk down the aisle in the processional as Mass got under way. Macie poked me in the ribs, knowing exactly what I felt. I'd made it through the service and when it was time for communion, I asked my aunt if she needed my help in walking up to the altar to receive hers. I wouldn't be taking it myself. After everything, I felt unworthy.

"Aren't you going?" Aunt Kathy asked.

"Not today, but I can help you walk if you want."

"That would be nice." I stood and held her hand and arm as we made for the altar. I wasn't sure how I didn't notice earlier, but there he stood, in the front of the church, handing out communion.

Merciful Jesus, get me through this, please. He looked like a gift from Heaven, with his dark hair and deep green eyes. Dressed in his vestments, though not the ones he would wear to say Mass, he was still regal looking. As I neared him, I didn't dare look at him for my shame at what I'd done to this chaste man made me feel the true sinner that I was. My body trembled with horror over the disgrace and dishonor I had brought upon his soul and I didn't know what to do to make it right. Or even if such a thing were possible.

Aunt Kathy had received her communion and I was in the process of turning when I heard my name.

"Haven?"

I sucked in my lower lip to keep it from quivering as I raised my eyes to meet his. He offered me the communion host, but I only shook my head and turned back, leading my aunt toward our seats. My chest rose and fell with the air I silently sucked in as I swallowed the sobs that were lodged in my throat.

"Haven, can you slow down a bit?" my aunt whispered.

"Sorry." The word was as broken as I was.

When we got back to our pew, Macie's raised brows had me shaking my head in response. I knelt down and rested my head on my arms. I needed to pull my act together and fast.

When I finally heard, "Go in peace," I perked up and looked at Macie.

Whispering to her, I said, "I hope he's not outside greeting people." She nodded.

"You looked like a ghost coming back after communion."

"I felt like one. A very damaged one anyway."

Then I took Aunt Kathy's hand and asked if she was ready to go. We walked outside, where it was unusually warm for a November day, and Father Cernak greeted us. He was talking to my aunt while Macie and I stood in the background and out of the corner of my eye I saw Canaan. He'd just stepped out of the church. What happened next was like dominoes falling in slow motion.

He walked up to us and greeted my aunt first.

"Kathy, how are you feeling?"

He cupped his hands around hers and gave her all the attention I longed to have.

"I'm doing all right."

He nodded. "Nice to see you, Macie, right?"

My bestie bobbled her head while her eyes nearly bulged out of her face.

"Should we expect to see you around more Sundays?"

Her blush was in full bloom.

"Forgive me, Father, I know I've sinned. I should be a better Catholic."

I almost laughed at her confession until he turned those green eyes on me. To say I was tongue-tied didn't come close. I wanted to do so many things, none of which were within reason.

"Haven." The way he said it felt like a prayer, one for forgiveness I imagined for the sinner I was. Instead, I stood there awkwardly, realizing how out of place I was. It was a mistake to have come here, though I didn't have much choice. My aunt needed me, so I couldn't very well refuse her, nor could I tell her why.

When Father Cernak spoke my name, I had to plead my guilt of not paying attention and that made me appear to be an even bigger fool. I turned away, wondering if everyone noticed how I hadn't answered Canaan, only stared. So, quickly, I moved over to Father Cernak and said our goodbyes. Stupidly, I chanced a glance at Canaan and my stomach gathered in ropes as I noticed the way his brows knitted right before he squeezed his eyes shut. That was my cue to get the hell out of here.

There was only one thing that could distract me, so I dove head first into the topic and prayed my aunt would take the bait.

"Aunt Kathy, you know I'm leaving next week. I can't bear the thought of not being here and you still living with him. Please, I'll get on my knees and beg to get you to move away from him."

Macie jumped on board with, "I'll help. You know the company I'm with can find you a nice studio apartment. I can look right away."

"We can have you out of the house in no time flat, nice and secure in your own place. Please think about it," I added.

Then Macie said, "I have an idea. Why don't we go to breakfast?"

"Great idea. Aunt Kathy?"

"Sure, that would be nice."

So the three of us went off to a local diner and ate while Macie and I did our best to persuade her to our side. By the time we were finished, she promised she would let us know that night.

"Really?" I asked.

Nodding, she said, "As long as I can move into something safe and affordable. I don't have much of my own money. Kent keeps a tight rein on the bank account."

"Don't worry. I'll help you out until you get on your feet."

The art gig had paid enough I could assist her, not indefinitely, but we'd worry about that later. I wanted to fist bump Macie, but waited until after we dropped Aunt Kathy off. As soon as we did, Macie started blabbing about all the studios she had been checking out already.

"You have?"

"Yeah, I figured she'd end up doing this before you left."

I hugged her for being such a great friend. "I guess we'll have to rent a truck for the move."

Macie's head rocked back and forth. "I don't think so. We'll borrow Mom's SUV. The places I found are furnished. All she'll need to get is a bed. So we'll only be moving kitchen and her personal items."

"You are a genius."

She blew on her fingernails and rubbed them on her chest. "Yep, I know."

I punched her shoulder.

Then a serious look descended over her. "So, Canaan."

"Don't even go there. My heart was blown into bits and pieces. You didn't see them scattered all over the parking lot?"

"I could almost feel your tension. Honestly. I knew him being there was killing you."

"I'm the biggest douche ever. Now I know how women feel who have been trampled on by men."

"Haven, you are being way too hard on yourself."

I picked on a loose thread that was dangling from my coat. "Can we not talk about this? I have to figure out how to deal with this one way or another. I'm leaving so hopefully, out of sight, out of mind."

"Uh, right. If you believe that, then I have a lake for sale. It's a really big one. The city of Chicago is situated on it."

"Shut up." I punched her shoulder again.

"Ow!" She rubbed the sore spot.

"You only have yourself to blame."

Her eyebrows shot up in cartoon-like fashion and I couldn't help but laugh. "Okay, it is my fault, but I'm owning it, and I'm not buying Lake Michigan."

"Let's look at the bright side. The solid news is that your aunt is going to move. And that really is something to be happy about."

"There is truth in that. At least I don't have to lie awake at night worrying about that asshole beating her to death."

Once we got home, Macie logged into her company's

website and did a complete search for rental properties and came up with a decent selection of places. We narrowed it down to one great option that was close to my aunt's neighborhood.

"Do you want to check it out?" Macie asked.

"Today?"

"Yeah. I could make some calls and we could get in this afternoon."

After agreeing, Macie worked warp speed miracles and in a couple of hours we were back on the train, heading to inspect what would hopefully be my aunt's new home.

When we walked inside, I knew my aunt would love it. "This is perfect," I breathed. "Look at the view." It overlooked a green park. Though it was almost winter now, I could imagine how pretty it would be in the springtime.

"Oh, Haven, this is awesome. And it's like brand new. She's only a few blocks from church. If she continues to improve she could even walk. And if she doesn't, there's off-street parking, so maybe you could get her a car. I love it has an interior entrance so it's extra safe, and lots of room. It's almost a one-bedroom."

"I know. We need to grab this."

"But don't you think we should talk to her first?"

I chewed on my nail for a second. If I called and the devil was home, I'd have to hang up. My aunt would never talk if he was there. But I couldn't waste any time.

Her line was ringing before I had any other thoughts.

"Hello."

"Aunt Kathy, can you talk?"

"Yes, what's wrong?"

"Are you alone?"

"Yes."

"Macie found you the perfect apartment and we're looking at it right now. We need to grab it right away because it won't last."

"Uh…I don't…oh, Haven. I'm scared."

"I know, but it's going to work out. And once you're here, you'll see."

"But what if I can't afford it?"

"You can. I'll help," I reassured her. "I don't want you to worry about that. Just say yes and we'll do the rest."

"Come on, Kathy," Macie called out.

Kathy chuckled into the phone. I could hardly believe it. "Did I just hear you laugh?"

"I think you did," she said.

"Is that a yes, then?" I crossed my fingers and held them up in the air for Macie to see.

"Okay. Let's do this."

Macie and I jumped up and down. "I swear you won't regret this, Aunt Kathy."

Three days later, after Kent left for work, Macie and I waited for about an hour and then we pulled up in her mom's SUV. It didn't take us long at all to throw her clothes into several suitcases and plastic bins that I had previously purchased. We also grabbed some kitchen items, pictures, and linens. I told her after she was settled whatever she was missing we could go and buy.

Right before we walked out the door, I grabbed my aunt's hand and said, "Take a look around because we won't be coming back. If you forgot anything, consider it Kent's."

She nodded, wearing a grim expression. "I should feel a bit remorseful, but I don't. I do feel afraid though."

"That's why we need to make sure you have everything." I watched her scan the house until she seemed satisfied and then we left.

"When he comes home and finds me gone, he's going to have a stroke."

"One can only hope," I muttered.

"Haven, don't say such things."

Shrugging, I said, "I'm sorry, but I don't have a single kind thought for that hateful man."

Macie shut the back hatch. "Let's go. We don't need to be hanging out here." We climbed into the SUV and drove off.

Our first stop was purchasing a bed that would be delivered around noon. Afterward we went straight to the apartment. When Aunt Kathy walked inside and saw her new home, her eyes lit up like sparklers. I couldn't remember ever seeing her look so happy before.

Macie grinned. "Kathy, why don't you have a seat and let Haven and I bring everything inside?"

"Yeah," I agreed. "Relax and soak it all in. We'll have this taken care of in a few minutes."

With the two of us going nonstop, we had her settled in no time. And soon I was saying goodbye.

"I'm leaving, but I'll be back for Christmas, Aunt Kathy."

She flung her arms around me, telling me how much she appreciated everything I'd done for her. It made me happy to know I was able to help her, and I told her as much.

"You can call Macie if anything comes up, but I'm sure Father Cernak would also help or get you in touch with some of the church members."

"Haven, your mother would be so proud of you, of the kind and lovely young woman you've become."

My eyes instantly stung, and I swallowed the burning in my throat that usually foreshadowed a serious episode of sobbing. I'd already done enough of that. Only Aunt Kathy's words left a bitter taste in my mouth because she was so wrong about me. My mother wouldn't be proud at all. She would be every bit as ashamed of me as I was.

"I'll call to check on things," I promised as I walked out the door. What started out as a lovely day had soured into something awful.

Macie's voice brought me back to the present. "You're going to have to figure out how to get over this, Have. He had a choice. He's an adult and could easily have pushed you away."

"Oh, Macie, you don't understand. It's not that simple." There was no getting over this. Canaan was one in a million. I had done the unspeakable to him by trying to heal him, and now I was paying the price for those actions.

"You're overthinking..."

"There's more to it and that's all I'm saying. I'm just going to have to find a way to deal with this. I'm the one who dug myself into this hole, so I'm going to have to dig myself back out of it. And it's not going to happen in a day."

"Okay."

We were both silent for the rest of the drive to her mom's and then most of the train ride. I didn't want there to be any tension between us during my last couple of days, so I suggested we go to dinner. She countered with the better idea of staying in and ordering pizza.

A week later, with my giant suitcases and a huge box filled with my art supplies, I headed to the airport. Macie borrowed her mom's SUV again to drive me. When she dropped me off, we both hugged like I was leaving, never to return.

"I'm coming back in what? Three weeks?" I asked.

"Yeah, I guess. Are you sure?"

"Yes. Christmas. I'm not spending it alone."

"Okay. I love you, Haven."

"Love you too, Mace. Keep an eye on Kathy for me. I know that jerkoff is going to cause problems."

"I've got it covered. Mom is going to check on her too."

When I boarded the plane, it struck me as funny how things had changed during the time I'd been here. My artwork had soared in popularity. Jonathon was in love with me as an artist and I had it made. A job was waiting for me if I wanted it. Money wasn't an issue for the time being. Kent was still an asshole, but I didn't have to worry about Aunt Kathy, although her health wasn't great. And I was deeply in love with a priest. How fucked up was that?

As I watched the skyline of Chicago disappear in the distance, I wished it were as easy for Canaan's image to vanish from my mind. Only I knew different. In all likelihood, it would take the rest of my life for that to happen.

Thirty

CANAAN

Seeing Haven at communion was like watching a scene in a movie. Only I wasn't an actor and the church wasn't a theater. Her cerulean eyes were dulled with what? Sorrow? Regret? And the darkening patches beneath her eyes saddened me even more than I already was. I didn't want her to feel remorse or guilt for what had passed between us. I could have stopped it but chose not to. The fault was mine to bear, not hers.

My request for a leave of two weeks had been gently denied. Bill requested I delay it until after the holidays, which I understood. Burdening him with my issues wasn't an option. He had enough on his mind with his aging and sick parents. He didn't need an added problem. January would be here soon enough and so would my visit to see my mentor, Father Tony. It would mean a difficult month, but hadn't my life thus far been difficult? What were another few weeks in the scheme of things?

Time coasted by. Haven hadn't returned to church. What

should have been a blessing felt like a curse. I did my best to show good faith, to be the man—the priest—I was supposed to be. At night, my self-flagellation and oratory diatribe of memorized prayers did nothing to ease my inner burden. Tears and blood didn't cleanse my soul as my dreams were filled with heated memories of things I shouldn't want with a woman who wasn't mine to have. But my routine continued on and I did what I could with half smiles and few words.

When Thanksgiving arrived, I spent the time with my parents feeling like the fraud that I was dressed in priest's clothing as I blessed the food. Mom noticed and kept asking me how things were. As much as I tried, they both observed my behavior was off. My attempt to cover up my emotions failed.

Before I left, Mom pulled me aside and wanted to know if it was Holy Cross I wasn't happy with. When I tried to convince her otherwise, she asked if maybe I was dissatisfied with the priesthood altogether.

My jaws snapped shut so fast, my teeth clattered. I didn't quite know what to say. So I did the only thing I could think of without telling a lie. I answered the question with a question. "Mom, why would you ask that?"

"Well, sometimes people make mistakes. They think they want something and when they get there they realize it wasn't quite what they expected. I can imagine being a priest is lonely. No one to share your life with and a lot of responsibility."

She was right on both accounts. But I hadn't found myself lonely until I'd met Haven. "It's a burden I willingly took on."

"You're not an island, you know. You should visit more. Your dad and I would love to see you."

I was an island, but only for Haven, though I could never divulge that secret. "I'll try. I'm so busy, there isn't much time." Which was pretty much the truth. "I have been under some stress with a few things going on that I'm not able to discuss. But don't worry, Mom." I pulled her in for a hug. "I'm fine."

"I'm your mother. I'll always worry."

If she only knew the truth, her anxiety level would shoot to the stratosphere.

"At least growing up I wasn't running around drinking and getting into trouble."

She ruffled my hair, like I was ten again. "No, not my Canaan Michael. Always a saint, you were. But too serious at times. Promise me something."

"What's that?"

"If you find you need to talk, you'll come home. I'm still your mom, you know."

She was my mom. And I loved her enough to not burden her with the shame of what I'd gone through. I couldn't imagine ever telling her what a sinner I truly was. It would crush both of them, and I simply couldn't do that.

"I do know, Mom. And I love you too."

God had blessed me with great parents, indeed. Now if I could be the man I masqueraded as instead of the sinner I truly was, maybe God would forgive me.

Back in my room, I sat staring at the painting Haven made of me. What remarkable detail she was able to capture in each pane. I was more than a man, more than a priest in her eyes. For the first time in my life, I felt like someone saw the true person I was. She saw me. Had that been the reason I'd confessed to her? I hadn't told my parents or my mentor, and I'd known them for years. Yet somehow, she'd stripped down every wall, and I'd unburdened myself on her. And for that reason she showered me with kindness and affection. She gave me what was so precious in God's eyes, a gift only to be shared between husband and wife.

I shouldn't want that again and did my best to expel those thoughts and memories from my head. But being joined with her had made me feel alive, made me taste life for the first time in years. The moon and a sky full of stars suddenly had meaning. She was my North Star when I stared into the night. I wanted to pray that she was well, but I felt like God wouldn't hear me. Not when my thoughts of her were at best impure.

How could I continue to walk the line of priest when my heart desired coupling with her again? Fornication was no longer a dirty word on my tongue. It was the dawn that brightened my day and filled my dreams at night.

What I could do and did was pray for forgiveness for thinking ill of the dead. Father O'Brian had been right about me all along. I should have heeded his warnings about my carnal inner nature and the effect it had on others. I didn't deserve to walk with God. I was a sinner, nothing more and nothing less.

Thirty-One

HAVEN

The weather turned bitter cold bringing in winter on a sled. My trip back to Chicago was in ten days. I would arrive on December twenty-fourth and stay until January third due to Macie's urgings. It wasn't like I had anything going on here anyway. I was still vacillating on what to do. Staying in New York seemed to be a good choice because it was far away from Canaan. Far away from the temptation of seeing him and shredding our hearts into fragments, even more so than they already were. Returning to Chicago worried me because every corner or restaurant would bring back memories, even if I hadn't been there with him. The fact that he was so close would be a reminder that it was possible for him to show up any time. On the other hand, my success as an artist would improve greatly by returning to the Windy City. And now that I was supporting Aunt Kathy, I had that financial burden to think about.

The plane ride back to New York and lack of sleep had to be the cause for why I hadn't felt well over the last week. People and their germs. And guess who didn't get their flu shot? Macie gave me crap about it, but being sick made me not want to make a decision either. What made things worse was thoughts of Canaan induced a serious case of insomnia. When I dragged my normally energetic but now exhausted ass out of bed for the eighth day in a row, that was what pushed me over the edge, sending me to a doctor to get some meds.

—

Macie met me at the airport on Christmas Eve. She picked me up in her mom's SUV because we were spending the evening with her family. They'd even invited Aunt Kathy to join us, which was awesome. We had a sumptuous dinner that Macie's mom had really gone all out on and it was wonderful. Around ten, I took my aunt home. I asked her if she wanted me to take her to church the next morning, but she informed me she'd gone to the five-thirty Mass earlier in the day. She was getting along great living by herself and her health had improved. Even her cheeks were rosy and she'd gained some much needed weight.

"Then I'll be over tomorrow in the afternoon to spend Christmas Day with you. It's great seeing you looking so good." I said my goodbyes around eleven fifteen and headed toward Holy Cross. I was going to Midnight Mass.

As usual, the church was packed. It was beautifully decorated with Christmas trees on the altar along with lots of greenery and poinsettias everywhere. The manger was adorned with evergreens as it sat prominently poised on the altar, and I thought how symbolic it was. I was not comparing myself in any way to the Virgin Mary. The thought itself was laughable and sacrilegious all at the same time. But I did feel that sense of isolation and loneliness that Mary and Joseph must've felt the night Jesus was born in the stables.

The processional began with the many altar servers,

deacons, and then the two priests. I'd taken a chance in coming, because I didn't know for sure if Canaan would be here. I assumed only because Midnight Mass was so well attended, and I was counting on that.

He looked splendid dressed in the pure white vestments with gold trim. And I could barely pull my eyes away from him, even from my distant seat in the corner. My responses during the Liturgy were automatic, as I supposed any Catholic's would be, after years of attending church as part of my education at a parochial school. The Christmas hymns were a nice distraction and I sang along as they lifted my spirit in celebration. All too soon, the Mass had ended and the attendees filed out. Cheerful as they were with the holiday spirit, I was left alone in the empty church. The altar servers came and went as they cleared everything as part of their duties. I lit a vigil light in memory of my mother and said a prayer for her as I thought of my upcoming conversation.

At last it seemed I was the only one around, and I heard muffled voices in the sacristy, which I presumed were Father Cernak's and Canaan's. I pretty much hid as I watched Father Cernak leave. I was counting on Canaan locking up. No, I was praying for it.

When he exited the sacristy and walked up the center aisle, I stepped out of the shadows. He didn't see me at first, not until I entered the light.

"Haven. What...why are you here?" He glanced around nervously.

"It's not what you think." The ache in my throat grew to a painful level, but I shoved it aside. "I need a few minutes with you if I can. And then I'll be gone. I promise."

His mouth, his beautiful mouth, opened and closed, and then he nodded. With an extended arm, he gestured toward one of the pews. But I declined.

"I'd rather stand, if that's okay."

"Sure."

My hands were clasped tightly together, held in front of me as I began. "First off, I want to tell you how terribly sorry I am for what happened...for what I did." He held out his hand to stop me, but I ignored it. "I should have never allowed things to, well, you know. That was beyond wrong of me. But that night, for whatever reason I had in my head, I thought I was helping you. Now I can clearly see I was mistaken. Here's the thing, though."

I stopped for a moment and inhaled a bucketload of air. I concentrated on my clutched hands. I was afraid if I chanced one look at him, everything I planned to tell him would turn into a jumble of messy words.

"For every action we take, there are always consequences. And my biggest one was I allowed my heart to get wrapped up where it had no business being. But then there was another one. I was stupidly careless. Our night together resulted in something that will have a lasting effect." I glanced at the manger near the altar again and hoped to sustain my bravado, which I sensed was slipping through my fingers. My arms wrapped around my body and I hugged myself as I hunched over. *Deep breath, Haven.* "You see, Canaan, I'm going to have a baby. The reason I'm telling you is because you have a right to know and not for any other. I have no expectations of you whatsoever. This secret is safe, so you don't ever have to worry about it. I won't come back here, unless my aunt asks me to bring her to church. She won't know who the father is. That's my solemn oath to you. I won't cause you any more grief." I had to stop because my voice cracked and I forced back the tears that stung my eyes. "I won't cause trouble since I've pretty much ruined you as it is. And I won't interfere in your life anymore. Again, I can only say I am sorrier than I can ever express." I didn't wait for him to respond. I spun and walked as quickly as I could and met the car that was waiting for me in the parking lot.

The Uber driver must've thought I was crazy because I wept all the way home and was so thankful Macie was spending the night at her parents'. There wouldn't be any questions or interrogations. I crawled into my bed and sobbed myself to sleep, hugging my pillow, worried about what kind of a mother I would be.

Gray skies greeted me in the morning when I woke up to my usual round of morning sickness. Rushing to the bathroom, I wondered how much longer I would be praising the porcelain god each day. I wasn't the sickly type, but this was ridiculous. When the doctor informed me that it wasn't the flu but pregnancy that was causing my illness, he projected I was about seven weeks along. And that was a week ago. This could go on for twelve weeks or more. Ugh.

Crackers usually helped, so I pilfered the cabinets until I found some saltines and nibbled on them for breakfast. Then I worried about what Macie was going to say when she learned of this. And Canaan. I couldn't stand the thought of what he was going through. A small part of me smarted over the fact that he hadn't called to check on me. Then again, it was for the best. What could he do or say?

When the afternoon rolled around, I pulled myself together and went to my aunt's. She had promised to cook an afternoon dinner and when she let me in her apartment, the aromas of the food punched me in the gut. I cupped my hand over my mouth and sprinted to the bathroom.

When I resurfaced, concern was sketched in her eyes. "Haven, what's wrong? You don't have that stomach bug that's going around, do you?" Her hand automatically landed on my forehead.

"No, I think I ate something that disagreed with me."

Her shrewd eyes weren't buying it. "You're positively green."

I felt green. The smell of the food was nailing me, but I didn't want to tell her that. This sucked.

"I'll be fine. I'm going to walk outside a minute."

She gave me a look that suggested I was losing it. And I was. "You can't go outside. It's freezing out there."

I couldn't tell her I needed to get away from the odor in here, but if I stayed, I'd be throwing up all afternoon.

Then she let out a hearty laugh, which was nice to hear. I couldn't recall ever hearing my aunt laugh like that. "Did you go back to Macie's last night and have too much to drink?"

This was as good of an excuse as any, so I tried to give her my very best sheepish look. "Well..."

"Well, I'm just happy to see you having some fun for a change. Let me make you a club soda with lemon and ice. That should settle your stomach, and I have some crackers."

Jackpot! "Thanks, Aunt Kathy." Now if she could turn on the exhaust fan and get the smell out, I'd be golden. Unfortunately, she never did. The soda and crackers helped though, and I was even able to eat some of her dinner.

"So, tell me, what's going on in New York?" she asked after we ate.

"Well, I'm going to be moving back here." I'd decided to break the news to her today.

"You what?"

"I've decided to take the position Jonathon offered me and make Chicago my permanent home." I left out the other *real* reason. No need to tell her that now. That nugget of news could wait until *my* nugget was further along.

"Oh, Haven, this is the best Christmas present you could've given me." She folded me in her bony arms and hugged me. Seeing how happy she was solidified my decision even more. Maybe her health would hold out and she would be around to see my nugget as a grownup. That thought brought tears to my eyes, but I hid my face on her thin shoulder so she wouldn't catch sight of my emotions.

"You think so, huh?" I asked.

"You know it. It'll be great having you around more, especially since, well, you-know-who isn't here anymore."

That brought a few things to mind. "Has he bothered you at all or come around?"

"Not once. I know he has to have figured out where I am, with all his access to police stuff."

I thought about this for a minute. "Maybe he hasn't figured out the apartment is leased in my name."

She shook her head. "I don't think so. He's sly like a fox. He would've checked that, I think. No, he's left me alone, and I thank God for that."

Kent had something up his sleeve; I was convinced. What it was, I couldn't guess. I'd have to be prepared for the worst, and to be honest, it scared the shit out of me. He was capable of so much more than anyone gave him credit for.

Later that evening I could see that my aunt was tired from having a visitor for the afternoon, so I set up an Uber and headed home. By the time I walked into Macie's apartment, she was already there.

"Wow, you look like hell. What happened?" she wanted to know.

Two questions and she had me in tears.

"What the hell did I say?"

Because she was my best friend and I had to tell somebody, I explained. After, she sat there in silence before she wrapped herself around me like a blanket. No judgment, no scolding, just my bestie there giving me the support I so badly needed.

"I really did it this time, didn't I?"

"So...you're going to have a baby, which means you definitely have to move here. It all makes perfect sense. You'll have a strong support group. Kathy, my mom, and me. Your job too. I'll find us a new place to live."

"Okay, stop. I've thought about that. You're right. I'm keeping this nugget. I can't get rid of it. I think about what if my mom had done that. I wouldn't be here, you know? And I've never felt that would be the answer for me anyway. So that's out. I couldn't give it up either. But, Macie, I need my own place." I watched her face drop as I said the words. "Think about it. Having an infant in the house is not conducive to being single. I love it that you want to do that, but I can't possibly let you." I swiped my face because there was a constant dribble that leaked out of my eyes. "But I do need that support network around me. And the job. So Chicago will be my permanent home. I already told my aunt and you should've seen her face."

Macie's jaw hit the floor. "You told her about the baby?"

"No, silly, I told her about moving here. You know I wouldn't tell anyone before I told you. Except the father." Then I waited for her reaction.

"You told him?" she whispered. I wasn't sure if it was from shock or because she thought I was an idiot, but I knew I was about to find out.

"Yeah, I told him."

A V formed between her brows and she asked, "When?"

"Last night after I left your parents', I went to Midnight Mass. Afterward, I waited in the church for him. It was a long shot, but I took a chance that he would be the one to lock up, and he was. That's when I dropped the bomb."

Her hand wrapped around my wrist and squeezed. "What did he say?"

"Nothing," I whispered.

"Nothing? You told him he was going to be a father and he said nothing?"

"You don't understand. I didn't give him a chance. Right after I told him, I basically ran out of there right to the car that was waiting on me to take me home. It was the only way. I couldn't even look at him when I told him."

Macie jumped up and paced back and forth, then crouched in front of me. "Why did you tell him? It's not like he can do anything."

I stretched the cuffs of my sleeves and used them to wipe my cheeks. "I don't want him to do anything. He had to know, though. It wouldn't be right not to tell him. What if my dad never knew about me?"

It wasn't something I thought about often. But with my little nugget growing inside me, I couldn't help but think about it. It was one thing I planned on asking my aunt about. She might know.

Macie offered me a handful of tissues. I greedily grabbed them and blew my nose. "You should definitely ask your aunt. What else did you tell Canaan?"

"I also apologized for ruining his life, sullying his soul, tarnishing his previously chaste life. I've made a shambles of the priesthood for him, so he deserved an apology from me. Not that it would change anything. Shit, Macie, I feel like a true Jezebel. Honestly. I've earned all of this by rights."

"It takes two, Have."

She was right. It did. But in this instance, I clearly had the advantage over him and had used it unfairly.

"Yeah, but this was different."

I was more than a little surprised when she didn't argue but instead said, "So, you need me to find you an apartment?"

"Yep, a three bedroom. I need one for the baby and one for me to paint in when I can't make it into the art studio. The ones you found before I could afford because we had planned to split the rent. Since the circumstances have changed, that won't work."

"And you're positive you want to do it alone."

What was supposed to be a laugh but sounded more like a croak came out of me. "Want? I wouldn't exactly say that I want this. But it's what I'm going to do. I'm going to make the best home I can for my little nuggie here."

"Nuggie?"

Rubbing my belly, I smiled and nodded. "I keep thinking of my mom. I wonder how she did it all those years ago. I guess she was every bit as scared as I am. At least she didn't have to worry about the father."

Macie patted my shoulder. "How will you handle it? When your nuggie starts to ask about their daddy?"

"I'm not sure yet. I'll have to figure something out when the time comes. Maybe I'll just tell her the truth. That I loved him but it was an impossible situation. I would have to wait to tell her that though, until she is old enough to understand. And pray she will understand."

"But you won't tell her who he is, will you?"

"Never." I wrapped my arms around my stomach and hugged myself. "Macie, you're the only person who will ever know the truth. And swear to me right now you'll never tell another soul. I know how close you are to your mom, but this can't ever leave this room. It would ruin Canaan, and God knows I've already done enough of that."

"I swear. I won't breathe a word of it."

Macie knew every single one of my secrets, but she didn't know about Canaan's past. That wasn't mine to share and I would carry that to my grave. But I could trust her not to speak of him fathering my child to anyone. She had kept her lips sealed about my awful existence with Kent during my years growing up. She often begged me to tell the teachers, only I knew it would be worse for me if I did. Eventually, I persuaded her to my thinking, and she became my shelter when I needed her the most. Hers was the only house I escaped to for a reprieve from my terrible existence. I envied her for the relationship she shared with her mother and father, the closeness they had with each other. The few times I was allowed to spend the night at her house, I soaked it up like a sponge, not even wanting to sleep, because I basked in the warm and cozy environment. This was the real meaning behind family and love. What my mom tried to show me but couldn't because her life had ended all too soon. And that was how I planned to raise my child. Even though my nugget would be fatherless, I would shower her with so much love, she would barely notice.

"You're the best friend I could've ever asked for. I doubt I'd be alive today if I hadn't met you." And even though I told her that all the time, it was the damn truth.

"I love you too, Have. And I'm going to be the best aunt in the world. Just call me Aunt Spoil. Okay, maybe not. That sounds like I never clean out my refrigerator."

Leave it to Macie to make me laugh.

All of a sudden she belted out, "Oh my God!"

"What?"

"Here we are acting like it's a girl. What are we going to do if you have a boy?"

I gave her my slyest grin. "We, my dear, are going to raise the greatest guy in the history of all mankind. One who knows exactly how to treat women."

Holding her fist in the air, she said, "I'll bump you one on that. Hey, can I be in the delivery room with you, holding your hand?"

"I'm counting on it."

Macie began her search for my apartment the week after Christmas. I handed her the reins and told her if she found something after I went back to New York to snatch it up. It wouldn't be wise to sit on something. My budget was fairly strict. While I was doing super with my work, I wanted to take some time off after the baby came, which would mean no income. So I had to factor all that in. There was also Aunt Kathy's rent, and then I would need a nanny to watch the nugget when I went back to work. Being rent poor was the last thing I wanted.

Since Jonathon was way past ready for me to be in Chicago full-time, the news about my pregnancy would wait until I was at least twelve weeks or maybe even sixteen. Many pregnancies didn't last, and I wanted to be sure mine did before I told him. My decision was to let him know upon my return, which would be around the third week in January. His part of the deal was to procure a studio outside of his gallery and my home where I could work without any distractions, away from prying eyes. He said everything would be set up by the time I returned. It had better be because I had a list of orders that was growing daily and I was starting to freak. I suggested to Jonathon that he shut it down until I caught up, but he said he would consider it after the first of the year. Fortunately, that had arrived so I would be calling him to give him a reminder.

On New Year's Eve, I spent the night at home alone. Macie had a date, and I couldn't party, so I watched movies and ate popcorn. With the crazy fatigue that didn't want to leave me alone, I never made it to midnight to watch the ball drop. Oh well. It was only another night for me.

I made a promise to my aunt that had me cringing the next day. I was taking her to church for New Year's Day. It was something she had done as long as I could remember, and she asked me if I would mind. How could I say no? Holy Cross celebrated a five o'clock Mass on the evening of New Year's Day that she loved, so I prayed Canaan wouldn't be there.

Much to my surprise and relief, he was nowhere in sight. I relaxed during the service and then afterward when I knew Father Cernak would speak to us. Church had been much more crowded than I remembered, and the parking lot was full of parishioners as we made our way out of the door, chatting with the priest. It was dark, cold, and what happened next caught me completely off guard.

Out of the darkness I heard his snarled words over my shoulder, directed at my aunt.

"Did you think I couldn't find you? I know all of your habits, where you go, what you do."

It was obvious by his slurred words that he'd been drinking. Cruel Kent had come out to play. Fearing for Aunt Kathy's safety, I placed myself between them. "Stay away from her. I saw the bruises you left on her, and she doesn't want or need any more abuse from you."

His head whipped toward me. "Shut your mouth, you stupid slut. I'm not talking to you. And this was all your idea anyway, wasn't it?"

At the time, it seemed wise of me to get his attention away from Kathy. So I said, "I won't deny I had something to do with it. You're unstable and need help, like anger management and possibly medication." Well, that certainly was not the right thing to say.

"Why, you little whore. I thought I taught you better than that." I didn't expect him to react as badly as he did, but one minute I was standing in front of him, and the next I was on the ground, cradling my face. The fucker decked me.

The steps in front of the church and the parking lot turned into chaos. Somebody grabbed Kent and restrained him while Father Cernak crouched down to help me.

"Are you all right?" the priest asked.

Even though it hurt like hell, I grinned. "Oh, I'm much better than that." He helped me to my feet, and I stared at Kent for a moment, gathering my thoughts. Then I finally said, "For years, years, I've waited for something like this to happen. Now everyone here can see you for the man you truly are. An abusive jerk. This is your final blow. You will never strike us again, because now we have witnesses. Lots of them. And this time you can't use your cop status to save you. I hope you go to jail for assault and battery, not only for this, but for all the times you broke my ribs when I was just a kid and too afraid to say anything. You're nothing but a poor excuse of a man."

I glanced at my aunt and if I didn't know better, I would've sworn there was a hint of a smile on her face. "Aunt Kathy, are you okay?"

"I'm fine, dear."

The flashing lights of the police cars filled the parking lot and soon the officers put Kent in handcuffs. It was one of the best days ever.

Father Cernak came over to me after the police had finished. "Would you and Kathy like to come inside for a minute?"

I didn't really want to, but I thought it would be terribly rude not to go. So we followed him inside the rectory. It was weird being here without Canaan. I kept looking around in the hopes he would walk in. Crazy, yes, I know. But I couldn't help myself. That was why I needed to stay away from here.

"I told the police I would be your witness if you needed it, but I'm also telling you, if it comes to that. He could've really hurt you, Haven," Father Cernak said.

"He has really hurt me in the past. I have the scars to prove it."

"You were a student here. Why did you never say anything?"

I shrugged. "He's a cop. It wouldn't have gone anywhere."

Father Cernak reached for my hand. "Yes, it would have. We would've called in Child Protective Services. It wouldn't have mattered who he was. You were scarred and injured. They would've investigated and gotten to the bottom of it. They have all kinds of ways to figure it out."

"It's long passed now. And you weren't here then anyhow."

"I'm sorry you endured all of that. And Kathy, the same goes for you. I hope you understand you always have a safe place here, if you need help."

"Thank you, Father," my aunt said.

"Now, let me give the two of you a ride home."

"Oh, we couldn't..." I started to say, but he cut me off and insisted. Father Cernak dropped my aunt off and then drove me all the way home. I told him I was moving back and going to set up shop here for good. He was such a nice man, I could see why Canaan felt so at home here with him. When we got to my building, he patted my hand and reminded me of his offer to be a witness should I need one. Then he wished me a very happy New Year and drove off.

As I thought about the events of what happened, it was a good thing Canaan hadn't been there. I was afraid things would've escalated between Kent and him. That would not have been good. The way it turned out was for the best. Kent would pay, hopefully with some jail time for assault and battery, and maybe even domestic violence. We'd also told the police to put up an order of protection on both Kathy and me. We had to go to the police station the next day to sign the papers and then I was leaving the day after.

I never thought Kent's own actions would have this effect. I couldn't have asked for better. When Macie came in, I explained things, and she wanted to celebrate, so we did. I drank a virgin colada and she drank one all spiked up.

The following day was a breeze. I picked up Kathy and we accomplished everything we needed to. Kent spent the night in jail and then lawyered up. The funny thing about it all was it would cost him a pretty penny to defend himself and he was the cheapest sucker around. Oh, how I laughed over his demise. But if I thought about it too long, I knew whatever he got would never be enough for all the things he had done to me over the years. But I let it all go. My life was on track. I was in a good place. Not the best, of course. But I was happy, having a baby, moving back here with a solid job, doing what I loved the most. What more could I ask for?

Thirty-Two

CANAAN

As much as I wanted to follow Haven, my knees gave out as I grabbed the back of the pew and lowered myself to the seat.

I'm going to be a father, and not in the biblical sense.

New Year's Day couldn't come soon enough. I tugged at my collar, feeling it tighten against my throat. I felt like running and leaving the city behind, but couldn't leave Bill in a bind despite that being a charlatan in priest's clothing.

"Canaan."

Bill said my name so softly, yet it sounded in my head as if he'd spoken through a megaphone.

"Yes." The one syllable word came out broken, just like me.

"Are you all right?"

If he told me that Jesus Christ himself had walked through our doors unannounced, I wouldn't be more flummoxed than I was at that moment.

"I got some news." Taken for a loop, I hadn't exactly meant to reveal even that much.

"Good news, I hope."

"I'm not sure," I said. "I think I just need some time."

Finding my feet wasn't easy, but I managed it. Bill let me go without asking me any more questions. I made my way out the back door and into the moonlight, spotlighting me.

I was never more grateful for the darkness in my tiny room. I pulled the clerical collar free from my shirt. What a sham I was. How could I continue?

When I turned, I was confronted by Haven's painting of me. Clearly she'd missed the version of me with a red face and horns.

Falling to my knees, I prayed, and not for me, but for Haven and our unborn child. I begged God for forgiveness and mercy while I fought the strong urge to seek her out. How could I go to her when I didn't have answers?

Somehow I managed on autopilot with robotic movements to make it through the week. I barely slept. Many nights, I ran under the cover of darkness heedless of the many dangers. My back ached from the strap, yet it did nothing to ease my torment. When I was able to close my eyes at night, Haven's lovely face graced the back of my eyelids.

The New Year dawned and I'd finally said the last prayers. Would it be for the last time? I removed the robes and stood in the room of inequity, troubled by everything that should have been holy but was marred by acts I didn't want and one that I did.

"Father Canaan."

Blinking rapidly, I forced myself out of my head and into the present.

"Everything has been put away."

I nodded at Shelby.

"Can I leave?"

I nodded again, unable to find words.

She scurried out and I let the river fall from my eyes. So

much of my life centered around the church. I loved God and wanted to serve him for as long as I could remember. It had been His light that allowed me to overcome the scars of my soul and not let them deter me from my path. But what could I do?

It wasn't about me or even Haven. An innocent grew within her from our lovemaking. Our transgression had created the most beautiful sin. A child who had no choice in parentage, would he or she be tainted? Unmarried, in the eyes of the church, our baby would be considered a bastard. And how unfair was that?

My fist connected with the table until my knuckles were bloody and bruised. The same table that had seen my first blood, the table that had stolen my joy and recently had brought it back to me. Was there life outside of these four walls for me?

Haven meant to have our baby without my help. And what kind of man would that make me if I let her? I had no wages or means to take care of a family. All my worldly possessions had been rendered to the church, which hadn't been much to begin with.

Those were the thoughts I struggled with on the drive that felt longer than it truly was. The secrets I'd kept most of my life felt like rotten eggs in my gut. And if I didn't release the pressure, I was sure to go insane.

I made it to Notre Dame and sought out my mentor. Father Tony saw my distress and led me down a forgotten walking path to a secluded spot I'd sought on occasion during my years in school.

"There's something on your mind. You wouldn't have driven all the way here on this day otherwise. I'm sure your parents expected you."

I scrubbed my face, ready to unburden myself. It was a new year and time for new things.

"There's a woman," I began.

Father Tony was a good man in more ways than I wasn't. His expression didn't change as I told him the story from beginning to end.

"It was the first time Father O'Brien took me when she showed up. I had no idea what she was going through when I sent her back to the Hell she was living in. I thought I was protecting her from him."

Every ugly detail uncurled from my tongue as I pulled out the spike that had been embedded in my heart.

"Canaan," Tony said as tears fell from his eyes in the steady stream in which they fell from my own. He rested a hand on my forearm. "You can't believe you deserved it."

Father O'Brien's words were never far from my mind. *Sinner and tempter, corruptor of souls. I was the beast made flesh. My external covering was Hell-sent.*

"Didn't I? All my life people have looked at me as much as I wanted them not to notice. My temptation was too much for even Haven to bear. And it's led me to this place."

"Canaan, temptation is a struggle for each one of us every day. Even our thoughts aren't pure. None of us are perfect in the sight of God. But no one deserves to be touched, especially by a person you should have been able to trust. I can't begin to apologize that this happened to you. You were not the cause. He used those words to force you into submission."

"And wasn't I dumb to believe it...and still believe it?"

"You were an impressionable child whose trust was broken. What he did was unforgivable." His pause forced me to meet his eyes. "Maybe that's wrong to say. We are taught that all our sins will be forgiven. And that's what God does. He forgives, Canaan. And maybe one day, you will too. But never think you deserved what he did to you."

Everything he said wasn't a revelation. But to hear him say it broke through the protective walls I'd been hiding behind.

"Thanks, Father Tony."

"I'm not done yet. Though I can't fully understand you breaking your vow, I also can't condemn you for it either."

"She's pregnant," I blurted. His face registered surprise for the first time. I soldiered on. "I have to take care of my responsibilities. But I can't do that as a priest."

It pained me as if I'd lost my best friend to say those words. My relationship with God had kept me on solid footing when I thought life was too unbearable. And I had no choice but to give up my position. At the same time, I looked forward to the future and the possibilities.

"Once a priest, always a priest in the eyes of the church. If you want to leave, you have to walk away."

I nodded. "How do I do that?"

"You have to request a leave from the bishop so that they will install another priest in your spot."

"Do I tell them everything?"

"That is up to you. But it won't change anything."

"What do you think I should do?" I asked belatedly.

His earnest eyes pinned me, and I prepared myself for his late incoming condemnation. "It was just the once?"

"Yes," I admitted.

"Do you love her?"

It was a question that didn't really require thought.

"It's not how I love my parents. And I've never kissed anyone before her. If love means she consumes my thoughts or that I worry about her all the time, then I do. I wonder is she okay? Is she safe? And that was before I found out she was with child. I want to be there to protect her. Most of all, I want her happy. If that translates to love, then yes, I'm in love with her."

He sighed. "I myself wasn't a virgin when I made my decision to give my life to God. I'd had relationships in my youth. So I didn't come into this blind. That could be a good thing. I have no regrets from leaving my secular life behind. You, on the other hand, didn't experience the secular world. I wondered when you were here on campus if seeing life differently would change your path. But it didn't. And I thought, what an extraordinary man you were. With that said, I don't think any less of you for your choices. Maybe not having knowledge of the world meant you didn't get to make that choice with full disclosure."

"I have no regrets. It hurts to think about leaving the church. But I see no other option. My life has to be different. I'm going to be a father."

"You have options, Canaan. There are many faiths that don't have the same restrictions we do."

I couldn't fathom it. "I am a Catholic through and through."

He nodded. "There are other options."

And for a long time, we talked about what my options were. I walked away feeling free for the first time in my life. Father Tony made me see what I'd been unable to see before. God would forgive me, and I was only responsible for my own actions not others'. Something I'd counseled others about, but didn't believe true for myself. But I could walk the right path. And I could still be involved in my faith without the cloth. There were many things I had to do, including finding Haven.

Thirty-Three

HAVEN

Being back in New York left me an emotional wreck. My pregnancy hormones had me riding the sentimental rollercoaster to Crazyville. My landlord, who I never liked and was rude to me most of the time, told me he was going to miss me when I went to give him my notice. I broke down and cried like he was my best friend. What the hell was that all about?

Then I happened to walk by a Catholic church. So I slipped inside to light a vigil light for my mom. A priest approached me, and I started bawling for no reason whatsoever. I was a mess. I hoped this hormonal crap didn't last for the duration because I wouldn't be able to stand it.

Later that night, I told Macie about how emotional I was and she laughed. "Yeah, it sort of sucks like that."

"I wish it would stop. It's crazy. I feel loopy."

"I hate to break it to you, but you've been in the loopy line for quite a while, Have."

"Right. Okie dokie. Thank you very much and I'm out of here." I hung up and started scrolling through my phone to call the leasing people over at my warehouse. I needed to cancel that lease too. As I scrolled, Canaan's name popped up. Oh, hell. Not quite what I needed to see. I wondered what he was up to and if he felt at all responsible for this baby. And just like that, the switch flipped and there I sat, sobbing. I threw my hands up, along with my phone, and went to my bed to cry it out.

A few days later, everything was lined up for my departure. All I needed now was for the time to pass. I pulled my shitty self together and started a painting for the hell of it. No surprise, it turned out to be Canaan in an almost fighter's pose. The way he looked that night at the bar when he stood up to Kent. I never had anyone do that for me before; that was an image I'd always carry with me. When I visualized him, his intensity popped out, exactly like it did that night. Before I knew it, I had created an array of colors on my palette, and he was coming to life right before me on the canvas. He was magnificent. Every line and angle on his face spoke anger defined by protection. His stance, with fisted hands by his sides, mimicked control, but only barely. But most of all, I saw someone who was not afraid to show who and what he was, and his courage screamed a loud message. *Back the fuck off.* And I loved it. I settled into my work, knowing this one was all mine. He'd acted on his own, only for me, and this painting would remind me of that. This was the night my nugget was conceived, and I would never forget Canaan Sullivan.

A few days later Macie called with the good news. She'd found the perfect place. There was an extra room, not quite big enough for a bedroom, but it would be perfect for my studio. I told her it was a go.

Exactly two weeks later, the movers came and emptied out my apartment, I took a taxi to the airport, and that night I stayed at Macie's. The following morning, I officially moved into my new apartment. It was done. I was now a resident of Chicago, eager to get my life on track.

The studio Jonathon set up for me was perfect. It had all the elements I needed, especially the privacy. All my supplies had been delivered earlier that morning, so I was free to paint my heart out. And that was what I did. It pleased Jonathon, but it pleased me even more. My life had come full circle. Yeah, I missed Canaan, and would always miss him, but he had left me with the most precious thing in the world—a part of him. And I would have that part forever.

Since I hadn't seen my aunt, I figured it would be a good time to visit her before I got too involved with my work. When I walked in her door, I couldn't believe the transformation in only a few short weeks.

"Wow. You look...young!"

Her hands covered her cheeks. "Really?"

"Better than I ever remember." We hugged. "Kent in jail awaiting trial agreed with you."

She looked somewhat ashamed. "I hate to say it, but yes. It's the fact that now he has to behave, especially with the order of protection. I don't have to cower anymore. He's lost his status."

I preened. "I'm not one to wish bad things on others, but—"

She nodded in agreement. Then her eyes lit up. "Oh, before I forget, I've been meaning to give some things to you." She disappeared in her closet and came out with an envelope that was a bit yellowed with age and a box. "I found this after I got to feeling better when I went through my things. You know when you and Macie moved me, I just had you girls throw things in, and I honestly didn't know what was in that old closet of mine. Anyway, I had forgotten about this stuff, and I'm sorry, honey. After your mom got sick, she asked me to give these things to you when you turned eighteen if she wasn't able. But you'd left and I didn't know where you were for a while."

That was right. When I moved to New York, I broke off communications with her because of the devil.

"It's okay. What is it?"

"It's a letter from Juliana and some other things."

Juliana was my mom. My hand covered my heart as it clanged under my breastbone so hard I was afraid it was going to bust on through.

The letter was in her hand and it looked as though it floated in mid air as I stared at it in disbelief.

"Haven." My aunt's voice was only a whisper.

My hand quivered as I reached for it.

"You don't have to read it here if you don't want."

But I did. What if I had questions? My name was artfully written across the thick paper and I lovingly slid the tips of my fingers over the aged ink. My mom had written this. Hugging the envelope to my chest, I went and sat on the sofa. Then I tore the letter open. Thick folded pages were stuffed inside along with a photograph, but I didn't want to look at it until I read the words my mother had penned.

My Dear Sweet Haven,

I picked the perfect name for you the day you came into this world, for that's what you've been to me—my lovely haven. There are so many things I want to say to you, but the most important of them is that I love you. There isn't enough paper and ink in the world to allow me to tell you how much, so I hope by these words you understand how much my heart fills with joy whenever I look at you or hear your voice. You have been my sole purpose for living. And I only wish I could have been healthy for you. But don't worry, I'll be watching you from Heaven. I promise.

Now on to something you should know. I wanted to tell you who your father was, but I wanted to wait until you were old enough to understand. Unfortunately, my health didn't allow for that, so this letter will have to do.

He was a beautiful man, one who I loved from the top of my head to the tips of my toes. His name was Joseph Michael Evans. We met when I was only nineteen and fell hard and fast in love. He was in Chicago studying art. We dated for a year and secretly married because he valued my Catholic belief of no sex before marriage, and my parents wouldn't have approved of me getting married so young. But my life heart died by tragedy when he was killed in a fatal car accident. It nearly destroyed me until I found out I was pregnant with you.

The saddest part of it all was he never knew. He was killed on his way back home from an art show, and I never got the chance to tell him the exciting news. That's the other piece of the puzzle. You have inherited his extraordinary talent because he was an artist. I've watched you sketch over your few years and see the talent emerging from you. It reminded me of him so much. He would've been so proud of you.

We used to plan our future, and he told me he wanted to have children, and if he ever was so blessed, he hoped he or she would love art as much as he did. Wouldn't he have been happy to know that his darling daughter could draw such astonishing pictures at such a young age?

So, keep sketching, beautiful Haven. One day, you will be famous. But most importantly, be happy. Find someone to live your dreams with. I'm sorry I couldn't be there to watch it all happen for you. But know that I'm watching from above with your father.

I love you more than words can say,

Mommy

P.S. I'm enclosing two pictures I have that were taken of us before…well, before. Hugs and kisses.

The room swam as my tears kept flowing. I handed the letter to my aunt so she could read it. I studied the photos of my father. I'd thought I looked so much like my mom, but I saw him in me as well. I had more questions, like where was his family and why she'd never introduced me to them.

When my aunt finished, we both looked like rainspouts after a summer storm.

I showed her the pictures. My father was very handsome. No wonder Mom had fallen so hard for him. Dark hair and eyes, he was stunning.

"Aunt Kathy, what was he like?"

"All about her. She was like the sunshine to him. But they were only together for a little over a year when he died. And she changed after that. Her spark dimmed. Everyone thought she'd pop back after a while, but she never did. When you came along, you were her reason for being. She never had any interest in another man after him."

"Oh, that's so sad. Why didn't you ever tell me?"

She frowned. "Kent never allowed me to talk about her. I'm pretty sure he had a thing for her, if you want to know the truth. I never knew for certain, but that's my opinion. I heard them arguing once. They didn't know. I got the impression he'd asked her out repeatedly, but she turned him down. Looking back on it, I think he turned to me to be closer to her. That particular day he called her a whore after he found out she was pregnant, which was ironic considering. But, she never told him or anyone about Joseph or that they'd been married, except me and the priest at the church."

I was so disgusted by that thought I scowled. "I'm sorry you ended up with him, but the thought of my mom and him together makes my skin crawl."

"I know how much you hate him and you have good reason to. But something you don't know was I wasn't as devoted as my sister. I found myself pregnant and trapped. Kent married me because our parents gave us no choice. I lost the child and with complications I won't trouble you with, my ability to have more." When I gaped, she patted my hand. "God had his reasons. And Kent resented me ever since with no baby to tie us together, but being Catholic, no way out."

"I'm so, so sorry."

"It's okay. I'm blessed for having time with you. I wish I could have been a better replacement for your mom."

"No, we aren't going down this road. What's done is done. Let's change the subject. I'm happy to know who my dad was. For whatever reason, I always assumed it was some random man she hooked up with."

Aunt Kathy laughed. "Not Juliana. She was too straight-laced to do that. When she found out she was pregnant, she was devastated because she didn't have the chance to tell him because he'd died. Then she was so ecstatic to have a piece of him in you. But Haven, they wanted children. She was just shocked because it happened so fast after they were married. Aren't you going to look in the box?"

The box! I'd forgotten about it. I opened the lid and inside were all sorts of things, but I was shocked to see sketches I had done of my mom when I was young.

"Oh my God! I can't believe it! She saved these."

"She saved everything. I hid these so Kent couldn't throw them away. I also managed to save some of the ones you drew when you lived with us."

Upon closer inspection, I noticed how good they were for a little kid. Then I saw something else, and I almost shouted for joy. They were sketches my father drew. They were of my mom when they must've dated.

"He was so talented." Mom was seated on the grass in the park with the cityscape in the background. I knew what my next painting would be.

"Keep looking, Haven."

There were lots of photographs in there, of me and Mom, of Mom and Dad, and Mom, Dad, and Aunt Kathy. Of Aunt

Kathy holding a baby. "Is this me?"

"Yeah," she said. "You were adorable. We used to fight over you."

All of my attention was centered on all of this, my mom and dad, for the rest of the night. To be honest, it was a relief to learn that she wasn't a slut in any way, like Kreepy Kent had accused her of being. And the irony of it all was we had so much in common now, it was a shame she wasn't here to advise me. Being a single mom wasn't going to be easy and having her around would've been amazing. I fell asleep with the picture of my parents hugged to my chest.

Thirty-Four

CANAAN

My leave wasn't up even though I'd made my way back to the city. I had many tasks to perform. One of which was finding Haven. She hadn't returned my calls and I had no idea where she lived. I sought out her aunt, only to learn of the horror that had transpired at the church in my absence.

It was a good thing Kent was behind bars or I would have joined him. The idea that he'd laid a hand on Haven and I hadn't been there sickened me. It was further proof that she meant more to me than a friend. I would have sullied my name in the face of God to give the man the justice he deserved and couldn't be found in a courtroom.

I should have been worried about my thoughts. But I was human. And Kent was a monster who needed putting down.

"Father Canaan, it's lovely to see you."

Kathy ushered me into her apartment. When I'd called her, she'd invited me over.

"Is Haven okay?"

The woman looked over the moon when she smiled. "That

lovely girl. I don't deserve her kindness. She set me up here." She opened her arms to encompass the room. "And after all she endured under my watch. How I let her down." She shook her head. "She's certainly Heaven-sent."

There was no denying she was my angel of mercy. She'd shown me light where there had only been darkness before. But I needed to know about her physical wellness not her mental well-being.

"Has she healed?" I pointed to my cheek.

Her eyes opened in realization. "Oh, well, she's doing fine with Kent having to face assault and abuse charges. Besides, she's back in New York."

The words clouded my hearing. My breath caught in my throat as I dislodged my next words. "Is she coming back?" I choked out.

She put a hand on my shoulder. "Are you okay? You look pale."

I wiped my brow. "I'm fine. I just worry about her."

"You are a good man and a dedicated priest. She'll be back soon. I'll give you a call when she comes in town again."

Although I didn't see myself as a priest, in the eyes of the church, I was. I managed to hide my distress that she'd most likely returned to New York when she said that she'd be back. I said parting prayers with Haven's aunt, and I did them for her, not for me. God would understand and bless my words. I believed that with all my heart. I left with many more things I needed to accomplish.

In the days to come, I met with the bishop. After, my next stop was to see Bill.

"You're back early."

"Not exactly," I began.

Bill deserved the truth as it related to me. I told him that I was leaving the parish as a priest and shared my experience with Father O'Brien. There may be others that had been harmed by his hand. I needed Bill not to have any doubts about anyone who came forward.

"Thank you for telling me. I felt that something was troubling you. I'm sorry to hear that one of our own was responsible for these horrors. I never thought something that happened at other parishes would happen here. How could I have been so blind?"

He didn't say that he wished he'd known sooner so he could've stopped it. That was a burden I would have to live with myself. I didn't tell him about Haven. That was her secret to share.

When I put on the robes for the next few weeks until my replacement arrived, I didn't feel like an imposter. My faith was renewed. God had plans for me, just not in the ways I'd always assumed. I would continue to serve him, just in a different way once my duties were done.

In some poetic justice, my torment as a child earned me a quick settlement from the church. I hadn't asked for one, but apparently Father Cernak had applied for restitution on my behalf along with the few others who had come forward. The archdiocese, not wanting a scandal, made quick work to offer up money to keep a lid on what took place in our parish.

I wouldn't have accepted it if not that I had nothing to live on. I would be forced to move in a week or so. Tony thought I deserved the money. I wasn't going to be rich, but I would have enough to begin again. I applied and got credit easier than I thought and used it to start my new life knowing money was on its way.

The apartment was small but clean. I would have been fine with a studio, but I got a one bedroom instead. It was all I could afford. I made sure to get a comfy sofa for times when I would have a guest if Haven let our child come for a visit because I couldn't hope for more.

The next several days were a whirlwind. I checked off each

item on my list. When the call finally came, I donned plain clothes—blue jeans and a shirt that was neither black nor white, but a light blue.

I rang the bell, having no idea what I was going to say. When she opened the door, I moved in. "Mom."

"Canaan, it's good to see you. We missed you on New Year's."

"I'm sorry about that. Is Dad home?"

She shook her head. "Not yet, but he will be home soon. I'm cooking dinner."

"Let me help."

The house looked much the same for as long as I could remember. It was always spotless.

"I have to ask, you look different. Is there something going on?"

She shifted the cutting board over to me and I began chopping vegetables on autopilot. "There is something I want to talk to you and Dad about."

"You're scaring me."

"It's not anything to be scared of."

When Dad arrived, I waited until after dinner was finished and the dishes cleaned and put away before I told them the truth. Even though I never thought what Father O'Brien had done to me would ever be revealed to them, I knew I owed them the totality of why I was leaving the priesthood behind. It hurt to see my mother wrecked over it. Even Dad shed a few tears.

"It's not all bad. I found Haven. She helped me and without her, I may have taken the secret to my grave."

I held back on the news about my impending fatherhood. Mom barely made it through my other truths. That joyous news I would share when I was sure about where I stood with Haven and our baby. My heart was lighter as I drove away, knowing my parents accepted what I had planned to do. I had never taken their love for granted, but having their support now meant the world to me. Deep inside was the knowledge that I was truly blessed.

My heart beat with fear and anticipation when I knocked on the door.

It was as if God's light shone down on me when it opened and she stood there with a grand smile.

"Canaan."

My name was but a whisper upon her lips.

"Haven," I said equally taken aback by the overwhelming feelings I'd held at bay for so long.

There was so much to say, yet I was powerless against the urges that bubbled inside me. I reached out and cupped the back of her neck as I closed the distance between us. Her stunned lips gave way a second after I pressed my own to hers.

One of us closed the door, but we both used touch to express our feelings. Clothes fell away like dust in a storm until we were bare. I acted on instinct as we stumbled into her room, me falling on top of her. She didn't seem to mind as she used her parting legs to draw me closer. Somehow, I found myself inside her once again.

Joy filled me as we made love for the second time. Each time I moved within her brought a stroke of pleasure that seared me all the way to my heart.

This time I explored. I kissed and sucked her breast, which made her gasp.

"Canaan," she cried out as her insides fisted me like a vice.

It was as if angels sang with every glorious thrust. The pleasure that had built up inside me for weeks with no release shot off like a cannon. I could say nothing as I found release for the second time in my life. I poured my love into her, knowing she was my beginning as much as my end. I was sure I left her overflowing. There would be no other woman for me but her, ever.

As we lay side by side panting from exertion, Haven laughed. "Why did you come?" She laughed again, covering her eyes, and I was confused for a second. "That didn't come out right." Then she was full-out doubled over with laughter. "I'm sorry."

"It's okay. I came because…" I paused because she seemed to laugh harder if that were possible. I didn't let that stop me from saying the next words. "I'm in love with you, Haven."

She stopped her giggling. Her face grew serious as she stared at me. "What?"

"I'm in love with you."

Her eyes lost their smile. "Canaan, if this has anything to do with the baby…"

"It has everything to do with you and our baby. But I was in love with you before I found out you were with child."

"But you can't love me *and* the church. You've said that many times."

"And I meant it. But I don't only love the church. My love is for you, our baby, and God. And I don't have to be a priest to love Him. But I can't be a priest when I love you more than any faith."

Tears sprang to her eyes and she covered her mouth.

"Don't cry, Haven. This is supposed to make you happy."

"What are you going to do? How will you live?" she yammered. Her eyes brightened. "You can stay with me. I have a three-bedroom apartment."

I shook my head. "What happened between us, however beautiful, didn't happen the way it should have. I may be new to this, but I'm not ignorant. I need to court you. I need to prove to you that I'm worthy of your affections."

Her lips curved in a sly smile. "We're in bed. We just had sex." A second later, she added, "And he blushes. My God."

The word died on her tongue. "It's okay. God is a forgiving God. We sinned. And it was a beautiful sin. But going forward,

I will take you out on dates. And walk you to your door. I will leave chaste kisses on your cheeks until the day you agree to marry me."

"I'll marry you," she said.

"I hope you will. But we aren't there yet. I've never lived on my own. Never had a job that paid enough wages to support me. Never have I dated a woman...let alone one who made me the happiest man alive. But the day will come when you will wear my ring. And I will be worth the man you call husband. And our child will see me as a role model, not a charity case."

Thirty-Five

HAVEN

My phone rang and Macie's name popped up. "Whatcha doin' chica?"

"Getting ready for my date," I said.

"Oooh. Where are you guys going tonight?"

"No idea. He wouldn't say. Our last date was to the aquarium, and he kept pulling me into all those dark little alcoves and sneaking kisses. And then he took me to the museum where he showed me all his favorite pieces of art. He loves art. It's so weird, Mace. He loves literature too. He's freakishly smart. And witty. It's like there's this super cool guy hidden inside of him who's just now emerging."

"Hmm. Sounds exactly like someone I know."

"Oh, you think you're funny," I said.

"Think about it, Have. You never got out much because of Kreep face. So what did you do? You read and studied and got super smart too. Just like Canaan. I can only imagine what your conversations are like."

"Mmmm."

"Oh, gawd. Spare me."

I busted out a laugh. "Okay, but I've got to finish getting ready. He's taking me somewhere nice. So I have to apply a little makeup."

"Interesting. Okies, call me tomorrow."

I scurried around to finish up and the doorbell rang. It wasn't possible to get used to looking at Canaan. And when he walked in, he grabbed me and kissed me like there would never be another day. But all his kisses had become that way. When I asked him about it, he only said that he would never take what we had together for granted, so I supposed it was his way of showing that.

"You look gorgeous," he said. But then he told me that when I had on flannel pants and a T-shirt.

"So do you."

"Haven, men don't look gorgeous."

"Says who?"

His brows pulled together, like they did when he was thinking hard about something, and then his shoulder lifted as he said, "I don't know."

"Exactly. I'm a woman and I know a gorgeous man when I see one. You are it." I leaned in to kiss him again. I ran my fingers across the planes of his cheeks and watched his forest green eyes latch onto my own.

"You make me want to stay in tonight."

My brows waggled. "Who said we had to go out?"

He ran his finger from my ear to my shoulder. "I do. You know the rules. Besides, I have some things planned. It's really cold out so you'll need your heavy coat." His eyes strayed to my feet and he frowned. "Can you wear boots or something? I don't want you to get chilled."

"But they won't go with my dress."

"But..."

"Canaan, are we taking a car or walking?"

"A car."

"I'll be fine."

He scratched his head, and then looked at my feet again. "You might fall on the ice."

"I'll have you to hold on to. Let's go." I grabbed my coat and started to put it on, but he grabbed it and helped me. He was such a gentleman. Then he spun me around and buttoned it all the way to the top.

"Do you have a scarf?"

I went and dug one out of the closet. I already learned he was too protective so it was no use arguing with him. Handing the scarf to him, he wrapped it around my neck and off we went. A car was waiting for us right outside, and I laughed at him.

"I didn't even have time to feel the winter air."

"And that's a good thing."

The drive to our destination was brief. It was a restaurant. An upscale one. I raised my brows and elbowed Canaan. "What's up with this kind of fancy?"

He didn't respond but flashed me a smile I would've paid good money for. He gave his name to the hostess and we were led to a very private table in the back corner.

Dinner was amazing, but what happened afterward was even better. When our dessert came, Canaan pulled a letter out of his suit coat pocket and slid it to me.

"What's this?"

Grinning, he said, "Just read it."

So I did. And when I finished I couldn't believe it.

"Is this the real deal?"

"It is. I start immediately."

It was a letter confirming his position as a professor at Loyola University. And he explained that the position he would be taking over was for another professor who had unfortunately fallen ill and was going to resign. They needed someone to come in immediately, and Canaan, with his Ph.D.

in Theology, fit their requirements perfectly.

"Do they know about you and me?"

He nodded. "I was brutally honest and was surprised I got the position. But the dean who hired me said he thought my honesty was refreshing and also thought I could bring some new air into the program. I'm not so sure, but the youth of today don't necessarily share the beliefs that I do, so I may have a tough job ahead of me."

"But you're smiling."

"Oh, I love a good challenge when it comes to debating the presence of God."

"So what exactly will you be teaching?"

He tapped his head and chuckled. "Ha, I forgot to tell you. The name of the class is *Does God Exist*."

"Hmm. Isn't that something I may have mentioned to you in the past, about my thoughts?"

"Oh, don't worry. That's one of the things on my list of *To Dos With Haven*."

I grabbed his wrist. "Your what?"

"I'm making it my mission to change your mind about your thinking. But not tonight. I have something else in mind."

My hand was still holding his wrist, but he flipped his hand over and laced his fingers with mine. "Do you remember what I said when I came to visit you after you moved back here?"

"That you loved me?"

His mouth curled into a beautiful smile. "Well, that, but something else."

"That you wanted to marry me."

"Yes, but that I wanted to court you. And I have." A worried look gathered his brows. "I have, haven't I?"

"Yes, and it's been amazing."

The worry lines disappeared. "So, I've been thinking. About us, a lot. And I'd like to ask you to become my wife. Will you honor me and become Mrs. Sullivan? We can't marry in the

Catholic Church, or I'll have to speak to Bill or Father Tony about that. Once a priest, always a priest, so I'm sure we'll have to marry in another church. If that's okay. And I won't be able to afford a—"

"Canaan, I'll marry you tomorrow at the court house."

His mouth opened and he practically recoiled at my words. "I…we…not get married in a church?"

This was absolutely the wrong thing to say to a priest. "You're right. What about getting married in the Episcopal or Lutheran church and asking Bill or Father Tony to officiate the ceremony?"

His stiffened posture relaxed and he smiled. Nodding, he said, "I think that would be very nice. A merging of the two. Blessed by the priests and in a church. And you would be okay with this?"

"It would be perfect. Did you have a date in mind?"

"Any time before the baby arrives would be great for me, but the sooner the better. You?"

I giggled like a schoolgirl. "Tomorrow?"

"Oh, I nearly forgot." He reached into his pocket. "I'm still learning." He placed a small black box on the table. "If you don't like it, you can exchange it for something else."

Shock didn't describe what I felt. Inside the box sat a ring. But not just any ring. It was a ruby surrounded by diamonds. And it was perfect.

"It's stunning." I slipped it on my finger and it sparkled by the light of the candle.

"I chose the ruby because of how we are connected. In a way, our blood was mingled before we even knew it. Maybe it was a sign we were meant to be together. God does work in mysterious ways."

"Hmm. I never thought of it that way."

"He does. I never thought I'd be sitting at a table in a restaurant, with the most beautiful woman in the world, who has just agreed to be my wife. And who has also changed my life and turned it into heaven."

"Canaan, you're the one who's changed my life. You brought love into it and you allowed me to trust again." I leaned in close to him. "Can you take me home now? There's something I want to do when we get there."

He stood up so fast he knocked his chair over. I doubled over laughing. But then he sat back down after righting it.

"Haven," he admonished. No matter what I did, he was sticking to his *no more sex before marriage* rules.

We barely got the door to my apartment opened when his mouth slammed onto mine and we clumsily grabbed for each other. My bulky coat was in the way, along with my silly scarf, and Canaan in his haste tugged it off, but in the process started choking me. I grabbed his hands to stop him and when he saw what he was doing, he shook his head and let go. I rid myself of the damn thing and shrugged off my coat.

"Will you unzip me, please?"

"Are you sure you trust me not to tangle you up?"

"Um, if you want me naked, I'm going to have to."

"You know I can't have you naked. I'll unzip you then close my eyes so you can change."

"My man with the self-control of steel," I teased.

Two months later, in May, we stood in the Episcopal Church. Both Father Tony and Bill were there to officiate. Our only guests were Kathy, Macie and her family, and Canaan's parents, who I was already very fond of. It was plain to see from where he had gotten his kindness. His mother and father had taken me into their arms on our first meeting and welcomed me into their family.

When it came to our vows, we gazed at each other without a prewritten script, having written our own vows. On my turn, I spoke simply from the heart, telling him how much he meant to me and how much I loved him.

But Canaan's blew me away. Of course, being on the hormonal roller coaster, I wouldn't be able to stop crying throughout, and Macie offered me the giant box of tissues she'd thoughtfully brought with her.

"Haven, I don't know if you know this or not, but they misspelled your name. They left out the *E*. It should be *Heaven*, for that's what you are to me. But then again, maybe not. Because you are also my Haven, my safe place, my sanctuary, my oasis. They say God works in ways beyond our understanding, and he certainly did with us. If anyone had told me a year ago I would be standing at an altar getting married, well, I would've called them crazy. And now as I look at my life, at our lives, I can't think of anything any better than this. A love so true and all-encompassing that it makes me thank God every day over and over that He led us to each other.

"So, on this day, our wedding day, I can't give you my heart, because you already own it, and I can't give you my soul, because you already share it. But instead, I give you all of me until this life of mine or yours has ended, because you possess every single bit of me, and I know you will cherish it as much as I will cherish yours."

Then he leaned in to kiss me, but I stopped him. "You can't kiss me yet."

"Yes, I can. And I'm only kissing your cheek."

I sniffled back tears but didn't do a very good job of it.

Father Tony pronounced us husband and wife, and Canaan finally got his big kiss in. He held my face, dabbed at my tears with his thumbs, and kissed me long and deep to the chuckles around us. "I hope those are happy tears," he said.

"Yes, but your vows were so amazing."

"I love you, Haven. You're amazing. Do you have any idea what you've done for me? You've changed my life, brought real meaning into it. You've given me joy that I never had."

My arms, which were wrapped around his neck, hugged

him even harder. "It's crazy to think how empty my life was without you."

"Psst. I think the natives are restless." Macie poked my back.

We turned to face the small group and they clapped. My cheeks heated because I was sure they'd heard us.

"Shall we head to the house?" Canaan's dad asked.

"Sure," Canaan said. His parents were giving us a small reception.

On the way over, Canaan asked, "So, wife, you never told me what Jonathon said about your pregnancy."

There was a reason for that. I didn't want him to be angry. "He didn't say a whole lot except not to forget about all the orders I had to fill."

"Figures."

In the short time Canaan had been in my life, he didn't have a great fondness for Jonathon. He thought Jonathon took advantage of me, and when my current contract was up, he wanted to renegotiate it so Jonathon would earn less or maybe nothing at all. We would see. But Jonathon was a big name in art. So I planned to hire a well-known attorney to make sure my interests were protected in the contract renewal or I would threaten to go elsewhere. And this time, all the fine print would be spelled out for me.

"Did I tell you how beautiful you are?"

"Yes, and you look quite gorgeous yourself." I leaned across the seat and kissed his cheek.

"Nothing will ever be as special to me as you are."

After the reception, which, thankfully didn't last too long, we headed for our hotel for the night. I was much more than eager to get my man undressed. In fact, I was downright horny.

At the front desk, I had to suppress multiple giggles as Canaan fumbled with his credit cards during check-in. There was a good reason for this. My hand had snuck under his coat and was pinching his ass. And oh, I couldn't wait to see that naked ass again.

He slid the card in the slot and the door clicked. When I turned the handle, he pushed it open so hard it slammed against the wall. When my mouth opened in surprise, his was there to take advantage of it. Warm lips pressed mine as his tongue tested out the waters. He was still unsure of himself, but everything about him was perfection. I cupped his cheek, and not the one on his face, and squeezed. He wasn't used to anything sexual yet, but it was going to be fun watching him learn.

"Canaan, do you mind unzipping me, please?"

Large hands reached around me and expertly did the job. I slipped the dress off and stood before him in my bra and panties.

"Oh, good heavens. I am so glad I didn't know this was all you had on underneath that dress. I would have never been able to get through the ceremony, much less the reception."

"Your turn." My eyes never left him for a second as he freed himself of his clothing. He was absolutely magnificent, standing there in nothing but his boxer briefs with his straining erection. I tugged those off of him and put my hand around his velvety cock. He automatically reached to take off my bra, which he was still clumsy with, and as soon as it was unhooked, we moved into each other's arms.

His kiss was like fire, flame in my veins. But it always was. Heat roared through me, and I was sure he could feel it. All I wanted was to feel him inside of me. He pulled away for a second, crouched down, and slid my thong off. Then he stood and cupped me, sliding a finger inside.

"You're so warm and soft. And wet."

"You make me that way."

I took his finger, circled my clit with it, but I wanted him.

His lips found mine, and moments later he lifted me and planted himself inside of me.

"Is this okay?" I loved how he checked to see if I was good with whatever he did.

"Oh, it's perfect."

His hands grasped my cheeks and moved me to a perfect rhythm as he backed me into a wall. Canaan's face as we made love was an artist's dream—this artist's dream, and one I would never share with another. The V between his brows, the creases on his forehead, the opening of his mouth, all came together to create a striking view. And that was only his face. His body could've been a sculpture. And when I heard the words, "I'm going to come," it was all over for me too.

Afterward, he carried me to the bed. Then he went to the bathroom and brought back a cloth to clean me up and also a glass of water. He was so considerate.

That night, Canaan didn't merely show me how much he loved me. He worshipped me with his mouth, hands, tongue, and body. He shared his heart and soul with me and kissed me until my body tingled from lack of oxygen. We fell asleep, him curved around me, whispering how much he loved me.

I woke later with large hands resting on my swollen belly as he gently placed his lips on it.

"You awake?" he said softly.

"Yes."

"I can't believe we've created this beautiful miracle, you and me. A miracle of life. I'm humbled by the gift we've been given. God has blessed us with something more precious than gold. I'm just so awed knowing a tiny person who could look like me or you or maybe both of us grows inside of you. There is nothing I wouldn't do for either of you."

Tears of joy spilled from my eyes, because he was right. There was no greater gift and the only thing missing was my mom, knowing she would never see my nugget. But there was something else Canaan had given me. Faith—faith that somewhere she was watching over me and hopefully she would approve of the changes I'd made in my life.

As he stroked my baby bump, he tenderly kissed me and it was the most beautiful and precious moment, something I would commit to memory and paint one day.

Epilogue

CANAAN

The rumble of the truck grew louder and came to a stop just as I parked in my driveway. I met the crew as they carried it inside. I opened the door and told them just where to position it. When they left, I went in search of my lovely wife.

Soft music played in the background, and I found her, covered in paint, as usual.

I wrapped my arms around her and held her tight as she jumped in my arms.

"Canaan," she said, slapping playfully at my hands, but I didn't let go.

Nuzzling her neck, I breathed her name. "Haven."

Gliding my hands down her sides, I knew she was on board with what I had in mind. I dipped my hand past her elastic waistband and cupped her sex.

"Canaan," she moaned, writhing against my back.

I molded her heavy breast in my other hand.

"I thought you Catholics couldn't have sex unless it was to procreate."

The fact that she could talk only made me work harder. I slipped two fingers inside her and she cried out.

"The Catholic Church isn't always right. Besides, the Bible requires a husband to keep his wife happy. Are you happy, wife?"

She nodded frantically as I pumped my fingers inside her. Oh, how much I'd learned and fast. I hadn't told her I'd used my research skills to learn more so I could keep her satisfied.

"On your knees, love."

She turned in my hold and my fingers left the silky depths of her heat. Her eyes flashed with anticipation as she glided to the ground, her paintbrush forgotten. She unzipped my pants as she went and fisted my cock before sliding her tongue around the head.

I loved her mouth. "We don't have time for that. On your hands and knees."

Her wicked smile did all sorts of things to me as I pulled off my shirt and kicked my pants to the side. On my knees, I slid deep inside her, forcing her back to arch in response. I ran my fingertips down the length of her spine before curling my fingers in her hair. I leaned over and kissed her neck.

She was wet and warm. And thank God we were married, because I didn't have to confess my baser desires in confession. I was allowed sinful thoughts of my glorious wife and her lustful body.

"Canaan, stop teasing me. Your parents will be here any time now with Hannah."

As much as I loved my daughter, I didn't want to think about her in this moment. So I sped up my movements.

"I love your breasts. I love being inside you."

Her response was indistinguishable as I hit that sweet spot. Leaving her breast, I moved to rub her clitoris because I was close. It only took her clamping around me in a vice grip to have me shooting off.

I didn't want to pull out, but the doorbell rang.

"They're here," she sang.

Kissing the smile off her mouth after helping her to her feet, I quickly put on my clothes.

"You have paint on you," she teased.

"And you should be in labor by now. The doctor said having sex would coax our wayward child out of his mother's belly."

"And how do you know it's a boy?" Haven asked.

"It has to be. I'm sorely outnumbered. God will have some mercy on me."

She laughed. "Clean up, my dear. Somehow I don't think my parents will see the beauty in our sexual activities."

When she stuck her tongue out, I added, "And I'm looking forward to lots of your mouth during the six weeks I'm deprived from being inside you."

"Were you ever a priest?" she called out after I left the room.

That part of my life felt so foreign to me. Though I had many occasions to call forth the prayers I knew like the back of my hand.

The doorbell rang again. "Coming," I called out and shook my head, remembering how Haven had shared with me the colloquial uses of that word.

I chuckled more to myself when I pulled the door open. Kathy and Ed greeted me with wide smiles. "Come in." I laughed again. Good thing Haven hadn't heard me.

"Oh my, the house is beautiful."

It had been a labor of love. We'd purchased a fixer-upper in a good neighborhood. Father Tony and Bill helped me along with contractors for the things that were out of my novice's hands. Macie's father was a contractor and had showed me how to do things like drywall and tile.

"Just in time. Haven should give birth any day now."

"And where is my granddaughter?" Kathy asked.

She and her husband, Ed, were Hannah's honorary grandparents since Haven's mother had passed long ago.

"My parents should be bringing her any minute." I gestured toward the door just as the bell rang.

Macie and her parents entered the house with oohs and aahhs. Father Tony and Bill weren't too long after. Haven had just come from the back freshly dressed when my parents arrived.

"Daddy," my daughter called out.

Haven frowned, so I kissed her cheek before taking my little princess from my father.

"Mom," I said, greeting her with a kiss on the cheek.

"Daddy's little girl," Haven muttered. Then she saw it. "What is that?"

Her words and eyes were full of astonishment. I nodded at Father Tony, who'd helped me procure it.

When the drop cloth was removed, Haven sucked in a breath.

"How?" she asked in wonderment.

Macie beat me to Haven's side. "He got it back."

Tears spilled from Haven's eyes and Kathy's too. The pair shared a hug and a private word I overheard.

"He's still in jail and he's lost his badge. He can never take this away from you. And your husband, a true man of God, got it back for you."

I understood the *he* was Kent. He had gotten the maximum time behind bars, which wasn't enough time if you asked me. Still, he'd been stripped of his badge, pension and other accolades.

Haven turned her glorious gaze on me. "How did you do it? How'd you find the painting?"

There was something very private in her eyes that let me know I would be given many, many wonderful and personal wifely gifts for accomplishing what she hadn't been able to.

"Father Tony helped me talk the buyer out of letting it go at a hefty price tag. And I might have promised him you'd paint something spectacular. But I didn't think you would mind."

"Is that grandma?" Hannah asked, reaching for her mother.

"It is. I painted that, but Jonathon sold it."

Before Haven could take our daughter, her face tightened in a grimace and her hand found her belly.

"What is it? Is it time?" Macie asked.

She nodded. "I've been having contractions all day, but I thought they were the false kind. My water hasn't broken yet."

It didn't take long for all of that to change. Leaving our family and friends in our house along with our daughter, we knew she'd be in good hands. I threaded my fingers through Haven's as I drove gingerly to the hospital, trying not to break any speeding laws.

"Do you ever miss it?" she asked quietly from her seat during one of the breaks between contractions.

"Being a priest?" I chanced a glance at her and she nodded while squeezing my hand.

It was a topic that had come up over the last few years since I'd made my decision to leave. I'd had talks with Father Tony and Bill about it before.

"No. I loved being a priest. But I love being a husband and father more."

"And being a professor, does it fill you the way being a priest did?"

Her eyes looked pained. She still felt guilty for my choices.

"It fills a different place in my heart. I enjoy the questions and debates over the text. I enjoy how the younger generation challenges the archaic views the church has on topics of the day. I enjoy the freedom of questioning the church as well. But there will always be a part of me that is a priest."

She nodded. At a stoplight she leaned over at a considerable contortion and kissed me.

"What was that for?"

"For being you."

Our daughter was born a few hours later. I thought Haven was asleep with her eyes closed until she asked, "Can we name her Juliana Susan after our mothers?"

"Yes. I was going to suggest the same."

"Are you sad we didn't have a boy?"

I laughed. "Of course not. God only gives us what we can handle. And I can't say I won't enjoy trying for a son soon."

She groaned. And it would take another daughter, Ava, to be born before our son, Joseph, would unleash his holy cry into the world. But at that moment, it was just the three of us.

"Maybe it's just the hormones," Haven began. "But are you sure you have no regrets?"

I didn't hesitate. "Absolutely none. And as much suffering as we endured to get here, I would do it again knowing it would bring us together. I love you so much more each and every day. You are my heaven, my angel of mercy on this earth, and no one will convince me otherwise. And maybe our love and our Hannah might have been created in sin. But oh, what a beautiful sin it was."

THE END

A Thank You

We'd like to thank you for taking the time out of your busy life to read our novel. Above all we hope you loved it. If you did, we would love it back if you could spare just a few more minutes to leave a review on your favorite e-tailer. If you do, could you be so kind and **not leave any spoilers** about the story? Thanks so much!

Acknowledgements

Every day we are amazed by the number of readers who follow us, contact us, or speak to us through Facebook. The messages you all leave us totally blow us away. We are humbled by this because we never dreamed this would ever happen, especially to two hermits like us. So a big shouty thank you to everyone who loves our stories. We honestly can't tell you how much we love you all.

We started writing A Beautiful Sin way back in the fall and it's been quite the process for us. We had to juggle it between the release of Cruel & Beautiful, and then the writing of A Mess of a Man. We have a few rewrites too, that complicated everything, but Canaan stole our hearts and we hope he steals yours as well.

There are so many people we'd like to thank but first off, here's a huge thank you to are beta readers: Kristie Wittenberg, Kat Grimes, Andrea Stafford, Heather Carver, and Jill Patten. You all have been with us since the beginning so thanks for putting up with us! A thousand hugs and smoochies!

Next, thank you Nina Grinstead for *everything* you do—all the marketing, keeping up with the ARCs, the beta reading, OMG, what DON'T you do? You are *da best*!!! There aren't enough words to say it here.

Sofie Hartley at Luminos Graphic House—thank you for the AHHH-mazing cover. You knocked it out of the park, girl. And we have been crying ever since you told us were retiring from covers. We took to our beds for days. We'll never get over that piece of news. If you ever change your mind, let us know. We'll be here waiting—impatiently, of course.

A big thanks to Max Henry for making everything on the inside just as pretty as the outside.

We'd also like to give a big shout out to the RedCoatPR team (A couple of crazy Brits and the rest Yanks!) for everything they do. Newsletters, Ads, FB posts, Tweets, and all the behind the scenes things too. Love you all to pieces.

Finally, thank you Lisa Christman of Adept Edits for all the editing and Emily Lawrence for proofreading.

About the Authors

A.M. HARGROVE

One day, on her way home from work as a sales manager, USA Today bestselling author, A. M. Hargrove, realized her life was on fast forward and if she didn't do something soon, it would be too late to write that work of fiction she had been dreaming of her whole life. So she made a quick decision to quit her job and reinvented herself as a Naughty and Nice Romance Author.

Annie fancies herself all of the following: Reader, Writer, Dark Chocolate Lover, Ice Cream Worshipper, Coffee Drinker (swears the coffee, chocolate, and ice cream should be added as part of the USDA food groups), Lover of Grey Goose (and an extra dirty martini), #WalterThePuppy Lover, and if you're ever around her for more than five minutes, you'll find out she's a non-stop talker. Other than loving writing about romance, she loves hanging out with her family and binge watching TV with her husband. You can find out more about her books at www.amhargrove.com.

TERRI E. LAINE

Terri E. Laine, USA Today bestselling author, left a lucrative career as a CPA to pursue her love for writing. Outside of her roles as a wife and mother of three, she's always been a dreamer and as such became an avid reader at a young age.

Many years later, she got a crazy idea to write a novel and

set out to try to publish it. With over a dozen titles published under various pen names, the rest is history. Her journey has been a blessing, and a dream realized. She looks forward to many more memories to come.

You can find more about her books at www.terrielaine.com.

Stalk

Terri E. Laine

If you would like more information about me, sign up for my newsletter at http://eepurl.com/bDJ9kb. I love to hear from my readers.

www.terrielaine.com

Facebook Page: /TerriELaineAuthor
Facebook: /TerriELaineBooks
Instagram @terrielaineauthor
Twitter @TerriLaineBooks
Goodreads:/ Terri_E_Laine

other books by Terri E. Laine

<u>Chasing Butterflies series</u>

Chasing Butterflies
Catching Fireflies
Changing Hearts
Craving Dragonflies
Songs of Cricket

<u>Him series</u>

Because of Him

Captivated by Him

Standalones and novellas

Ride or Die
Thirty-Five and Single
Money Man

Sex, Love, and Alcohol (Beer Goggles Anthology)
Honey (originally in Vault Anthology)
Sugar (Part II of Honey & Sugar Duet)
Married in Vegas: In His Arms
Absolutely Mine

other books co-authored by Terri E. Laine

Cruel and Beautiful
A Mess of A Man
One Wrong Choice
A Beautiful Sin
Sidelined
Fastball
Hooked
Worth Every Risk

Stalk

A.M. Hargrove

If you would like to hear more about what's going on in my world, please subscribe to my mailing list on my website at http://bit.ly/AMNLWP

You can also join my private group—Hargrove's Hangout—on Facebook if you're up to some crazy shenanigans!

Please stalk me. I'll love you forever if you do. Seriously.

www.amhargrove.com
Twitter @amhargrove1
www.facebook.com/amhargroveauthor
www.facebook.com/anne.m.hargrove
www.goodreads.com/amhargrove1
Instagram: amhargroveauthor
Pinterest: amhargrove1
annie@amhargrove.com

Other Books by A. M. Hargrove

For Other Books by A.M. Hargrove visit www.amhargrove.com

The West Sisters Novels:
One Indecent Night
One Shameless Night (TBD)
One Blissful Night (TBD)
The West Brothers Novels:

From Ashes to Flames
From Ice to Flames
From Smoke to Flames

Stand-Alones

For The Love of English
For The Love of My Sexy Geek (The Vault)
I'll Be Waiting (The Vault)
Sabin, A Seven Novel

The Men of Crestview:

A Special Obsession
Chasing Vivi
Craving Midnight

The Edge Series:

Edge of Disaster
Shattered Edge
Kissing Fire

The Tragic Duet:

Tragically Flawed, Tragic 1
Tragic Desires, Tragic 2

The Hart Brothers Series:

Freeing Her, Book 1
Freeing Him, Book 2
Kestrel, Book 3
The Fall and Rise of Kade Hart
The Hart Brothers Series Boxset

The Guardians of Vesturon Series

Co-Authored Books

Cruel and Beautiful
A Mess of a Man
One Wrong Choice
A Beautiful Sin

The Wilde Players Dirty Romance Series:

Sidelined
Fastball
Hooked
Worth Every Risk (A Spin-off of The Wilde Players Series)

Made in the USA
Lexington, KY
15 August 2019